MYTH✸S SEAS
ALARM IN THE ARCHIPELAGO

BOOK TWO

MYTH✵S SEAS

ALARM IN THE ARCHIPELAGO

JEREMY J. DAVIDSON

To my friend Tupp, whose enthusiasm and insights helped these books get published.

This is a work of fiction.
The story, all names, characters, and incidents portrayed in this production are fictitious. No identification with actual persons (living or deceased), places, buildings, and products is intended or should be inferred.

Identifiers: ISBN 979-8-9891162-2-5 (Paperback) | ISBN 979-8-9891162-3-2 (ebook) | Library of Congress Control Number: 2023919969
Printed in the United States of America
Dayton, NV.

Check out Mythosseas.com

Design by Jeremy J. Davidson
Cover design by Jeremy J. Davidson

CONTENTS

CONTENTS

CONTENTS

CHAPTER ONE
DREAMS AND DISASTERS

Jackson anxiously gasped as he ran around several flooded and abandoned buildings while dark clouds grew thick above him. "GRANDPA? MOM? DAD?" He called out worriedly. "Where are you?"

The flooded buildings reminded him of something, but what exactly, he wasn't sure. He reached out, putting his hand against a door that had been shoved open by the waves swirling around his ankles before he leaned inside the empty building. Lightning flashed across the sky above him, making him jump and take a step backwards! "Where is everybody?"

"Lost."

Jackson flipped around; his legs trembling nervously while he cautiously crept around the house to see a flooded pathway that led to the broken walls of a strange town. "Hello? Is someone there?"

"The lost are in danger."

"Who's there?" Jackson asked nervously as the moon broke through the thick rolling clouds above him. When a glowing form shot over the walls and vanished into a building behind him, he stumbled after it. "Hey, who are you!?" He called.

"Your family wish to be found, please help them."

"I can't find my family!" Jackson exclaimed, but stopped when memories came flooding back. Memories of his family being trapped in stone, meeting the Sonaekian Medians, his journey through the ocean to find a way to save his tribe, and of his new friends he'd made along the way.

This is just a dream. He thought quietly while thunder rolled above him. *Then why does it feel so real?*

"Save your family before it's too late, darkness is growing on the waves and in the seas."

"I'm trying to save my family! What do you think I'm doing?" Jackson looked around desperately until a glowing white bird flew by, turning its brightly glowing head towards him. Someone started shouting his name as the moon flashed and dimmed in the sky above him. "Who... are you?"

"JACKSON WAKE UP!!!"

"GAHH!!" Jackson yelped when Daychaser threw him off his bed, sending him spiraling into the water towards the wall! Startide swooped around to catch him on her large head, her quick reflexes saving him from crashing into the wall of Mistsurge Outpost.

"You ok Jackson?" Startide, a large female oroca asked, lowering her head to let Jackson float off. "You were shouting and yelling in your sleep."

"I was having a crazy dream..." Jackson rubbed his eyes only to blink when the magical orbs that lit the room suddenly dimmed, only to brighten a few moments later. "Uh, what's going on with the outpost?"

"We weren't sure..." Daychaser made a nervous whine-squee when the lights dimmed again. "That's part of why I threw you off the bed to wake you up; you're the only one here that really knows anything about magic."

Jackson went and placed his hand against the wall, closing his eyes while he felt around for the magic within the outpost. He took a quick breath, the flow of magic ebbed and faltered, getting weaker by the moment as if it was dying. "Something's wrong all right." Jackson opened his eyes. "I think we'd better go try to contact Oceaono and the others while we still can!" He shot out of the entrance to the resting quarters and hurried across the main area of the outpost towards the Communication Chamber, his friends hot on his tail.

"Where're Zepherdust and Avavo?" He asked, while he rushed over to the large teardrop shaped communication crystal and reached out to lay his palm against it.

"They went off with some of Avavo's friends to explore around Mercenary Beach awhile ago." Startide looked back towards the entrance of the outpost worriedly. "I thought they'd be back by now."

"Oceaono!" Jackson called urgently. "Are you there? Somethings wrong with the outpost's magic, its fading."

The crystal flickered for a moment before the magical form of Oceaono—a tall blue sapphire golem—appeared, the forms of a small whale and a large dolphin quickly flashing into view next to him.

"JACKSON ARE YOU IN HERE?"

A voice interrupted anything Oceaono might've said when a large white sea lion flew into the room with a wild look of fear in his eyes. "Oh thank currents, there you are! Zepherdust's flipper got cut by a broken mercenary blade and I'm worried she's poisoned!"

"Can never just have one emergency at a time, can we?" Seanel the whale median asked wryly. She gave a tired shake of her head when three more sea lions came swimming into the room. A light gray and a dark brown sea lion helped Zepherdust—a light cream gold-colored sea lion—over to Jackson. Zepherdust was struggling to swim, since she was using only one front flipper while she favored the other, which was torn and bleeding slightly.

"Jackson, take a look at her flipper while you explain what's going on, if you please." Docion, the dolphin median, looked around the room worriedly once the lights dimmed again. "Although, I have a fairly good idea of why you contacted us."

Jackson hurried over to check on Zepherdust's flipper while he explained that the magic of the outpost seemed to be weakening and ebbing, as if dying.

"Ooo…" Jackson stopped his explanation once he saw how deep the cut was in Zepherdust's flipper. "What happened, Zepherdust?"

"I slipped on a large piece of wood and fell into one of the craters left over from the battle." Zepherdust winced when he gently took the flipper in his hand and started healing the wound. "There was a broken spear at the bottom that my flipper landed on when I hit…"

"That's not going to heal very quickly, even with your knowledge of healing magic Jackson." Seanel said, after inspecting the wound thoughtfully. "The nerves will take some time to recover enough for you to swim without pain Zepherdust."

"Time is what we don't have." Oceaono looked around the room worriedly as the magic suddenly dimmed and the magical murals on the walls faded away. He looked over at Startide. "Do you remember the seamounts and currents you'll all need to follow to get to Starkelp Strand?"

"I think I have them memorized." Startide seemed a bit unsure. "Seanel and Sharval have been showing me the way to the strand with their magic for the last four days. I think I know them all."

4

"I hope for your sakes, you're right." Docion looked around with an unhappy squee when the magic of the floor started to dim. "I think we only have a couple more minutes with you before you'll be on your own again." He looked over to Oceaono worriedly. "Shouldn't the outpost's magic have lasted longer than this?"

"Yes, either something is draining it, or someone had used some of the magic before Jackson and the others got here." Oceaono's features were strained in worry, and he looked over to Jackson who had paused his healing spell to listen better. "Get to the strand as quickly as possible and ask for help along the way if you get off track or lost." His voice was firm. "Don't make the same mistake the Lost Ones did."

"The Lost Ones?" Startide asked. "Who are they?"

Seanel the whale median crooned sadly. "The Lost Ones were the last group of loyal Sonaeko that escaped the effects of the Great Petrifying all those centuries ago…"

"And the only group that survived the next two years afterwards…" Docion added grimly.

Jackson's mouth dropped open as magic suddenly coursed out of his hands and into the water around him. Bright blue shapes began to appear, taking on the appearance of humans and other creatures that morphed and moved, playing out the scenes Seanel continued to describe.

"After the Great Petrifying the Lost Ones gathered along the shorelines of an island to the west of the capital and discovered another group of Sonaeko called the Ironcurrent who had also escaped the petrifying."

"However…" A figure came into focus. "The leader of the Ironcurrent was a wicked and selfish man and refused to allow the Lost Ones to reach out to us, or the other ocean life, for help. He claimed that the creatures of the sea were responsible for the Great Petrifying, and that he alone could fix the damage that was done."

"That man and his followers forced the Lost Ones to go with them across the Void of the Deep, a giant underwater chasm that separates the lands and waters of the Sonaeko from yours. All the while, the Ironcurrent refused to accept help or guidance from any creature of the seas." Seanel let out a keening cry. "Their pride was to be their destruction, for lurking in the void was a darkness that emerged from the depths in horrible silence as it viciously attacked!"

Jackson yelped in fright when cries of fear and sorrow vibrated the water around him while Seanel's voice turned grave. "To the horror of the Lost Ones, the leader of the Ironcurrent tried to strike a deal with the darkness. When the darkness rejected the leader's offer, their horror turned to terror, and they fled for their lives. In the ensuing confusion, while the darkness drove the Ironcurrent into the depths of the sea and consumed them, the Lost Ones were able to escape."

Oceaono took up the tale. "Free from the Ironcurrent's oppression, the Lost Ones sent messages on the waves for help, even contacting us in their desperation. With the help of some ocean creatures, they were able to flee as far as the great barrier ridge before the darkness caught them..."

Jackson shuddered as he watched the scene unfold.

"However, their calls to us for help came too late, and we were too weak to do more than watch through the Star of the Sea as the darkness attacked. With the help of the Star of the Sea the Lost Ones fought off the darkness long enough to escape through the cliffs lining the Great Barrier Ridge." Oceaono shook his head as his eyes glistened with unshed tears. "Sadly, their last stand ended with many of them wounded and bleeding, and a couple drifting towards death. There was still magic from the Great Petrifying in the oceans in those days, and the remaining Lost Ones harnessed that power to freeze their wounded comrades in stone, saving them from certain death."

"Sadly, what we know of the Lost Ones after they escaped is very little." Seanel added with a mournful bellow as the magic in the water vanished. "The Star of the Sea was damaged from harnessing the chaotic power of the Great Petrifying, and after we saw the Lost Ones petrify their wounded brethren, the star's power faded, preventing us from seeing anything more."

Her tone turned remorseful as Jackson looked around in confusion before he realized no-one else had witnessed what he'd just seen. "We only know that those who survived fled to the northern continent, passing by the Starkelp Strand and the other Sonaekian cities where they might've found help." She seemed to sigh. "The legends told by the great whales say: that after a time the Lost Ones returned to the ocean and became petrified of their own free will, choosing the same fate as their nation."

"How sad…" Zepherdust gave a mournful bark. "Do we have any idea if any of them remained?"

Oceaono pointed to Jackson. "Perhaps, we suspect at least a couple remained on the shores of the northern continent and became Jackson's ancestors. That would be the only reason why his family would've had the Star of the Sea and the Book of the Sonaeko with them."

"Now back to business." Docion interjected. "When you get to Starkelp Strand, call for Leavementee, she is the Guardian of Starkelp Sanctuary." He got a funny look in his eyes. "She's a bit moody, but she's mostly all bellow and no bite."

"Mostly?" Daychaser gave Docion a worried look.

"We're out of time to explain." Seanel interjected when more of the magical light died. "You must leave at first light, get to the strand as quickly as you can. Time is of the essence and the longer you stay in one place unprotected, the more likely dishonored will find you there."

"Good luck." Oceaono said before the magic in the room suddenly flickered out, like a candle being blown by a strong wind.

"Oh spells…" Jackson whispered as the whole outpost went dark.

CHAPTER TWO
INTO THE OPEN OCEAN

The next morning Jackson and his friends gathered next to the rocky beach right outside the entrance to the outpost: which was now stuck open as Jackson couldn't summon enough magic to close it.

"Are you sure you aren't going to come with us?" Jackson asked Zepherdust and Avavo sadly before he gave Zepherdust a hug around her neck. "You could ride in my bag for most of the trip until your flipper feels better. Daychaser and Startide have been bringing me extra fish to store for the journey, so you'd have food to eat."

Zepherdust hugged him back with her good flipper before she shook her head and pulled away. "I would only slow you down, and you'll need all those extra fish for the journey." She looked over and bobbed her head to Daychaser and Startide while she favored her wounded flipper. "And I think I'll heal faster here: where I can breathe the cool ocean air and rest on the shore."

Avavo barked his agreement. "Not to mention finding food when traveling over the deep ocean is hard, especially for those of us who are used to hunting in coastal waters."

"I won't be around to help heal your flipper if it gets infected though…" Jackson protested worriedly.

Zepherdust gave him a gentle shove towards Startide and Daychaser. "I'll be ok, this isn't the first time I've been wounded like this. Avavo and the other sea lions will be looking out for me and helping me find food."

Jackson was quiet for a moment before he nodded reluctantly.

"We'll miss you." Startide came over and gave Zepherdust and Avavo gentle, friendly shoves with her snout. "It won't be the same without you guys."

"We're going to miss you too." Zepherdust said quietly. "Be careful out there, ok?"

"We will, and you guys stay safe here." Daychaser gave a sad howl. "And maybe stay away from Mercenary Beach for a while."

Zepherdust laughed quietly. "You don't have to tell me twice."

"We'd better get going." Startide made a sad creaking sound before she turned to lead them out of the lagoon and towards the open sea beyond.

"Come-on." Daychaser gave Jackson an encouraging nudge when the boy hesitated.

"By you guys." Jackson said quietly. "Thanks for everything."

"Good luck! We'll be rooting for you!!" Zepherdust called while Avavo barked his encouragement as Jackson and the others followed the shoreline out of the lagoon.

The three friends silently traveled down the rugged, rocky coastline for the rest of the morning until they entered the shallow offshore waters. Daychaser and Startide decided to stop before they reached the end of the shallows for one more hunting trip, and Jackson quickly teleported into his bag for a quick lunch of seaweed and some frozen eel.

When Startide shook the bag to get his attention, Jackson teleported out to anxiously follow his friends as they swam towards the darker waters beyond. He gulped nervously, stopping quickly when the seafloor below them suddenly fell into the foreboding dark depths.

After taking a long, shaky breath, Jackson looked out into the deep water while holding back a dread-filled groan. This was going to be a long trip.

Startide bopped him on the shoulder, giving him a toothy smile. "Ready?"

Jackson sighed. "No, yes, not really…"

Daychaser swam over with an encouraging squee. "We can do this!"

"It'll be fine!" Startide said and began swimming off to the east. "Let's go."

Daychaser rolled his eyes at her impatience and Jackson managed a weak smile. Letting out a happy sound, the seawolf spun after Startide, while Jackson hesitantly followed them into the endless expanse of dark blue liquid.

Jackson felt his pulse quicken once he lost sight of the drop-off. He firmly tamped down the panic striving to seize him as he glanced around and was faced with nothing but water! Endless and never-ending water filled his eyes: the only change in scenery was if he looked up to the sky or down into darkness.

I'm going to be looking up an awful lot his trip… Jackson shuddered after he'd glanced down at the darkness below him, *and avoid looking down as much as possible!* He hurried to catch up with the others before they vanished from view.

Jackson rushed up beside Daychaser, breathing heavily while butterfly fairies spiraled around in his stomach. The fairies whirled around faster and faster with each glance into the depths below and Jackson closed his eyes anxiously. Daychaser gave him an understanding look; the seawolf knew him well enough to know when he was getting anxious, and why. Startide was still working on understanding why deep dark waters scared Jackson, and gave him a long, concerned glance.

Daychaser began asking Jackson a bunch of different questions—ranging from the many types of magic, to what living on land was like—while he tried to help Jackson focus on something other than the dark depths below. As the sun rose higher into the sky Jackson's nerves calmed considerably, and he was grateful for Daychaser's support. Around noon, Startide slowed her pace to join the conversation Jackson and Daychaser were having about the different types of barriers you could make with light magic.

The group stopped for a bit so Jackson could pull some fish out for them to eat, as Startide insisted that they keep up their strength. Once lunch was over, Startide started drilling Jackson on different types of ocean creatures with Daychaser throwing in a comment here and there while they swam. They saw nothing for the rest of the day, except for a couple small schools of fish that vanished the minute they saw Startide.

When the sun began to set—making the water darken around them—Jackson began to fidget nervously, earning him another confused look from Startide.

Once darkness had covered the sky, Jackson gave a shaky sigh and tried to concentrate on the brightly gleaming moon and stars above. He tried his best to ignore the dark water around him and was relieved the stars at least provided something bright for him to focus on.

They stopped for a moment while he worked with his color changing spell, covering his white tail with a dark gray on top, but a lighter shade on the bottom. Their old friend Sandfang had suggested this color combo, claiming that it would provide him with some degree of camouflage. Finally, he insisted that he needed to sleep, teleporting into the bag where he managed to get some rest for the night.

As a day turned into five, Jackson thought he might go insane from seeing water—and only water—day after endless day. He tried to keep himself occupied with working on his spells and talking with his friends. Although it didn't help that Startide still seemed concerned about him getting so antsy every time it got dark, but she was keeping her promise to try and be more patient and understanding with him. However, she still seemed a bit perplexed as to why he insisted on going up to look at the clouds so often.

While the sun set on the fifth evening, Jackson took his place above Daychaser and Startide to make him less visible to any creatures below. The arrangement was fine with Jackson, since he could look up at the stars until he went into his bag to sleep. Every now and again he'd tentatively look into the deep, his heart skipping a beat each time he saw a small flicker of light or some other sign of the deep-sea creatures coming to higher waters with the fading sun.

They traveled quietly for a time until Startide gave a concerned squark, making Jackson jump when something big swam under them.

"Good evening to you deep diver… can we help you?" Daychaser asked once a large shape moved ahead of them.

"Sorry, didn't mean to sneak up on you." A deep male voice replied, "but seeing a lone oroca and a cadolin swimming together was too strange to ignore."

Jackson squinted, making out the shape of a large dolphin, or was it a whale? *Wait…* His eyes widened when the creature moved near enough to be seen in the faint moonlight.

A beaked whale.

Jackson had only heard about them from the ocean creatures, they were strange looking animals that spent most of their lives hunting deep in the oceans depths.

"No harm done, although you did surprise me a bit." Startide said calmly, although her eyes were still wary.

Jackson let go of the breath he had been unconsciously holding when he got a look at the beaked whale's eyes, they were kind. This was an honorable creature.

The whale's eyes widened a bit when he caught sight of Jackson, and he slowly looked the boy over.

"Is there something you wish, deep diver?" Daychaser asked, still acting leery as he moved to block Jackson from view.

"Only proof of the current's songs about a lightborn Sonaeko returning to the seas…" The deep diver looked directly around Daychaser at Jackson. "And if the currents bring truth, to offer some help for the night."

Startide gave a curious croon while she moved her body to help block the whale's view of Jackson before she spoke up. "And who might you be?"

"I am called Depthstride, I am an elder among the black-backed diving whales."

"You are an elder of the divers?" Startide asked cautiously, yet respectfully. "Could you list me the names of your first mothers and fathers by singing their names on the currents?"

"Ah, you seek greater proof than my word alone. That is wise in these waters."

Jackson peeked around Startide and saw a look of approval in Depthstride's eyes. "Very well, young oroca, I will give it to you." The whale slowly began singing a series of long flowing names that Jackson had a hard time following as Depthstride weaved his ancestry into song. Startide moved in time to Depthstride's song and

Daychaser's fins swayed to the haunting rhythm while a slight
glisten of magic danced through the water. Once Depthstride
finished, Startide repeated a few of the names respectfully and
Depthstride let out a series of approving creaks and bellows.

"Your names and voice on the currents are true." Startide said,
and some of the tension in her jaws released. "Forgive my distrust,
but these waters aren't known for the kindness of their creatures."

"No need for an apology young oroca." Depthstride gave a long
whale-ish chuckle. "I know very well how harsh these waters are."

Daychaser spoke up. "You mentioned you had an offer?"

"Ah, yes." Depthstride flicked his pectoral fins. "If indeed you
travel with the one the currents speak of, would you perhaps like for
I or some of my kin to escort you for a time? You are headed east to
the Starkelp Strand if I'm not mistaken?"

Daychaser tensed defensively, a look of fear in his eyes. "Did
you hear that on the currents?"

"No…" Depthstride gave Daychaser a slow shake of his head.
"But it fits with the old stories, the medians would want a lightborn
Sonaeko to travel to where they could speak with him more freely."

Daychaser relaxed, looking relieved. "Thank the lights. I was
worried that perhaps the currents carried news of our trip eastward,
and we'd have every dishonored in the sea looking for us here."

Depthstride made an odd noise. "Be that as it may, you have
already been seen many times in the last few days. While these
oceans don't appear to be filled with creatures, news still travels fast.
Although…" He looked around Startide at Jackson. "Perhaps the
currents were wrong about a lightborn…"

Jackson swam around Startide and let his color spell break, and
Depthstride's eyes widened when the boy's white tail flashed into
view.

15

Jackson opened his mouth to introduce himself but was beaten by Startide.

"Depthstride let me introduce Jackson Growingstar, born of the light and water." She inclined her head towards Jackson a bit.

Ugh, why more formalities? I was hoping they'd stop after we left the coast. Jackson rolled his eyes.

Depthstride stared long and hard at Jackson. "By the deep currents, you **are** a lightborn."

"Indeed, he is!" Daychaser said happily before he bowed. "My name is Daychaser, and this is Startide. We've been assigned by our pods to accompany Jackson on his journey."

Depthstride let out a sound that was almost like a loud gurgle. "You have been given a great honor and responsibility."

"Yes." Startide said. "We have."

Depthstride nodded, looking back at Daychaser. "While we are still over our feeding grounds, my kin and I could escort you for a few weeks or so." He pointed with his beak to the depths below.

Daychaser looked at Startide who bobbed her head approvingly before he glanced over to Jackson who nodded.

"We accept your offer Depthstride." Daychaser said humbly. "We would be grateful for you and your kin's assistance on our journey."

Depthstride gave a happy bellow. "We are honored young lightborn and friends! Continue your journey eastward, and we will join you soon." He let out a farewell bellow and slowly dove into the deep, vanishing from view.

After Depthstride left, Jackson felt a wave of exhaustion sweep over him and winced, rubbing his head tiredly. "I… I think I need to rest a bit."

"You do look a bit paler than normal..." Startide gave him a concerned look. "We'll let you know when Depthstride and his kin join us."

"You ok?" Daychaser asked.

"I... I think so." Jackson shook his head. "Just... really tired."

After teleporting into the bag Jackson flopped onto the floor with a groan, all this traveling was wearing him out again. He sighed as he closed his eyes. "We just started this part of the journey, why am I already feeling so exhausted?"

He shook his head and slowly opened his eyes; he'd been feeling more and more anxious and tense over the last few days. Staring into an infinite expanse of water from morning till evening was starting to drive him stir-crazy, and he was feeling distressed and discouraged. "What would you say Grandpa?" He closed his eyes and sighed sadly, thinking longingly about his family while tears stung his eyes.

Memories from his strange dream haunted him while he rested and he finally rolled over onto his chest, crossing his arms beneath him. *I wonder what that dream was talking about?* He thought with a frown. *I'm already on this whole journey to try and save my family... and who's lost? The Lost Ones maybe?* He shook his head. *No, I doubt it's them... that happened almost two hundred years ago, and Seanel said that most of them returned to the sea and became petrified.*

After a few more minutes he twisted around, put his arms against his sides, and rolled across the floor to his chest of personal items. He rummaged around for a journal and writing wand, grunting when the wand he found slipped into a crack between the stacks of books in his chest.

"Lovely." He grumbled and dug into the pile to find it. As he lifted an old book on light magic, the wand clattered onto the bottom, landing next to an old silver amulet.

Jackson paused when he saw the amulet, his mouth twisting thoughtfully. Slowly he reached out to pick it up, opening it carefully as he bit his lip, feeling his heart throb. A few tears formed in the corners of his eyes while he smiled warmly at the portrait of his whole family. A friend of their tribe had drawn the portrait less than a year ago and it was the only picture Jackson had of his whole family. Longingly he ran his hand over the side of the metal casing, not registering the knocking sound made by Daychaser, who was trying to get his attention. He slowly read over the words engraved along the edges of the amulet, whispering them quietly.

"Every tree has many leaves, each their own shape and size.
To the tree, each leaf it needs, bringing joy as it will higher rise.
For every leaf brings strength unseen, the light of lifting lives."

It was a saying he often heard his mother use to comfort him when Jackson had felt down or lonely.

"Each leaf is needed, and important."

His mother's words echoed in his mind and he sighed, leaning his head back against the wall. He found a tiny bit of encouragement from the memories and was just about to fall asleep when a question woke him.

"Where did you say the lightborn went?"

Jackson jumped at the sound of Depthstride's voice; he'd completely forgotten the beaked whale was supposed to return with his kin!

Quickly placing the amulet back into the chest, Jackson shut the lid and teleported himself back into the ocean. A chorus of surprised bellows from the whales blasted his ears once he popped into view next to Startide, making Jackson wince.

"GREAT STEAM VENTS! Where did you come from?!" A large female beaked whale gave Jackson a shocked look, while a couple other whales let loose streams of bubbles in surprise.

"Jackson is able to… what do you call it again?" Startide gave him a questioning look.

"I'm able to teleport, or go to another place using my magic." Jackson said with a small smile. "I can teleport to a specific place my family is magically connected to. After I teleport there, I can return to where my backpack is." He tapped his backpack with his finger as the whales watched incredulously.

"Tel… aport…" Depthstride rolled the word around on his tongue a few times before shaking his head. "Magic is a strange thing… can you teleport wherever you want too?"

Jackson shook his head. "I wish I could. It would make this journey a lot faster, but I only know of a handful of people who could teleport to different places on a whim. Although, I think they had to have been there first, or worked with someone who had been where they wanted to go."

"Makes a strange sort of sense I suppose." Depthstride said, still looking slightly confused. "Very strange indeed, but why do you go to this place?"

"If you don't mind, could we answer those kinds of questions in the daylight hours?" Startide suggested worriedly. "There are so many creatures active at this depth at this time of night…"

Depthstride's eyes widened. "Forgive us. We let our curiosity get the better of our good judgment. Indeed, let us continue our course and not speak of this till the morn!"

And so began the next couple weeks of Jackson and his friends' journey with Depthstride and his family. The first night they traveled together, Depthstride had proudly introduced his family: a gentle female whale, their youngest calf, and a full-grown male calf from a past season who was staying with them, all of whom were quite friendly and kind.

As the days ticked by, the group would occasionally run into different open-ocean creatures. The animals ranged from ocean-going sharks, huge cream-colored oval shaped fish, schools of rays, curious seabirds, and spinner or yellow sided dolphin pods that would happily join them for the day.

The copper-colored sharks they met weren't particularly friendly, though they were curious and patient, they were truthfully a little ornery. Despite that, a couple shivers traveled along with the group for a short time, wanting to talk to Jackson and ask him questions. One group made the mistake of rudely demanding to see some magic. The sharks were quickly put in their place by Startide, who had snapped her jaws so loudly it made Jackson's ears hurt. The display scared the sharks so badly that most of them fled for deeper waters, while the remainder humbly apologized before requesting to see a few spells.

Depthstride and his mate also taught Startide and Daychaser about hunting for food in the open ocean. This often seemed to entail a lot of deep diving, which neither Startide nor Daychaser seemed thrilled with or good at. Startide was more adept at deep sea hunting than Daychaser and often found herself some squid, fish, or something else to fill her stomach.

Daychaser on the other fin, usually returned empty mouthed and hungry, mumbling something about not being able to dive deep enough for the good stuff. Depthstride and Startide soon took pity on the seawolf and began searching for ways to calm his aching belly. Much to Daychaser's relief, Startide began bringing back any extra fish she caught to share with him. Between Startide's generosity, the frozen food in Jackson's bag, and the nightly hunting trips

Daychaser took with the whales, the cadolin's belly was full enough he didn't grumble **too** loudly.

Jackson had long talks with Depthstride and his mate about the currents and a host of other topics as the days went by. However, as time passed, these conversations dug up a problem that quickly morphed into a bigger issue: Jackson's fear of the dark.

After Depthstride and his family had discovered Jackson's fear, Jackson did his best to avoid the topic entirely while they traveled. Despite the perplexed looks and slightly prying questions Depthstride and his kin asked, Jackson largely kept quiet or quickly changed the topic. He hated to bring up the memories of... that night. Depthstride and his family, however, weren't so keen to leave well enough alone and kept bringing the topic up, much to Jackson's chagrin.

Finally, late one evening, after much prodding from the whales, he'd let Depthstride and his kin convince him to take a tentative dive into the dark water below to try and hear the voices on the deep currents. As Daychaser had worriedly predicted, Jackson only got just deep enough for the light to completely vanish above him before he panicked. With the light gone, a light bump from Depthstride's calf had sent Jackson into such a wild terror that he'd shot to the surface, going so fast he flew through the surface and high into the air above the water before landing with a giant splash!

Daychaser and Startide had hurried over to Jackson, who was breathing heavily and shaking from the fright, while the startled whales came rushing up from the depths.

"What on the deep currents?" Depthstride asked in surprise. "What was that about Jackson? It was only our little calf who bumped you."

Startide held out a fin to quiet Depthstride as Jackson trembled. "Leave him alone a moment and let him get his breath back."

21

"What's the problem? It's only dark down there…" Depthstride's son said.

"He can't sound like we can." Daychaser looked over with a frown. "How would it affect you if you couldn't hear or see anything around you in the darkness?"

"I'm sorry Jackson, I didn't mean to scare you." Depthstride's calf said meekly while Jackson took a few deep breaths.

"Are you ok Jackson? Whatever could've caused you to be so frightened by a simple touch?" Depthstride's mate asked worriedly.

Jackson took a few deep calming gasps before he quietly answered. "We were attacked."

He shuddered while the memories spiraled around in his head. "When I was really little, me and my family were being hunted by the Toxicshade, and they attacked us on a really dark night." A shiver wracked his body. "It was completely overcast and dark and I fell behind the others in the confusion…" He shakily pulled up his shirt to reveal a set of long scars on his right side. "I got hit by the attack of a shadow mage before my grandpa was able to rescue me and we were able to get away."

Another shiver sent his body shuddering and he let go of his shirt. "I nearly died from my wounds, and ever since that night…" Jackson shook his head and looked up at the sky. "I can't handle being in the dark, and the darkness of deep water is even darker than that night was." He took another long breath to try and steady his nerves. "I'm sorry, I just can't go into the depths right now."

There was a long moment of silence before Depthstride spoke.

"It is we who should apologize, Jackson. Had we known, we never would have pressured you like we did."

"We only wished to share part of our world with you." Depthstride's mate shifted as is uncomfortable. "And the truth is, the old tales speak of Sonaeko like you who were afraid of the dark, even some of the lightborn." An embarrassed look crossed her eyes. "We thought perhaps you just needed to adjust to the dark waters and that we could help you. The old stories speak of our kind helping Sonaekians with such a fear to overcome it, allowing them to explore the world hidden below the layers of light ocean. There are many beautiful things you can discover deep below the surface waters."

"I guess we were hoping to help you overcome your fear." Depthstride's son said quietly. "Like our ancestors used to."

A sad smile touched Jackson's lips, though his body still trembled. "I appreciate you wanting to help." He paused, looking over at Depthstride's mate. "I'd never heard those stories about the Sonaekians who were afraid of the dark." He shivered. "I guess it's kinda nice to know that others had a problem similar to mine."

Jackson fidgeted a bit before giving Depthstride and his mate a shy look. "Maybe you could tell me more about the old stories and the wonders of your world, it might help it seem less..." He looked down into the dark and shuddered. "Terrifying, if I heard about the beautiful and wondrous things of the deep."

The whales exchanged a long look before they all seemed to smile.

"That sounds like a wonderful idea." Depthstride's mate agreed.

"Then let's start with the unique life that we can sound around the deep crevasses of the deep waters." Depthstride began.

"Or perhaps the undersea coral reefs we find around the undersea mountains and hills." His mate added with a wistful whistle. "They truly are a wonder to sound, though I'd love to know what colors they are, if they have any."

Daychaser gave Jackson a wink before the whales began regaling them with stories about the deep, and Jackson sighed in relief. Maybe now the rest of the trip would be a bit less stressful. Maybe.

CHAPTER THREE
WHIRLPOOLS

The next morning the group was surprised by a large group of tan colored seafaring rays who soared through the water towards them on their large fins. The diving whales aided Startide and Daychaser in forming a protective circle around Jackson when the fever of rays changed directions, coming closer to inspect the odd group of creatures.

"What'cha hiding in there?" The largest ray inquired once the group came closer. "You divers normally put your calves in the middle, but yours is helping hide something."

"And good morning to you too." Startide said somewhat primly.

The rays swirled around warily for a moment when Startide moved closer.

"You must be daft to travel with a killer whale Depthstride." A smaller ray said in surprise although her eyes held a disgusted look. "She'll lead the rest of her pod here to eat their fill and leave the rest to the depthfeeders."

"Sailin, mind your tongue please." Depthstride quickly spoke when Startide got a shocked and deeply insulted look in her eyes. "She is an oroca, not a killer whale."

"Aha, then you must be protecting the Sonaeko." Another ray crooned. "We heard he'd been spotted heading east with an oroca and a cadolin."

Jackson unintentionally locked eyes with the female ray, Sailin, when she peeked through the wall of whales trying to block him from view. He felt his heart skip a beat once he saw a worried look flash across her eyes. "You all best start hurrying your pace." She warned. "A new pod of killers has been spotted in these waters, they've barely stopped to eat and have been heading steadily east."

Daychaser, Jackson, and Startide all exchanged a frightened look.

"How many are in the pack?" Daychaser asked.

"Are there any calves?" Startide added.

The rays mumbled amongst themselves for a moment before the largest one answered for the group. "There are around seven in the pod, no calves."

"Daggerfin and Sharkflayer..." Jackson gasped while his friends groaned.

"Who?" Depthstride asked, looking troubled.

"A pod of dishonored killer whales that attacked us before." Jackson bit his lip worriedly. "They planned to kill and eat Daychaser and one of our other friends before capturing me."

"They believe the false myths about a lightborn restoring honor and power!" Startide made a revolted face. "Stupid to think that holding someone hostage against their will would restore lost honor."

"We don't have time to worry about that now." Daychaser interjected, looking back at the rays. "Do you know how close behind us they are?"

"They're probably less than a day or so behind you." Sailin said emphatically. "If I were you, I'd head south towards the whirlpools.

Their strong currents and the magic that courses through them might help throw the killer whales off."

"I don't know the seamarks as well there…" Startide said uncertainly, "and I've heard enough to know the whirlpools often create horrible storms."

"If you continue your present course, they'll catch up to you soon. You haven't been traveling very quickly." The large ray pointed out and Jackson colored up in embarrassment, knowing full well he was the reason for the slow pace.

Daychaser flicked his fins before slashing his tail determinedly. "Then we'll have to take our chances with the whirlpools. They are only a couple days south of us."

"And the change in direction could throw the killer whales off long enough for us to gain some distance." Depthstride added before turning to his mate. "I think you and our dear daughter must leave us for now. We'll try to meet up with you at Mawtooth Canyon once we've gotten Jackson and his friends safely out of our feeding grounds."

Depthstride's mate crooned her agreement, giving her calf an urgent nuzzle before she squeed a hasty goodbye to Jackson and the others. "Travel safely lightborn and friends, may the Creator of the currents light your way."

"May the Creator light your way as well." Startide said, dipping her head as Jackson waved and Daychaser squeed his farewells.

"Will you be coming with us?" Daychaser asked the rays. "We could really use your help."

The rays mumbled amongst themselves for a moment before they shot off at high speeds, vanishing from sight and leaving nothing but only a trail of bubbles.

"Cowards." Depthstride's son said with a whale-ish frown.

"I can see why they fled; they don't have any good defenses against hunters such as killer whales." Depthstride said, although his eyes held a disapproving look. "I thought perhaps Sailin would've helped though."

"We don't have time to worry about it." Daychaser said, taking charge. "Jackson, grab hold of Startide's dorsal fin. We'll travel that way for a time until you get tired and need to rest in your bag." He looked over at Depthstride. "We'll go southward as fast as you can travel. Once we've gotten a little distance between us and Daggerfin's pack, maybe you could tell Startide and I some of the seamarks along our route while we swim. That way we can hopefully regroup if we're separated." He began moving forward. "Let's go, we don't got a moment to lose."

Jackson held tight to Startide's fin while the group swiftly changed course and fled southward. Everyone was as silent as possible as they flew through the water, sometimes skimming along the surface so the whales, Startide, and Daychaser could take quick breaths as they swam. As the day turned to two, Jackson started using the seaweed growing from his bag to form a thick rope that he tied around Startide's middle to help him hang on. Once night finally fell, he'd collapse into the bag to sleep, exhausted from the smart pace the others had set.

The third morning he was woken by Daychaser urgently tapping the bag and Jackson practically flopped out into the water, having teleported from a laying position.

"What's wrong?" Jackson asked quietly while he quickly tried to rub the sleep from his eyes.

"Nothing terrible yet." Startide whispered as she urged him forward. "Take your bag and hold onto my fin, we'll talk as we swim. Quietly though."

Jackson slipped on his bag and latched onto Startide's dorsal fin before they took off again. "Where's Depthstride?"

"Father went deeper so he could try to figure out where the killers were without them noticing him as easily." Depthstride's son said in a hushed voice. "We're used to dealing with killer whales. They're our main predator, unless we swim further north, then we have to deal with being hunted by the Fallen."

Jackson felt Startide shudder at the mention of the Fallen and noticed a faint symbol form on his hands which petered out after a second. *Wonder what that was about?* He thought.

After a bit, Startide and the others quickly surfaced for a breath and a quick break. Jackson took the chance to poke his head above the waves and felt a firm breeze blow past him. *Cloudy up ahead...* He thought when he saw the swirl of dark clouds beyond as a heavy feeling of foreboding settled on his chest. His brows shot up when bright blue energy skyrocketed up from the sea. The magic coursed through the clouds and made him jump when his hands suddenly flashed with the strange symbol once again.

"Uh, you guys?" He said, sticking his head underwater. "There's a storm brewing up ahead, and it has some strange magic affecting it..."

"You sure?" Daychaser asked, turning around from sounding behind them to check for danger.

Jackson nodded. "And the Star of the Sea keeps making a strange symbol form on my hands, but I don't know what it means."

"It means danger!" A voice said urgently in Jackson's mind and his eyes widened.

"We don't have time to figure that out now. We have to get closer to the whirlpools while we still can." Startide said hurriedly. "Depthstride said the magic flowing around there messes with sounding calls. That'll give us the chance to hide before we move towards the strand."

Jackson looked back at the clouds when another charge of magic rippled through them. "I don't know Startide…" He said hesitantly. "That magic seems pretty potent, it could be more dangerous than the killer whales."

"Will it kill us and hold you hostage?" Startide asked firmly.

"It could kill us, but I don't really know." Jackson's tone wavered.

"We'll take our chances with the whirlpools." Depthstride's son shot forward. "At least they offer us an unknown fate."

Jackson looked back and gave Daychaser a meaningful look before he pointed at the storm and made an alarmed expression. Daychaser looked down at the depths for a moment in thought before he shook his head and pushed forward.

Jackson's shoulders slumped once he saw another pulse of magic hit the clouds, creating a pseudo thunder-like noise. "If something bad happens when we get there, no-one better say I didn't warn them." He mumbled while he grabbed Startide's fin, knowing full well the others would hear him.

Depthstride joined them not a moment later, his eyes wild with fright. "Hurry my friends!" He cried. "The killer whales are not but five whale lengths behind me!"

"GO!" Startide's eyes bulged as Daychaser shot forward! The group surged through the waves, straining to make it towards the storm as quickly as they could. While he was dragged along, Jackson started feeling a powerful current pull them eastward and saw another pulse of magic up ahead, traveling from the east through the water. "Don't go into the magic!" He warned while his friends charged towards the pulse as it coursed westward.

A triumphant and haughty sounding squark made Jackson grimace and he quickly looked back to see the killer whale pod charging headlong towards them! He scowled when the long thin gray eyepatches of Daggerfin and Sharkflayer flashed into view.

"We'll hold them off! You flee further into the vortex!" Depthstride called before he and his son flipped around, barreling back towards the large killer whales while making strange bugling calls.

"Depthstride!" Jackson cried when the two whales, who were only slightly larger than the largest killer whale, slammed into two of the pursuers! Four of the seven killers slowed to attack the two whales who lashed the water around them with their tails before they dove into deeper waters, leading the main part of the pack after them.

Three of the killers kept on with their pursuit and Jackson shuddered when he saw the dark slitted eyes of Daggerfin and her sister as they shot closer! Behind them was their nephew, Shadowtorrent, who was pushing himself to get beyond his aunts.

"Startide they're gaining."

"I know, I know!" She gasped while she and Daychaser shot to the surface for a quick breath as they pushed themselves to go faster.

They truly are used to hunting other dolphinkin... Jackson shivered, feeling disgusted when he saw Daggerfin give her version of a smirk as she and her sister took a quick breath.

"Oh no..." Jackson whispered once he saw other dark shapes start closing in from the west.

"I don't even want to know!" Daychaser said, making Jackson pause before he clenched his fist which began to glow.

"Blades of evening sun."

Jackson's right hand began glowing brightly as he seemingly pulled light from the water and fired! Multiple beams of light flew from his fingers, slashing through the water in cutting spirals as they sliced towards the pursuing killers! Daggerfin barely dodged the one aimed at her while her sister got caught by another, making her screech in pain when the light cut a long burn mark down her side before barely cutting Shadowtorrent's dorsal fin. The other beams were dodged by the other member of the pack but the whole display made the group falter, which is what Jackson was after.

Daggerfin's sister slowed considerably but didn't stop, leveling Jackson with a glare that was a frightening reminder of their plan to bite his fins off when they captured him.

Jackson started the spell again but held it at the beginning stages, making small eddies of light spiral around him. The killer whales moved side-to-side nervously, but continued forward while Jackson and his friends were suddenly pulled eastward by the strengthening current of the whirlpool.

"Whatever you're doing I hope it made them leave." Daychaser gasped as he went up for another breath.

"No, they're just nervous about charging head on." Jackson said as a couple of the whales' broke formation to skirt the sidelines. "They're trying to trap us against the whirlpools."

Startide squeed in frustration and Jackson felt her muscles tense before she snapped her jaws angrily.

"Do I need to teleport you into the bag Daychaser?" Jackson asked, seeing his friend was starting to flag.

"You said there wasn't water in there." Daychaser said.

"I can change that really quick; I know you haven't got your landform figured out yet." Jackson said. "Just make sure the magical artifacts don't get banged up too bad."

"I'm not done yet." Daychaser said stubbornly, "and I promised to help protect you."

"We all promised to protect each other." Jackson responded when Startide started to slow as well.

"Surrender now and just maybes we'll spare your friends!" Daggerfin's sister yelled.

"Or maybe we won't." Jackson heard another whale laugh. "I haven't eaten cadolin in ages!"

"Maybe I could teleport them all into my bag and let them sit there awhile!?" Jackson ground out tightly before he shook his head. "Nevermind, I have to have permission from the creature, or at least a friendship."

"Neither of which apply in this situation." Startide snorted as the current got stronger and pseudo thunder suddenly boomed above them.

"You could just give yourself up now lightborn, it'll give your friends a chance. We'll make sures to keep you well fed until our honor returns." Sharkflayer gave a sinister snicker. "Course we might eat them before getting you a snack."

Jackson's eyes flashed before he catapulted seven light arrows at Sharkflayer, five of which hit their mark, cutting deep into her head and sides. The whale screamed and lashed about in pain before she stilled when the arrows faded.

While Sharkflayer tried to shake off the pain, her sister gave Jackson an icy stare. "Try that again and–"

"I'll level you all with a second, more powerful, round!" Jackson interrupted, his eyes flashing. Daychaser and Startide both gave him a surprised look when his tail faintly flashed. "I've lost enough, I don't plan to lose more to the likes of you!"

The killers all hesitated uncertainly for a moment before Daggerfin and her sister sneered and moved in closer.

"Prove it little pup." Her sister hissed.

"Wait." Shadowtorrent moved in front of his aunts. "This is going nowhere."

"What's gotten into you Shadowtorrent?" Sharkflayer chided. "We was generous enough to keep you in our ranks after yous mother left for another pod, don't stand in the ways of our honor."

"Think for a minute! If we kill his friends, what will that do? He already hates us; do you seriously think he'll let himself stay caught. He'd likely just keep attacking us until we either kill or almost kill him." Shadowtorrent said, his firm voice almost pleading. "And if we almost kill him, then he'll likely just die! Then we're right back where we started! HONORLESS!! Hated by every creature and the ocean itself."

"Don't be ridiculous, once I's bite off his fins he'll be not able to do anything." Daggerfin's sister snarled.

"Listen to your nephew." Startide hissed. "Kill him and us and your pod will continue to suffer, as well as the whole ocean."

"Don't you even realize I'll die if you bite my arms off?" Jackson added with a blank look. "You know nothing about human anatomy, don't you?"

"We'll be fine, his sharp things don't even hurt that bad now." Sharkflayer grinned darkly. "I'm sure we'll figure out something." She said as she started forward. "Like who will taste the best first."

Daggerfin and her sister began moving forward, shoving Shadowtorrent out of the way. The young male's eyes hardened while his aunts and Uncle closed ranks. Suddenly the young whale charged forward, crashing into them and violently throwing them aside.

"SWIM!" He yelled when Jackson and his friends stared in shock. "GET OUT OF HERE!"

Startide shook herself, snatching Jackson up in her mouth as she and Daychaser dove into the lashing current while the whales tried to fight off Shadowtorrent's attacks! As some of the other whales joined the fray, Shadowtorrent bit down on his uncle's dorsal fin while slapping one of his aunts across the face with his tail.

Some of the other killers shot after Jackson and his friends while another whale slammed into Shadowtorrent, making the whale's bite loosen. The young whale was promptly thrown off by his uncle who smacked the younger male so hard across the snout it left him stunned, hanging limply in the water while his aunts, uncle, and the rest of the pod tore after Jackson and his friends.

"Oh no…" Jackson said again.

"You said that already!" Startide gasped.

"No, OH NO THAT!" Jackson cried, pointing towards the bright blue light that soared towards them!

Jackson grimaced when the magic hit, crackling through him and the others while thunder crashed above them. He felt the magic around them suddenly shift upwards and a crack formed in the water itself before bright beams of energy shot into the clouds! As another crack formed in the air above them, there was a mighty roar before the whirlpool surged, snatching Jackson and his friend into its grasp!

As Jackson was sent spiraling out of control, he somehow saw the pursuing killer get torn into the vortex, spiraling away while Daychaser spun closer to him. Jackson managed to grab onto Daychaser's tail when he was pulled past while Startide somehow managed to gently bite down harder on Jackson's chest as they were dragged away. "HOLD ON!!" She yelled through her teeth!

"I CAN'T MUCH LONGER!!" Jackson cried, tears streaming from his eyes.

Just when he lost his grip on Daychaser's tail, the Star of the Sea came flashing forth from his hands. The star spun around them before enveloping him and his friends in a drop-like sphere before they faded out of consciousness.

CHAPTER FOUR
QUESTIONS AND CORAL REEFS

U gh…" Jackson groaned as he rubbed his head and shook himself, blinking a few times before his eyes shot open. "DAYCHASER? STARTIDE?"

"Over here!" Daychaser grumbled, rousing himself from his spot at the surface and looked around uneasily. "Startide?"

"I'm ok." She slapped her head against the surface a few times, like she was trying to shake off a suckerfish. "I think."

Jackson gave a relieved sigh and then glanced around anxiously. "Uh, where are we?" He shivered when he noticed the swirl of the whirlpools not far off.

"Uh…" Both Daychaser and Startide followed Jackson's gaze and inched away from the swirling waters. "Wait!" Daychaser suddenly looked around urgently, his eyes wide. "Do you see any of the dishonored?" His question made them all whip around and scan the area nervously.

"What a relief, I can't sound them anywhere." Startide let out a stream of bubbles in emphasis.

"Me neither, perhaps they got sucked into the whirlpool or got away: they weren't as far in as we were when the current increased." Daychaser gave Jackson an apologetic look. "Guess we owe you an apology for doubting your warning about the magic."

Jackson shrugged. "It's ok. Not like we were safe outside of the whirlpools either…" He shook his head. "We were trapped between a rock and a hard place."

"I think you mean, stuck between a wave and a hard place." Daychaser gave Jackson a teasing smirk.

"Whatever." Jackson rolled his eyes. "Same thing." He smiled wryly and repeated his earlier question. "Anyone know where we are?"

"At the moment I'm betting we're lost…" Daychaser sounded relieved and worried at the same time, "but at least we got away from the dishonored."

"The whirlpools must've carried us a long way from where we were." Startide commented while slowly rotating herself around in a circle. "I haven't been able to find any seamarks or currents I recognize, and my grandpodmother or the medians didn't mention any of the seamounts or the canyons I can sound." She whistled worriedly. "The water feels a lot warmer and tastes quite a bit different too, so maybe we got pulled southward before we managed to get ourselves out of the spiraling currents."

"You mean the Star of the Sea got us out of the currents." Daychaser interjected. "Don't you remember it flashing out of Jackson's hands?"

Startide paused for a second. "I… do…" She looked over at Jackson. "Before I fell… asleep? Is that what it feels like when you sleep? Not being aware of anything?"

"Basically." Jackson smirked. "Glad you guys finally understand what it's like for me every night."

"I don't know if I liked it…" Startide frowned uncertainly, "but at least we're all here together and we're safe." She gave a longing glance at a passing school of fish. "But wherever here is, there are plenty of fish, especially towards what I think might be an island to the south."

"An island?" Jackson and Daychaser both asked in surprise.

"I think so…?" Startide eyes squinted. "The currents have been a bit jumbled on what's over there, but they carry word of plenty of fish and some reefs over that direction." Startide tilted her head for a better sound. "Plenty of noise in that direction, which normally means a lot of fish, or a lot of rough water, but this sounds more like fish."

Jackson smirked mischievously. "Well, we can either get you some frozen fish from my bag, or we can head that direction to look for something fresh."

"Something fresh!" Startide blurted out before a sheepish expression crossed her snout. "I mean…" Startide began. "It will do us some good to have some fresh meat. It tastes better and has more nutrients than that frozen stuff, I'm sure. Although, it's still wonderful that you have the ability to store food for us on our journey."

Daychaser batted at Startide with a whistling chuckle. "He's teasing you Startide. I think he's more anxious to get to some shallower water and land, than you and I are to get back on a diet of fresh fish."

Startide laughed. "I can't guarantee the shallow water will be clearer, but I do think there is an island or maybe a small chain of them off to the south. I say we go there to rest before trying to figure out where we are, and how to get to the strand from here."

"I'm in, race you guys!" Daychaser took off with a happy squee.

"Hey wait up!" Jackson quickly reached out to grab Startide's fin before they took off after Daychaser. Jackson swam along as fast as he could so he wouldn't burden Startide, keeping the strokes of his tail in time with hers.

The three raced through the waves excitedly while they headed southward, the sky clear and bright above them. Jackson even dared to send a couple of beams of light shooting after Daychaser to try to keep the seawolf from getting too far ahead.

Eventually Daychaser slowed, still laughing from the chase and Jackson smiled. They were all feeling better now that they knew there was shallower water ahead, and the promise of food.

As the morning turned to afternoon, they neared the area where Startide thought she'd sounded an island and—to Jackson's relief— she was right. Jackson took multiple flying leaps above the waves to look at the growing speck of green until he finally let out a whoop and splashed back into the sea with a huge grin on his face. "Oh, thank heavens! It truly is land! Wonderful clear, green solid ground!"

Startide rolled her eyes. "Technically solid ground shouldn't be green, also we've been swimming over solid ground for weeks now."

Jackson gave Startide a mock glare while Daychaser chuckled. "Well, technically, I can SEE this solid ground, which will be the first I've seen in weeks!"

They all laughed, resuming their swift and cheerful pace towards the island as the first sight of the sandy sea floor came into view. Jackson and Daychaser exchanged a look before they both grinned and bolted down to the sandy bottom. Jackson swam close over the sand, bringing his tail down hard and sending a billowing cloud of sand in his wake while Daychaser made another one next to his. As the cloud of sand billowed up towards the surface, they both turned and bolted into it, laughing enthusiastically while they darted around inside the cloud as they tried to catch each other. Startide hovered a few whale lengths away, watching their antics with a dry look, grumbling under her breath about how silly males were.

"Oh, come on Startide, we're just having a bit of fun." Daychaser said with a brighter smile than he'd had for weeks. "That, and sand means I might be able to find some types of sand-dwelling fish, I've been craving one of those for ages now." He snapped his jaws hungrily. "Ooo, some side eyes sound delicious right now."

"Side eyes?" Jackson asked before he snapped his fingers. "Oh, your mean those weird fish you and your aunt love. Forgot that's what your pod called those."

"Well, their eyes are on the side of their head. Strange looking fish but delish!" Daychaser said eagerly.

Startide smiled. "I'm hoping the island has some streams big enough for some hookjaw fish, or even some trout. I'd about kill for a large one right about now."

"You will kill for some if we find any, you shouldn't eat them alive you know, that's just cruel." Jackson said with an impish smirk.

Startide gave an exasperated sigh while Jackson and Daychaser snickered.

They all resumed their course towards land, traveling in contented silence that was broken only by Jackson breaching every few minutes to get a better look at the island. To Jackson's delight the isle looked to be quite large, and was covered with bright green jungle. The sunlight was so warm and bright in the clear, shallow waters that Jackson even took a few deep dives down to explore the bottom, happily swimming after a couple schools of bright fish who scattered in a sparkling cloud of scales when he swam through them.

At long last, Startide could make out the sounds of waves crashing onto the rocky shores as the seafloor suddenly traveled upwards, morphing into a beautiful forest of brightly colored corals!

Jackson's jaw dropped open as shoals of beautifully colored fish swirled about him, weaving amongst gaudy colored corals as he swam further into the reef. When a large parrot fish and a group of brightly colored fish with fins like butterfly wings swooshed by, Jackson found himself wishing dearly that he could be sharing the sight with his family. He followed the line of large branching corals that reached boldly up towards the surface and blinked from the bright sunlight dancing on the waves. When he looked down, he saw strange brain looking corals and giant clams nestled amongst the more fragile looking lace and fan corals while sea slugs, sea urchins, crabs, shrimp, starfish, and other creatures meandered around.

Curious fish darted and billowed through the coral around him as a few sea snakes, a small porpoise, and some sharks took notice. Jackson grew slightly self-conscious when he heard the whispers and exclamations of the locals once they spotted his white hide traveling through the coral gardens.

"It's the lightborn!"

"The awakened Sonaeko?!"

"Why is it here?"

"Is it lost?"

Jackson stopped and turned around when Startide cleared her throat. She and Daychaser were hovering at the edges of the reef, unwilling to go into the shallower waters Jackson had swum into.

"Oh, sorry Startide." He quickly swam back over, making the schools of fish closest to him scatter away.

Daychaser looked just as awestruck as Jackson was by the sight of the brilliant coral forest and the seawolf's jaw hung open in awe. Startide's eyes were wide, and she looked like she was committing every part of the reef to memory so she could tell her pod about it later.

"I've never seen the reefs of the warm waters before." Startide said quietly. "I've heard about them of course, but I never thought they would be so colorful and bright."

"I know, and there are so many fish, thousands of them." Daychaser commented, only for Jackson to give him a dry look when the seawolf's stomach grumbled hungrily.

"Really?"

"What? I'm hungry ok." Daychaser said defensively. "I've never seen this many kinds of fish in one place in my entire life."

His comment sent many of the nearby fish dashing into the coral to hide while others hovered close to nooks and crannies they could dart into, if needed. Jackson noticed the whisper that was traveling through the reef died down slightly once the fish grew concerned over being hunted.

"Perhaps we should go look for those side eyes you were craving earlier." Jackson suggested, hating to see all the fish vanish into the crevasses of the coral. "And leave the reef fish alone."

At his comment he noticed some fish hesitantly poked their heads out from their bunkers.

Daychaser looked thoughtful. "Ok, most of these fish are too small for me right now anyways. I want a meal, not a snack."

Startide giggled. "Judging by the sound of your stomach you're wanting a couple meals, not just one!"

They laughed and slowly turned to head back towards the sandy flats they had crossed earlier. Jackson hung back to whisper an apology to the reef fish who shivered their fins in thanks. He gave them a quick wave goodbye before following after Daychaser and Startide.

"I think I might head off and scout the southern shoreline for a bit." Startide said after Jackson caught up to them. "I haven't heard any sound of oroca or killer whales on the currents, although killer whales are usually harder to detect unless they're hunting."

Jackson paused and listened hard for a minute. "The currents are clearer here. I can actually hear a little bit." He left out that he could mostly hear the reef life speaking about seeing him, which was growing ever louder by the second. However, he definitely didn't have Startide's ability to listen to and hear the currents.

Daychaser just shrugged his flippers. "I got nothing, but we know that's normal for me."

Startide had a thoughtful look on her face. "You make a point Jackson. I hadn't really noticed it at first, but it does seem like the currents are clearer here, unhampered even." She spun about and looked back at the island curiously. "It reminds me of something my grandpodmother used to talk about, but I can't remember what exactly…"

Daychaser's stomach rumbled again and Jackson and Startide snickered.

"Well maybe we'll all think a bit better on a full stomach." Startide said wryly. "I'll go check out the southern shoreline while you two find some food here; I'll meet you back here before sunset."

"Sounds good." Jackson glanced behind him. "Although, I might head closer to shore to look for a rocky outcropping to sleep on tonight. Sleeping under the stars sounds amazing after all these weeks of sleeping in a bag." He gave a happy sigh.

"I'll try to see if I can talk to any porpoises or dolphins that might be in the area, perhaps they might know where we are." Daychaser said, swishing his tail back and forth slowly while he mused. "Doubt there are any seawolves in this area, but if I run into any, I'll try to talk to them."

"Sounds like a plan, see you two later." Startide gave them a happy flick of her fins and set off to the south, whistling happily to herself.

Daychaser howled a quick goodbye before he swam towards the sandy bottom. "You comin?" He glanced back when Jackson didn't follow.

Jackson shook his head. "I'd like to go look at the reef for a bit before checking around the western shoreline. I think I saw some sandy beaches and maybe a sea bird rookery when I was jumping earlier, and I'd like to go explore a calm quiet area of the ocean for awhile."

Daychaser nodded, a spark of humor twinkling in his eyes. "Needing some time alone for a bit?"

Jackson gaped, embarrassed that Daychaser saw through him so easily.

Daychaser laughed. "Oh come on Jackson, I learned long ago that you like to go off and be left alone for a bit. You haven't been able to do that much for over a month now. Unless you count the time in your bag. Must be a human thing."

Jackson laughed. "I think it's more of a me thing, but yes, I'd like some alone time." He gave the rainbow-colored reef a wry look, "and I probably won't hang around the reef too long. Too many eyes and ears watching me." A thoughtful frown crossed his face as he lowered his voice. "You going to try and let out a howl to see if there's any other seawolves around?" He asked quietly.

A conflicted look crossed Daychaser's snout. "I might later, but I really doubt there would be any here." He looked around them with a small whine. "I don't think my kind come this far south…" He turned to leave, "but, I'll see if I can find some porpoises or dolphins to talk to. I'll catch up with ya later, unless I hear of some emergency or dishonored. Although, if the currents are unhampered here, I doubt there are really any that are hanging around." His stomach rumbled again, and he started swimming off. "I'll be coming to find you with Startide in a bit."

"Sounds good, good fishing." Jackson called, turning and swimming back towards the reef, his spirits lifting. Finally, some time to wander about alone!

Grinning wide, Jackson swam quickly back towards the reef and slowed his pace when he coursed over the brightly colored corals. He smiled warmly to the fish who gently billowed out of his way, flickering their fins in a friendly way. A large eel watched him intently when he passed, and Jackson gave it a nod in greeting. The eel poked its head out of its hole further to watch as Jackson dove around a gigantic fan coral while a group of bright orange seahorses danced around the huge branches.

Jackson was mesmerized by the menagerie of creatures around him; from the colorful sea slugs to the crabs who snapped their claws at him in greeting as he paddled past. Sea turtles, a small group of colorful ocean fairies, and a few sea snakes—that were either blue and black striped or dark purple and yellow—all seemed to pause when they noticed him, watching him with interest. A small amount of commotion caught Jackson's gaze and he looked over when several reef sharks lazily wove above the corals, the multitudes of local fish giving them a wide berth.

After a few minutes, Jackson slowed when he noticed he had a following of reef creatures tailing behind him. He let himself relax so his movements were calmer, hoping to put some of the more nervous creatures at ease. His relaxed pace had the desired effect, and after a minute many of the fish came forward to swim around him, eyeing him curiously.

"Hello," he said quietly, and a few of the fish darted back in surprise. "Sorry, I didn't mean to scare you." He apologized in a whisper.

The fish hovered for a minute before some beautiful yellow butterfly fish swam forward and drew closer to his face. "Are you the lightborn Sonaeko the currents spoke of? The one the message was about?" The largest fish asked curiously, its butterfly-like fins waving gently.

Jackson slowed to a stop before he answered, slightly apprehensive when he noticed the huge audience of reef creatures, all of whom were curious about what he'd say. "Yep, that would be me. At least as far as I know."

"Why are you here?" A small red grouper with purple stripes asked. "We thought you'd be heading somewhere else, not to these isolated reefs."

Jackson gulped nervously when more fish began crowding around as the coral itself seemed to lean in to listen. However, as he looked into the eyes of the creatures about him, he didn't see a darkened eye among them and felt slightly more at ease. "Well to be honest, I don't really know where here is. My friends and I were driven into the whirlpools by a group of dishonored and we were carried far off course…" He shrugged. "Once we woke up, we found ourselves here."

There was a collective gasp from the reef life, and a red-orange sea slug spoke up. "Dishonored? They didn't follow you here, did they?"

"They wouldn't have, you silly sea slug." A yellow seahorse said curtly. "Most of those driven into the great whirlpools are sucked into its great maw and lost forever."

A green crab snapped its claws. "You were incredibly lucky to have escaped to whirlpools with your life, did your companions survive as well?"

"Yep, we were all able to make it safely." Jackson said with a shrug that caused some of the more nervous fish to dart back.

"Those companions wouldn't happen to be the seawolf and oroca we saw you with earlier, would they?" A large blue and gold angelfish asked wryly.

Jackson smiled apologetically. "Those would be the ones, sorry if Daychaser made y'all nervous."

"We should be thanking you for encouraging him to hunt in different waters. Although I daresay the fish there won't be as thrilled." A cream and white unicorn fish said with a bit of a chuckle, its spiraling horn glistening in the sunlight.

"Y'all aren't his normal fish of choice anyways." Jackson said reassuringly. "There aren't any reefs like this where he's from, colder waters and kelp forests instead."

"Good to know, but most predators aren't overly picky when hungry." The eel Jackson swam by earlier said as it swam over. The eel's appearance made some of the fish promptly move around Jackson, so they were on the opposite side. "If you don't mind me asking, now that you're here, what are you going to do?"

Jackson stopped and bit his lip. "I honestly don't know. I guess we need to figure out where we are and then try to figure out how to get where we're going."

"Good luck leaving these chains of islands." A small shrimp said as it poked its head out from between some kelp fronds. "Haven't you ever heard of the lost reefs?"

"No... To be honest I knew very little about your watery world until a couple months ago." Jackson admitted sheepishly. "I lived on land all my life before then."

It seemed to take the reef creatures a minute to digest that information before a sea turtle spoke up. "It makes sense, the Sonaeko were lost to the seas before you suddenly popped up months ago."

"These reefs are known as the Lost Reefs or the Lost Jewels." A large green lobster said as it crawled over. "They were lost to the rest of the world during the Great War when rogue spells and magical weapons created the great whirlpools that cut us off from the rest of the seas."

"This used to be a sanctuary for the Sonaeko before the whirlpools were created, after that the Sonaeko fled along with many other creatures." A parrotfish proudly fanned its fins. "Those of us that stayed are the descendants of those that chose to stay and perish with their homes."

"You make it sound like the Sonaeko abandoned our ancestors." A small female octopus interjected disapprovingly, "but that's not what happened. Many Sonaeko's risked their lives trying to stop the whirlpools from reaching here. We know in the end they succeeded, although we don't know how, since the Sonaeko vanished right after the whirlpools were stabilized." She changed to a yellow color. "The knowledge of our reefs and the islands was lost not long after their disappearance. Although, we know about the outside world from the creatures that get brought here by the whirlpools, and from the gossip of the seabirds." She nervously looked up when a couple seagulls flew overhead.

"Oh...so there's no way out of here?" Jackson asked worriedly.

"There's one way out of here, but it's not a pleasant one." An old sea turtle said, swimming slowly around Jackson. "To the northeast there is a deep set of canyons, with sides high enough the whirlpools can't pull you away. But no one goes there, it is a place of death and stone."

"Death and stone?" Jackson questioned warily.

"Yes." The sea turtle's voice was grim. "Old magic from the Great War and the Great Petrifying still pulses through the canyons: or at least it used to when I was a hatchling, though that was many years ago."

He seemed to get lost in thought. "To those of us here, it is a forbidden place that's littered with the petrified bodies of those caught in the Great Petrifying or who carelessly wandered into the canyons and were caught by the old magic. It was also the place of a major battle during the Great War, or so the tale goes. The armor and weapons of fallen beasts and creatures are scattered amongst the stone figures, but enough of this..." He stopped and gave Jackson a long look. "You have had a long journey, and you look like you could use some rest and a good cleaning." He pointed to Jackson's backpack and clothes with his beak.

Jackson groaned. "I wish I knew how to get these things off, I could get them off my own skin but not my pack." He thumbed his pack and shirt, glowering at the abundance of little creatures and plants that had attached themselves to them during his oversea journey.

He heard a communal chuckle from all the gathered sea creatures before the small porpoise came swimming forward. "Say no more, we know just the thing!"

She swam off in a westerly direction, followed by the sea turtle, and Jackson hurried after them. The reef creatures ushered him through the coral gardens to a spot where there was a slight clearing amongst the coral beds. The elderly sea turtle swam down and tapped the earth with his beak while the rest of the creatures gathered around with knowing looks.

"Wait here." He said before swimming up for a breath.

Jackson felt a little silly while he patiently floated above the clearing. He was just about to ask what was supposed to happen when a bunch of small black and white striped fish began emerging from the cracks in the coral.

"Oh my, in all my years!" One of the largest black and white fish swam around him excitedly. "Oh my, my, my, my. I never thought I'd see the day when a Sonaeko would return to our humble reef. Oh yes this is a blessing indeed!" She stopped in front of his face and twitched her fins happily. "You aren't by chance needing a cleaning dearie? We would be ever so honored to clean for a Sonaeko, and a lightborn no less. Ah, such an honor indeed!"

She didn't wait for him to answer before she darted around to inspect him. "Hm mostly good, mostly good, the tail has a few parasites. OH, gracious me!" She swam frantic loops around his backpack and shirt. "You are utterly loaded with pests, oh dearie we must get to work at ONCE to remove these horridly delicious morsels from your shining self."

She turned and called out to the small school of striped fish that were hovering patiently below. "COME! Quickly, my dear family, we have ourselves a shark's maw worth of a job to do. Quickly now."

Jackson tensed when the school of fish suddenly disbanded and darted around him. He had to keep from twitching once a couple fish began busy working by gently nipping around on his tail while a couple swam up to his head and began poking through his hair. The fishes' little nips and nibbles as they removed small parasites and dead skin tickled like mad, and it took all of Jackson's self-control to keep from wiggling around. He noticed that five of the fish, including the large female, had dutifully set to work cleaning his bag while a handful swam around and snipped small creatures off his clothes. One, after a brief moment of inspection, looked at Jackson and pointed to his mouth with its fin. "Want me to clean your teeth lightborn?"

Jackson's eyes widened in alarm. "Uh… n-no, no thank you."

The fish fluttered its fins in acknowledgement before it went down to help clean Jackson's clothes. Jackson let out a relieved breath, the thought of having a fish swimming inside his mouth and nipping at his teeth was a bit too much for him to handle.

Though apparently, the reef fish don't seem to mind it… Jackson watched when a large grouper allowed another group of the small cleaning fish to swim into its mouth and begin purposely pecking at its teeth.

Much to Jackson's relief, the fish who had tail and hair duty finished fairly fast before they joined their brethren that were still busily working on his backpack and clothes. As the minutes ticked by, Jackson strained not to fidget nervously while the assembly of watching reef creatures seemed to swell as more and more animals came over to watch.

At long last, the cleaning fish dispersed, and Jackson gently took off his backpack to inspect it and was shocked by how well the fish did. "It… looks amazing!" He smiled as he glanced at his clothes, relieved to see they were clear of pests as well. He gave the little school of cleaner fish a deep nod. "You all did a wonderful job. Thank you, I really appreciate it."

If a fish could beam in pride, the cleaner fish were doing just that. "Our pleasure dearie, it was an honor!" The biggest fish swam around proudly. "Now where are you off to?"

"I'm thinking of heading down the coast for a bit to explore the shoreline there…" Jackson began before a loud shout interrupted him.

"AGH! NO! GET YER SORRY SCALED CARCASSES OUT OF MAH ALGEA PATCH!!"

Everyone turned to see a commotion as a distraught, but angry looking, tan and purple fish quickly darted past and began fighting off a small swarm of yellow reef fish who were quickly devouring a patch of algae. The little fish shouted and slashed the long spikes that had laid hidden against his tail while he drove the other fish away and Jackson heard an ocean fairy tisk sadly.

"Another day, another gardenerfish garden ravished." She shook her pretty little head sadly. "Poor things, they never seem to catch a break."

Jackson slowly went over to where the fish was mournfully swimming over a small, and very thrashed, looking bed of algae.

"Excuse me?" Jackson gently asked the pacing gardenerfish.

"EXCUSE ME!? Why ye darn—!" The gardenerfish stopped when it looked up from its algae patch and saw Jackson. "Uh... sorry yer lightborniness, thought you was another algae thief."

Jackson looked down at what had once probably been a fairly nice patch of algae that had been reduced to tatters. "Was this yours?"

"Yah. Ya see yer lightliness, ah had been hauling away of one of those horrahdly gluttonous spikay creatures that lahke to sneak ahn and stahrt eatan mah patch of algae, but ah had gone too far." He glared hotly in the direction of some yellow fish who were making a hasty exit.

"Ah got too fah away, and those CURRENTLESS algae aters rushed over and started devourang my weeks of harr wok and toil before ah could get back to defend mah lovely algea!" The fish yelled in the direction of the retreating fish before he sadly poked around at the small patches of torn looking algae. "Aht'll take mah weeks to get aht growin narly that good gain."

"I'm sorry." Jackson said sadly when a thought struck him, "but perhaps I can help you a bit." He kindly reached out and tapped the bare ground next to the remaining patches of algae.

The fish looked up and flared his fins grumpily. "No-fense, yer lightliness but what ya gonna do? Tand watch and distrac every fish tat comes by with yer pearly hahde." He motioned to the large audience Jackson had behind him.

Jackson laughed. "No, not what I had in mind." He gently shooed the gardenerfish back. "I'll show you what I was planning, if you'd please back up and give me a minute."

Jackson felt a bit embarrassed when the mass of reef creatures behind him moved in for a closer look as he spread his hands wide over the area where the algae had grown. He quietly started a nature spell and touched the shredded patches of algae with his fingertips before they began to glow. He smiled once the bright green glow covered the tattered fronds before they burst into action, growing quickly over the barren ground, and even spreading up the rocks around the gardenerfish's original patch.

"Aat! Ut how did?!" The little fish scurried over the patch with a look of complete awe and Jackson smirked. "Th-thank ye so uch yer lightliness, mah humblest apologaes." His voice choked with emotion. "Ye saved mah weeks of hard urk, thank ye!"

Jackson smiled. "No problem."

"How'd you do that?" The eel asked curiously.

"I can use nature magic as well as water." Jackson smiled when the happy gardenerfish went to cleaning the edges of his patch. "I'm just glad it works on water plants to."

"I've never seen anything like that." A parrotfish said while he and his friends drifted closer, giving the algae interested and slightly hungry looks. They were quickly driven off by the gardenerfish, who uttered a loud chain of angry words Jackson couldn't follow until the parrotfish were far away.

Jackson winced. *No need to get nasty...* He shook his head while the gardenerfish huffed and went back to his patch, though the rest of the reef life just seemed amused.

Jackson glanced away from the gardenerfish once he heard the movement of many fins and saw one of the reef sharks had come over to investigate. As a couple more sharks came over, many of the fish carefully edged away while the first shark eyed Jackson intently.

"Now that ya know where you are. What you planning to do now?" The shark asked as it came over. "Getting out of the canyon is no easy hunt."

Jackson paused, faintly surprised the shark had heard his earlier conversation. "I really don't know... my friends and I have to figure something out though." He bit his cheek worriedly. "We're supposed to be heading somewhere where we can talk to the Sonaeko Medians."

"Are your friends coming back anytime soon?" A school of small silver fish asked in unison as they nervously darted down towards the sheltering coral.

Jackson shrugged. "They'll be back later today, but by then they should've eaten their fill. They were both after something larger than reef fish." He gave the sharks a sideways look. "Although, Startide has a taste for shark, so I'd suggest you stay in the shallower waters if she's about."

A couple of the sharks hunched their backs in alarm.

"Thanks for the warning, we normally only have to worry about the large flathead sharks." One of them said as she calmed herself. "None of us want to be a snack."

"Think she'd go for any of us?" The old sea turtle asked.

"I doubt it, you aren't her normal type of prey." Jackson shrugged. "From what she's told me, her pod were mainly shark and fish eaters, and she's never strayed from that."

The turtles seemed quite relieved by that, although the local fish all seemed a bit nervous.

"You aren't all planning to meet here, are you?" A large bronze fish asked cautiously.

Jackson shook his head. "No, I was planning on heading west to explore a bit until they finished hunting, so they might pass by you, but they shouldn't stay for dinner."

"Not that we wish for you to leave, mind you." A blue and orange fish said, "but we would be grateful for a little less…" The fish gave the sharks and eel a wary look. "Hungry visitors."

"You know you don't need to worry about us until after dark." A shark said smugly, its eyes gleaming hungrily. "We don't like wasting our time trying to catch you during the daylight hours."

The smaller reef life seemed to give the sharks a collective glare, which only made a couple of sharks yawn in mock hunger, making some of the fish dart for cover.

Jackson shook his head, grateful he wasn't normally around when Daychaser and Startide were hunting. He knew his friends needed to eat, but he preferred to not meet the food before they began eating the food.

"We could chase you now, just for fun." A thin shark with white tipped fins teased as she roused herself from her resting place below a coral encrusted rock. A couple of her friends seemed to wake as well, making more of the reef life move away nervously.

"Now, now you lot." A huge green sea turtle said as she came swimming over. "Is this the image you all want to give the lightborn?"

A couple of sharks chuckled. "Oh come on Kelpbeak. We aren't going to go breaking old traditions, we're just having a bit of fun." One of the gray reef sharks assured. "We know the old laws, and we truly don't want to waste the energy it takes to chase fast prey in the daylight."

"We get enough to eat at night as is." The shark with white-tipped fins settled back down to rest. "It's just fun to make the fish nervous."

Jackson could almost feel the reef fishes grumbling while some of them moved off towards their normal territory, **away** from the sharks.

"Feel free to come by the reef whenever you wish, lightborn. I promise that despite the competition and the normal predator-prey conflict, that things are usually quite peaceful during daylight." Kelpbeak said, slowly paddling around him. "Although you being here has calmed things down considerably, usually the smaller reef residents are a lot noisier while they go about their afternoon."

"True, so maybe you should stick around…" Another one of the white tipped sharks said slyly, giving the remaining fish a sideways look. "Makes resting a lot more enjoyable when you can't hear fish arguing over who has the best spot for catching food on the currents."

Jackson snorted in amusement as he shook his head. "Thank you Kelpbeak, I would like to come back." He looked around at the colorful reef and smiled. "It's really a beautiful home you all have here, maybe I'll see you here soon." He gave the creatures a small wave before he swam off to the west towards the shore.

"Farewell lightborn!" Kelpbeak called as some of the sharks swished their tails in goodbye.

As the reef began to thin around him, many of the fish that chose to keep tailing Jackson started breaking away. However, it wasn't until the last outcroppings of coral were far behind that Jackson finally seemed to be all alone. With one last look at the stunning sight of the reefs, Jackson turned to continue down the coastline until he stopped to surface and look around.

While the waves gently washed around his chest, he saw a rocky outcropping up ahead and swam forward eagerly to investigate. The cry of seabirds rang through the air above as Jackson dragged himself onto the rocky outcropping and pulled himself to the top of a large boulder to get a better look at the rookeries of gulls and cormorants. The colonies of seabirds coated the cliffs and clogged the air as they flew around, vibrating the air with their cries. He watched the seabird colonies for a few minutes before slipping back into the water to explore further down the shoreline, keeping an eye out for anything dangerous.

He spotted a couple groups of small reef sharks who, like their brethren, were resting beneath rocky overhangs and outcroppings during the bright light of day. As he swiftly passed by, a couple of individuals flared their gills and fins in surprise, while others darted behind the rocks warily. Jackson didn't stop to chat, but a glance over his shoulder revealed that a few sharks had moved forwards to watch him, while the rest seemed more inclined to continue their half-nap.

Jackson encouraged the seaweed strapped to his pack to grow as he traveled, and he paused to look above the waves for somewhere he could stop to have a late lunch. He spotted a sandy section of beach next to a large, tilted spire of rock and made his way towards it. As he scrambled ashore, Jackson took a brief glance further down the beach at the small group of seals who were watching him curiously.

Crawling across the sand, he found a spot he liked and brought one of the few remaining frozen fish out for him to cook before he set to work on gathering a few pieces of sun-dried driftwood.

Once the driftwood was burning, and the fish was roasting on the small magically lit fire, Jackson began to pluck some fronds of seaweed from his bag. He rinsed the fronds off with some fresh water he conjured up, humming happily to himself as he got ready for a relaxing lunch on the beach.

CHAPTER FIVE

HORROR AT THE HARBOR

Later—after he'd finished eating—Jackson thoughtfully watched the smoke from his fire curl into the air as he settled down on the warm sand to rest for a while. Jackson had tossed his leftovers towards some crabs who were scavenging along the small beach, and he smiled contently when the little creatures gratefully dug into the food.

Enjoying the feeling of the sun shining above him, Jackson sighed, put hands behind his head, laid back on the sand, and listened to the sounds of the rolling waves as they lapped against his tail.

If we weren't lost, this would be like a vacation. He let out a calm, relaxed breath while he closed his eyes and rested.

After the sun had drifted a little ways across the sky, Jackson finally let out a quiet groan and pushed himself up. Somewhat reluctantly, he slid himself forward into the water and swam off. *I guess I should really go try to find out where exactly the Lost Jewels are, and how we're going to get to the strand."*

He noticed a few gray-brown seals swimming around a short distance away and made his way towards them, only to stop in confusion when they let out barks of warning and scattered.

Should've tried talking to the sharks. He thought once the seals vanished from sight. *Only shark that ever ran from me was that spotted shark in the kelp forest.*

Deciding against going back towards the reef just yet, Jackson moved further down the coastline where he could enjoy the quieter waters. He ran into some silvery fish, a couple stingrays, and even some small sharks, but they all fled in a panic when they saw his white hide.

What on Mythos is going on? He thought after a small tiger shark had fled at the sight of him. *Why are they swimming away like I'm going to eat them? I'm not a kraken...*

Jackson looked around uncertainly to see if perhaps he was being followed by some dangerous creature that was scaring off the other marine animals. He even used his light magic to try to detect something, but after a few minutes of searching or trying to hear something on the currents he couldn't find anything. *Odd...*

Finally, he decided to continue following the towering cliffs that jutted out from the main island, making a long, jagged peninsula that stuck out from the coastline. The sun was hanging low on the horizon when he rounded the tip of the cliffs, still puzzled as to why the different ocean creatures were fleeing from him. *It's just so weird, it's not like the reef life were scared of me...*

When another tall outcropping came into sight, Jackson decided he might as well try to see if he could get a better view of the coastline. *Maybe from up there I can get the attention of one of the seabirds' and ask them if they know a way to get out of here...*

Carefully he made his way towards the outcropping, using his growing water magic to try and keep the water calm enough that he could scramble onto a lower section of rock without getting smashed by the waves. Jackson slowly scraped his way up the large boulders, wishing he knew how to turn his tail back into legs as he climbed up to the tallest part of the outcropping he could.

"Finally." Jackson gasped once he reached the top of the outcropping and gazed over the rock-ridden coastline, smiling at the sight of verdant jungle plants dangling down the cliff sides and the tall, vine tangled, trees rising proudly into the air. Movement from further down the shore caught his eye as something big bobbed in the water and his heart immediately dropped when he saw something purple whipping around in the breeze.

"Nonononono! Please no." He whispered, a groan escaping his lips once a strong surge of wind gusted down the coastline, making a large purple and black flag fly open and flap in the breeze. Jackson broke out in a cold sweat while his chest tightened in horror. He hurriedly pushed himself backwards and quickly—but cautiously— slid down the rough rocks into the water below.

Please just be a trick of the heat! They can't be here too! Jackson pled while he snuck under the waves towards the ship.

Once he came within sight of a small dock, that had around five large vessels moored along its length, Jackson let out a long dread-filled moan. Each ship was marked with the bold markings of the Venom Nations. *Oh please, pleeeaaase don't be aligned to the Toxicshade!!!* He thought, slinking around one of the largest ships before poking his head out of the water for a better look.

A beautiful purple, black, and light green flag flapped brazenly in the breeze from atop a tall post next to the large building at the end of the pier. Jackson's tense muscles relaxed ever so slightly when he found no sign of the dark purple, red, and black of the Toxicshade's insignia anywhere in the harbor. He squinted as he stared at the flag, something about it looked oddly familiar... *It's the flag for one of the old venom clans that's for sure, but which one? I feel like I've seen it before...*

He dove under the boat to snoop around below the docks while he searched for something that might help him figure out which venom clans these were, and why the flag seemed so oddly familiar. To his surprise—and slight disappointment—whoever these clans were, they kept their harbor exceptionally clean, there wasn't any trace of debris or trash in the water around him. He'd finally given up on finding any trash or other items that could help him, and quietly surfaced next to the dock before he heard a shout.

The shout seemed to flip a switch and Jackson darted back under the water when the harbor erupted in chaos! He hastily pushed himself deeper as soldiers and mages charged onto the deck while men and women began shouting, the wooden docks vibrating with running feet!

Suddenly, glowing purple arrows hissed through the air and Jackson dove with a startled yelp once they pelted the water around him! In his fright, Jackson darted into the dark waters below while some long, glowing spears smashed through the waves and he felt the gathering of venom magic around him! He yelled, hastily throwing himself to the side when the venom magic condensed into a bright purple snakelike form and struck!

Jackson barely dodged the snake's lunge, desperately firing a series of light arrows through the coils, disrupting the magic of the spell just enough for him to dart out of the harbor into deeper water where he could hide in the shadows. As the dark waters closed in around him, Jackson heard—above the blood pounding in his ears— the sounds of men roaring orders while boats pulled in their anchors and more men fired their attacks into the waves!

"Dolphin that chases the sun, oroca of the stars and tides! HELP!" Jackson cried, magically condensing his words into a message which he sent flying on the currents while he continued his mad dash up the coastline towards the peninsula!

CHAPTER SIX
SPEARS AND SEA SNAKES

Jackson's frightened flight up the coast didn't stop until he'd rounded the peninsula and found shelter in a small cave where he collapsed onto the bottom with exhausted gasps! After a few minutes, his mind slowly began working again once his panic began to still.

Why did they attack me? And for that matter, why were they watching the water around the docks so closely? He wondered, struggling to calm his breathing when he remembered how close he was to getting hit. *I have to go find the others; they could be in danger too.*

"Daychaser, Startide!" He called out as he poked his head out of the cave, not knowing how best to find his friends in the darkening water. Forcing himself out of the cave into the shadowy seas, he used his water magic to help push his tired body up the coastline, calling for his friends every minute or two as he went.

After a while, Jackson stopped by a large boulder to rest, only to yelp in surprise when two purple and yellow sea snakes darted around it and hissed. "GAAAH!"

The snakes both snickered before the finer built one seemed to grin.

"Did we scare you?" The lighter female asked, her eyes sparkling.

"Yes!" Jackson's voice squeaked a bit from shock while he tried to calm his shaky breaths once again. "Don't sneak up on me like that, I thought you were another venom coiler spell!"

He heard the snakes laugh mischievously. "We couldn't resist giving you a bit of a fright, it's just too easy to scare you humans, Sonaeko or not." The darker male gave him a look that he was sure was the snake version of a smirk.

Jackson gave the snakes a slightly disapproving look. "Perhaps next time could you not scare the daylights out of me until after I've recovered from being attacked?"

"You were attacked? By who?" The female snake's amusement vanished.

"By the venom clans, err the humans that live further down the coastline." Jackson pointed behind him with his thumb. "I barely got away..."

"They must've thought you were the Shattered One." The male said, his features pinching ever so slightly in worry. "Around the time when the moon is new, he sometimes escapes the canyons and haunts the shoreline. I know the people here are terrified of him."

"Who?" Jackson asked.

The snakes exchanged a quick glance.

"We might not have time to explain..." The female said. "Did the humans send any ships out after you?"

"I'm pretty sure they did, although, I really haven't bothered to look behind me." Jackson said nervously. "I was trying to find my friends so we could all find somewhere safe to hide out..."

"Then we'd better hurry." The male said and started to swim off. "Come with us, your seawolf friend wasn't far from here. We'll help you find him and your oroca friend and then answer your questions."

Jackson quickly followed the snakes while they slithered quickly into deeper waters, casting a nervous glance behind him. After a couple of minutes, he was greeted with a relieved squee before Daychaser came sailing through the water towards them. "Jackson! There you are, I've been looking everywhere for you since I got your message. What happened?"

"We don't have time to explain, we need to find your oroca friend before the ships come this way." The male snake said urgently. "Quickly, and quietly now."

Daychaser gave Jackson a look that begged for answers, but Jackson shook his head while they followed after the snakes.

"Do you have any idea where our oroca friend might be?" Jackson asked the snakes.

The female snake paused for a second. "Last I heard, she was up near the old ruins looking around."

"Ruins?" Jackson asked in surprise. "Of what?"

"Oh!" The female snake said in surprise. "Right, you wouldn't know they're ruins of—"

They all turned when a loud angry razz-squeal sounded through the water.

"That's Startide!" Daychaser bolted off towards the sound with everyone else hot on his tail.

Jackson and the others dashed through the water after Daychaser as the sounds of Startide's tirade grew louder and louder. When he heard some distinctly human voices cry out, Jackson halted a moment before he let out a yell when Startide barreled into view, a long spear stuck in her side!

Startide flared her fins lividly as she charged forward, hurtling herself into a small boat slightly longer than she was! Her attack made the people on board shout in terror and Jackson held his breath when the boat tilted back and forth while arrows snapped into the water around Startide as she smashed the boat again. He saw the faint glow of a venom spell getting ready to cast and steeled his nerves, they had to get Startide out of there!

"Startide. Over here!" Jackson bolted forward towards the fray while Startide smashed into the boat again, sending it teetering dangerously to one side as a glowing dark purple spear splashed into the water! When Startide pulled away, the boat quickly swayed towards her, throwing several people overboard! Jackson's breath caught in his throat when he saw two kids, a boy and a girl, scream as they fell to the water while an older man desperately tried to grab them.

"Daychaser get Startide away from that boat NOW! Before she gets poisoned or killed. I'll handle the humans." Jackson called sternly and dove forwards, making Daychaser give him a shocked look at his stern tone before the seawolf charged towards Startide.

While Jackson shot under the ship, Daychaser rammed into Startide as she smashed into the boat again. "WE HAVE TO GET OUT OF HERE NOW!" He yelled, his call making Startide's eyes refocus slightly before she ducked out of the way of a venom spell that sent glowing green thorns cascading into the water above her. She shook her head and dashed after Daychaser into deeper water while Jackson rushed towards the two struggling kids.

Jackson quickly shot over to the kids, who looked to be around ten, as they desperately tried to swim towards the surface! Grabbing their hands in his, Jackson swiftly started dragging them upwards, and the children's thrashing stilled once they got a good look at him. Both the kids' eyes widened when he gave them a tight-lipped smile before they broke through the surface with a splash. He steadied the kids as they gasped and coughed while a man who had also fallen overboard was hefted into the ship.

Jackson quickly, and carefully, pulled the kids over to the damaged boat as an older man frantically paced alongside the railing, looking ready to leap in. He and some of the other people on board were desperately calling for the two children while others helped pull a couple of other people back into the boat.

The man cried out in relief once he saw the two children being pulled along by Jackson, and nearly fell out of the boat in his haste to get the two kids into his arms. He quickly lifted the little girl into his strong embrace before reaching down and pulling the boy onto the boat. As the boy's feet hit the deck, Jackson quickly sank down into the water and swam away to join the others who, thankfully, had stayed within earshot.

Startide's temper was still boiling when Jackson swam over, his fists clenched in worry as he apologized to Daychaser for his harshness before Startide gave him a glare.

"Why did you help them?" She demanded. "They tried to kill me!"

"There were children on board that boat, Startide, human calves." Jackson explained quietly, "and the men had poisoned spears that could've killed you really fast if they hit you with one. We had to break this up before you were killed, or the kids were hurt."

Startide froze at the mention of children and Jackson saw her anger slightly cool. "They had calves with them?"

Jackson nodded. "They fell in the water when you were ramming the boat, and a lot of human calves can't swim or swim well." He glanced back at the boat, "and neither can a lot of human adults for that matter."

Startide quietly looked over at the boat and made a strange sound. "But why did they try to kill me? And endanger their young ones?"

"I don't know…" Jackson had the same question burning in his chest, but he was more worried about Startide. "But right now, let me help you with that spear. I need to make sure you didn't get poisoned."

"We can understand them fairly well from here." The female snake spoke up. "So we should be able to listen while you help Startide."

Jackson swam over to inspect the spear that was loosely stuck into Startide's side and carefully started trying to see if it was poisoned. He couldn't find any traces of poison on the outside of the wooden handle and was just checking for a hidden venom bladder when someone started speaking on the boat.

"WHAT were you thinking Farren?! You could've gotten all of us killed!"

Jackson paused and glanced over Startide's side to get a better look whilst a middle-aged man, with dark brown hair and tough looking features, bore down on a stringy looking teenager.

"What? You heard the warning horns, what if that was the monster?" The stringy looking young man said defiantly.

The older man seemed to take a minute to calm himself before he replied. "Farren, even if that was the monster, throwing a spear at it would only have angered it enough to attack us. I specifically said that no one was to attack anything, and you have been told, **many** times, that you aren't to handle the poisoned spears. You nearly killed yourself and some of the other youths the last time you did. It's lucky you didn't manage to break the venom bladders in that spear before you threw it, or it could've poisoned the water everyone fell into!"

Jackson stopped his inspection as he and the other ocean creatures exchanged quick looks.

"The monster needs to be killed old man, or people will die again." The youth retorted.

"The killing of the monster isn't your business, especially not when we are in a boat with children on board." The older man ground out, letting out a terse sigh. "I realize you want to make an impression, but endangering others, especially children, is not honorable."

The young man sneered and started to say something else, only to freeze when a white-haired man started the chant for a very painful venom spell. The old man stopped before the spell could cast, giving the young man a stern look while bright green magic swirled around his fingers. The youth made a gurgling sound before looking down at the deck, balling his fists, and marching to the back of the boat.

As the young man sat down with a loud huff Jackson was finally able to yank the spear from Startide's side! When the spear sliced free, Startide cried out in pain, making the people aboard the boat jump nervously and the young man quickly scrambled back towards the middle of the boat.

"Sorrryyy…" Jackson quietly apologized to Startide as he teleported the spear into his bag before he gently started checking Startide's wound. Although, after hearing the old man's words, he wasn't very worried about poison. He soon let out a sigh of relief when he found no signs of poison.

"It's not poisoned Startide," Jackson whispered while he started his healing spells. "You're clear. You doing, ok?"

"It hurts like crazy…" Startide winced when Jackson's magic entered the wound, "but I don't think it got in too deep."

Jackson nodded while the wound began to close, it would leave a good scar, but he had a feeling Startide wouldn't mind too much.

"Chief Norven it's getting late, and I think I heard another warning call." A short stocky man with dark black hair said.

The man with tough features and dark hair nodded. "Do you think the boat will get us back to the docks Larsen?" He turned to a lean man with weathered skin and sun-bleached hair who was carefully checking the damaged Startide had given the boat.

Larsen nodded slowly. "We should be good enough to get back, but we need to be careful."

"Then let's go." The man waved his hand and the men set to work, even the stringy young man called Farren obediently grabbed an oar and began to paddle.

"Are we going to follow them?" Daychaser asked quietly once the boat began to fade away into the dark of night.

Jackson watched the men rowed away. "No... part of me wants to, but I think we'd better find somewhere safe to rest." He looked over to the sea snakes. "Do you know a good place where we could hide for the night?"

Elsewhere, Chief Novern bent down and pulled some towels around his two children, Terven and Leavan. "Are you two doing, ok?"

Both the children nodded, but the little boy, Terven, who had thick brown curly hair, looked out over the water with wide dark blue-gray eyes. "But who was that that saved us Dad?"

Norven stopped, *good venom spells is everyone on board?* He quickly turned and quietly whispered to his old friend and mentor, Toceth. "Is everyone here?"

The old white-haired man nodded slowly, a strange look in his eyes. "Yes Norven, everyone is present."

Something in the older man's tone made Norven pause, and he gave his mentor a long look as something in his mind clicked. "Then who was the young man that helped Terven and Leavan into the boat?"

"No one I know. Although his face reminds me of someone, but I can't think of who…" Toceth looked out over the waves. "Strange."

"Perhaps it was the monster, and he was just playing tricks on us." Another man suggested, a look of fear in his eyes.

"But his hands weren't cold…" Leavan looked up to her father with confused light blue-gray eyes as the night breeze dried the thick curly brown hair she shared with her twin brother, Terven. "I thought that Garrel said the monster felt cold…"

"Perhaps one of us just knocked our heads and don't remember helping the kids back in?" Another man ventured.

Leavan shook her head emphatically. "The boy who helped us didn't have legs, he had a tail."

Everyone on the boat within earshot stopped to look at Leavan in shock, making her hide head in embarrassment.

"That's… ridiculous." Larsen said with a disbelieving frown. "Leavan, people have legs not a tail."

"He had a tail!" Terven affirmed, a stubborn look on his face as he defended his sister. "I saw it too."

"I too thought the boy had something like a tail." Norven said thoughtfully, casting a quick gaze out to sea, "but at the time I was so worried about Leavan and Terven I didn't really notice."

"He definitely had a tail, a white one, and he looked like he was around Bennor's age." Terven said firmly.

The men on the boat exchanged slightly disbelieving glances.

"You sure you two didn't knock your heads together on your way off the boat?" The kids Uncle Derrek asked.

Elsewhere Jackson and his friend listened intently while the two sea snakes, who said their names were Spinescale and Deepbite, explained why the humans attacked them.

"There weren't humans here until many years ago when a few ships suddenly came through the canyon pass into our waters." Spinescale—the female sea snake—said with a quick look at her brother. "They seemed to be in a hurry, but when they entered the canyons, they found themselves in trouble. The canyons are full of wild and powerful magic from the Great Petrifying and the Great War.

"And it's also where the Shattered One lives." Deepbite added forebodingly.

"Who's the Shattered One?" Startide questioned.

The snakes exchanged a long look before Deepbite answered. "We don't really know, he appears to be made of cloudy, slightly clear stone, riddled with glowing magical cracks. He wanders the canyons, attacking anyone who comes too close." Deepbite's eyes slitted slightly. "When the humans entered the canyons, their ships were affected by the old magic and one of them began to sink. Some of the men saw the Shattered One and attacked him, but we don't know exactly what happened. We know one of the ships sank with a few men on board and that the humans say the Shattered One is responsible for its sinking and the death of those men."

"Their other ships almost didn't make it to the island as it was." Spinescale added. "And ever since then, around every new moon, the Shattered One will suddenly leave the canyons and haunt the beaches, as if he's looking for something. He will often scream and call out while he wanders the shores and attacks the humans, but no one can understand him."

"When he first started his hauntings, he went ashore and fought with the humans before they drove him off." Deepbite said. "He's targeted them ever since."

"Has anyone been killed when he's attacked the island?" Jackson asked, feeling horrified.

Spinescale shrugged her tail. "We don't really know. Some people were petrified, we know that much. Regardless, the humans are terrified of him, and the ocean creatures are afraid of him now too, since nearly every-time he comes a terrible storm hits not long after, and if he touches you, you'll turn to stone." Her tone was full of dread.

"And he does look a bit... unsettling." Deepbite added.

"I wonder who he is?" Startide wondered, "and what he wants."

"But why did the people attack me? They almost seem to be watching for me, and it isn't even close to a new moon." Jackson pressed.

"It's because it's monsoon season." Deepbite began, "and since the humans have begun associating bad weather with the Shattered One, they've been posting guards at the harbor. I'm assuming..." Deepbite gave Jackson a once over while he swam around him. "That they attacked you because of your white tail. I think the Shattered One is an off-white color, or light gray, I'm not entirely sure." He shrugged his coils. "I'd guess that your white and light cream hide looked too much like his."

Spinescale hissed in annoyance. "The people are on edge enough to shoot at anything that remotely resembles him. Even some things that aren't." She grumbled sourly. "Bout got blasted with a venom spell last week."

Jackson placed a hand against his head with a weary groan. "And here I was hoping we'd been dragged somewhere where things would be slightly less dangerous."

"O come on, people shooting poisonous attacks and a strange deadly creature—that seems to be enraged for no particular reason—seems like small fry compared to dishonored dolphins, small krakens, killer whales, mercenaries, and a raging ophiotaurus." Daychaser joked, earning him a glare from Startide.

"Um… So… What do we do now?" Daychaser asked after a minute.

Startide gave Jackson, who had started sinking from fatigue, a worried look. "Our next move is getting some sleep." She came over and gave Jackson a sisterly look. "We all need some rest after this evening, we'll worry about all this tomorrow."

Jackson simply nodded before he tiredly followed the sea snakes, who had offered to lead them somewhere safe to rest for the night. Spinescale happily took the lead in escorting them to a hidden lagoon on the northern side of the island, which was sheltered from the crashing waves and unwanted eyes. Inside the lagoon was a small sandy beach just large enough for Jackson to stretch out on and go to sleep.

As he looked up at the moon and stars above him, Jackson sighed contently and—for the first time in over a month—fell into a peaceful sleep under the stars.

CHAPTER SEVEN
DECISIONS AND DOCKS

Jackson didn't know how long he'd slept when something thwacked him smartly on the back. He groaned and flipped over, nearly crushing Spinescale who's alarmed hiss jolted him awake.

"Watch it will you?" Spinescale said in annoyance and flared out a beautiful pair of batlike wings.

"Sorry, I didn't realize you were so close I—?" Jackson's eyes widened. "Good spells you have wings!"

Spinescale snickered while she tucked her wings back against her body. "Of course I do, my species aren't just any ordinary sea snake you know, we used to be very strong magic users before the Petrifying."

Jackson shook his head in surprise only for a tired yawn to fight free from his throat. "Aah, sorry, how long have I been asleep?"

Spinescale flicked her tongue out. "Nearly a full day, you obviously were either sick or have really strange sleeping habits. Although, Daychaser and Startide said that it was normal for you to sleep so deep."

Jackson was feeling different for some reason, and he stopped rubbing the sleep from his eyes to stare at Spinescale. "I've slept for almost a whole day?"

"Yes." Spinescale said.

Jackson groaned. "Well, that is not normal; I normally just sleep for one night and I rarely sleep through the day... I guess I was more tired than I thought." He yawned again, why did he feel weird?

"Hmph, I still think you might be sick, that might be why your tail turned back into legs..." Spinescale said as she looked down at his legs.

"WHAT!?" Jackson bolted upwards in a flurry of sand, forgetting about the low rock overhang that protected the small beach and painfully smacked his head against it! The impact caused him to lurch forward, yelling in shock as he tumbled into the water while Spinescale quickly shot out of the way.

As he sank under the waves, Jackson clamped a hand over his mouth, feeling a warm sensation sweep over him while he scrambled towards the surface. He paused right before he broke through the gentle waves of the lagoon and gasped in relief when he saw his tail had returned.

"Hm, so your tail turns into legs when you are on land, and switches back to a tail when you're in water. Interesting." Deepbite commented as he swam over.

"I had no clue that it did that!" Jackson rubbed his very sore noggin gently in surprise. "I thought I'd have to do a spell of some kind to get my legs back." He looked over at Spinescale as she swam over. "When did my tail turn back into legs?"

"This morning actually, not long after you rolled over and pulled your tail out of the water completely." She sounded amused. "We weren't able to ask Daychaser or Startide if that was normal, since they've been off spying on the humans or talking to the elder creatures here."

Jackson stared at her for a moment. "And my tail turning into legs didn't concern you guys any?"

Spinescale gave a snake-ish shrug with her wings. "Didn't realize that it wasn't something new. Although, I was starting to think you were sick since you were sleeping so long."

Deepbite chuckled. "We tried to wake you up earlier, but you just mumbled something about your mom needing to let you have a few more minutes of sleep before you flipped over."

Jackson grinned sheepishly. "Sorry, I can be really hard to wake up." He looked up at the sand bank. "I wonder..."

He hauled himself onto the little beach, pulling himself entirely free of the water while Spinescale and Deepbite came slithering across the sand curiously. With the snakes watching, Jackson started drying himself off with a mix of wind and fire magic that quickly left his clothes and skin dry. After a minute he gasped when a strange feeling washed over him and his tail began to glow. When the glow subsided his legs had returned, pants, belt, and all.

He stared dubiously at his legs for a moment before carefully getting to his feet, taking a few shaky steps around the beach. The feeling of walking on solid ground was comfortingly familiar and brought a smile to his face.

"Missed being on land, didn't you?" Spinescale asked with a serpentine smile.

"Yes. I mean I was born and raised on land." Jackson said quietly as he held up his foot and wiggled his toes. "Although, being able to swim in the ocean is wonderful in its own way."

Deepbite smirked. "We understand the feeling."

Jackson smiled at him. "Are your kind born on land then?"

"Yes, we are born on land and must return to drink fresh water, to rest, and for the females to lay their eggs." Deepbite affirmed.

"Both the sea and land are our home, we are a part of two worlds." Spinescale gave him a friendly hiss. "Just like you are."

Jackson hummed happily. "We are, aren't we?"

"Yep. But..." Spinescale looked slowly out at the setting sun. Suddenly, they saw a burst of mist rise from the ocean when Startide surfaced to breathe as she and Daychaser swam into the lagoon. "Right now, we all need to take to the other half of our home. It looks like Daychaser and Startide are back."

Jackson slipped back into the water and followed the snakes through the lagoon, meeting Startide and Daychaser in the middle.

"Morning sleepy head." Daychaser grinned while he batted Jackson's shoulder with his snout. "We have a lot to tell you since you dozed off into the human sleeping realm."

"We've been talking to some of the local creatures and have found out more about the humans, although learning more about the Shattered One has been difficult." Startide said, looking uneasy.

"We learned that the humans have only been here for about ten years, and that some of them were killed when they came through the canyons." Daychaser continued. "We're also told that any creature who wanders too close to the canyons is almost always turned to stone."

"And that their stone bodies are arranged at the ends of the canyons by the Shattered One like trophies." Startide shuddered.

Jackson shivered. "Did he do that with the humans too?"

"There are human bodies at the end of the canyon." Deepbite answered. "A couple of whom were frozen during one of the Shattered One's visits to shore."

"Ever since that happened, the humans keep using some type of powerful magic to give their mages a boost of magic to use against the Shattered One. It usually drives him off." Spinescale added, "but like we said, we all keep a wide berth of the human settlements around the new moon, since the whole village is on high alert and occasionally fires at something that isn't the Shattered One."

Jackson sighed. "And we're stuck here in the middle of it all…"

"With no way to contact the medians…" Startide added ruefully.

Daychaser grumbled. "What can we do though? We gotta get Jackson to the strand somehow, the medians made it clear we needed to get there as fast as we could."

"The only way I've ever heard of anyone making it to the outside world has been through the canyons." Deepbite added thoughtfully. "Although, even that has become more of a myth to most of us who live here. Ever since the humans came, no one has even gone near the canyons if they can help it."

Spinescale's eyes brightened when an idea struck her. "Toxic, hey Morningshell would know about it, she's one of the oldest creatures in these waters." Her eyes slitted in an annoyed way. "She'd definitely know something about how to get out of here."

"Who's Morningshell?" Jackson asked.

"An old sea turtle who rattles on forever about the old days." Spinescale rolled her eyes. "Fit to drive one nuts with her stories, but I think she'd know more about the canyons than anybody else."

"Do you think we could talk to her?" Daychaser asked hopefully, not looking bothered by Spinescale's annoyance with the turtle.

"I ain't getting her, the last time I tried to talk to her I got stuck listening to her tales all afternoon, I couldn't even get away for a snack." Spinescale gave Deepbite a sly look. "Maybe Deepbite would go ask her if she would meet with you."

Deepbite didn't look very thrilled with the idea either. "How about I go find Slicetooth and see if he'd go ask her to meet Jackson and the others here tomorrow morning? Slicetooth seems to enjoy her tales more than most."

"Toxic, sounds good to me." Spinescale smirked, "and hopefully they'll get here by morning."

"I'm sure Morningshell will happily make time to meet a lightborn." Deepbite made a hissing sniff. "I'll go find Slicetooth then, I'll meet you all back here later."

"Thanks Deepbite!" Jackson called when Deepbite went swimming off.

As Deepbite vanished from sight, Startide went up to the surface for a breath and Jackson gave her a searching look when she grimaced.

"What?" She asked, sounding slightly sheepish.

"Is the spear wound hurting you today?" Jackson asked suspiciously.

"Yes, no. Um… maybe a little." Startide admitted, looking away guiltily.

"Is that why you kept lagging behind earlier?" Daychaser looked surprised. "I just assumed you were just tired, since we both hardly rested last night."

"I am tired." Startide said, "but the wound has been hurting pretty bad too."

"Let me take a quick look at it, I have a spell that might help dull the pain a bit." Jackson insisted, swimming over to hold up his hand while Startide obediently turned onto her side to let him get a better look.

"I wonder how those human calves are doing after their fall last night." Daychaser wondered while he and Spinescale watched Jackson use a healing spell on the wound in Startide's side.

"I've been wondering about them too…" Jackson said as he switched to another spell. "They sure looked scared; I don't think they really knew how to swim that well."

"I know a way we could go check on them…" Spinescale said mysteriously. "If you guys are brave enough to go back to the place where the humans keep their ships."

"The harbor?" Jackson stopped his spell. "Wouldn't it be dangerous to go there right now, after yesterday?"

"Hm, it might be for you." Spinescale hissed thoughtfully as she looked over his white tail. "You stand out too much."

"You could change your color to a shade of gray, like you did when we were traveling across the open waters." Daychaser suggested helpfully before he gave Spinescale a perplexed look. "Even then, why go somewhere we could be in danger?"

"A group of the human hatchlings often comes to the docks in the evening to watch the sunset." Spinescale explained. "Once it gets dark, they enjoy watching the sky for some reason." She swam towards more open waters and glanced back at Jackson. "Maybe the ones you helped yesterday will be there. If not, I'm sure the other human hatchlings will bring them up."

Startide made a disgruntled sounding razzchirp. "I'll stay here and rest thanks, I've had enough of humans for awhile." When Jackson gave her a wry look, she hastily cleared her throat. "I meant humans with legs, not you."

"If you're sure…" Jackson teased before his gaze returned to Spinescale. "I would like to know if the other kids are ok…" He moved after Spinescale before giving Daychaser a quick look. "You going to join us?"

"Sure, sounds like an adventure." Daychaser said with an impish glance back at Startide. "Better than lazing around here with nothing to do."

"I heard that!" Startide retorted, making the others chuckle before they swam out of the lagoon.

The group moved off down the coastline while Jackson changed his skin to a medium gray color. The sight made Spinescale's eyes widen ever so slightly before she smirked. "That's a cool little trick."

"It comes in handy once in a while." Jackson smiled.

"I think you mean it comes in handy a lot." Daychaser quipped.

Jackson and Daychaser stuck close as Spinescale led them further down the coast, the sea snake navigating through the shallows with ease. After a while, Jackson began to flag and gratefully hitched a ride with Daychaser by hanging onto his main dorsal fin. When they finally rounded the small peninsula of cliffs not too far from the harbor, the sun was setting behind them and Jackson felt a bubble of nervousness bounce around in his stomach.

Daychaser and Spinescale stopped for a quick breath break once they were within eyeshot of the harbor. When they'd caught their breath, they quietly slipped down near the bottom of the harbor as they snuck towards the moored ships.

"There." Spinescale flicked her tongue towards a group of around seven kids who were sitting at the edge of the dock, a few swinging their legs around while they talked.

"I can't get a good enough look at them from here…" Jackson whispered after a moment, "and I can't hear a thing that they're saying."

Spinescale looked around the harbor shrewdly and flicked her tongue out a few times. "Let's try between those two smaller boats. I don't think they'd look over that way, and we'll be hidden from the sentries on the larger ships." She slid backward before diving towards two smaller boats that were swaying in the waves.

Jackson followed after her while Daychaser, who momentarily forgot his dorsal fins could be spotted from above, swam up to the surface just long enough to be seen by some of the kids.

"LOOK!" One of the kids shouted and Daychaser made a zipping sound in surprise before he dove after Jackson and Spinescale.

"Was that a shark?" A boy asked excitedly.

"No, I think it was a dolphin." An older boy said. "The fin didn't look like a shark."

"I wish I had seen it." A girl pouted. "I love dolphins, and they've been too wary of the boats since Farren and his stupid friends shot at them when they thought they were the monster."

"I wish it was one of those seacows, they were so cute." Another girl said shyly while Jackson, Spinescale, and Daychaser slipped between the two ships. Spinescale gave Daychaser a chastising look for almost giving them away, to which he made an apologetic squee-whine.

"I wish we could go out and see the whales again, but my dad said we couldn't go until the soldiers and mages took care of the monster." The oldest girl said with a sigh. "I loved watching for them."

"Forget whales and sea-cuties, I want to go look for s'more sea snakes or a sea serpent! My grandpa let me hold a sea snake he caught in one of the nets a few weeks ago!" A little boy with spiky black hair boasted.

"There, those two kids are the ones we saved." Jackson pointed to the boy who wanted to see sharks and the girl who was upset over the dolphins.

Spinescale made a thinking hiss. "They and their friends and older siblings often go with the adults to explore the shoreline in the boats. I've seen them quite a bit when they go for a quick swim over the reefs. Avoid the little black haired one if you ever run into them."

"The one who loves snakes and sea serpents?" Jackson gave Spinescale a teasing smirk. "Were you the snake he got to 'hold.'"

Spinescale shuddered. "Last time I ever get that close to a fishing net, he nearly squeezed the venom out of me!"

"The two kids seem fine." Daychaser commented as they watched. "Although, I've never seen human calves up close before so I wouldn't know."

"Where are Dad and the others?" One of the girls asked. "Isn't anyone else on watch?"

One of the two older boys shook his head. "Nope, not tonight. Dad said between the clear skies this afternoon and the fact the soldiers drove off the monster yesterday, that the Town Council wasn't too worried about needing to have a watch tonight. The monster never comes two nights in a row."

"I wish Mom and Auntie had come with us, they usually tell us stories or sing songs when the sun goes down." Leavan frowned. "Everyone has been so busy because of the storms that no one comes to watch the sunset with us anymore!"

"Yeah, and Auntie would tell us stories, like the one about the young boy who sailed out to sea to catch a hippocampus but caught a drop of sunlight instead." Terven grinned, "and Mom and Dad would sing the old sun songs."

The youngest girl giggled. "Remember the night when Donner tried jumping off the docks to try and catch the sun and belly-flopped in the water?"

The other kids all laughed while the little spiky haired boy who liked snakes cried out. "Hey, that wasn't funny! I bloodied my nose when I did that."

"Why don't we sing a song tonight, even if our parents are off in a meeting with the other adults?" One of the older boys suggested.

"Oh! Oh, I know which one we should sing!!" The boy called Donner said, hopping up and down.

The oldest girl giggled. "Why don't you start us off then Donner?"

Donner excitedly began the song before the other kids started to join in. Jackson quickly found himself humming along to the tune, faintly surprised it was one he knew. He was so caught up in humming along that when the kids stopped, he failed to notice and kept humming while they looked around the harbor, confusion written on their faces. Spinescale hissed a warning when one of the boys spotted him, and Jackson clapped his hand over his mouth and sank down into the water when the whole group spied him.

"HEY! Who're you?" Donner yelled.

Jackson peeked over the surface but didn't say anything.

"Is that you Farren?" One of the older boys called in an unfriendly tone, apparently not liking the idea of Farren being around.

Jackson poked his head further out of the water and heard the kids gasp when they saw his gray skin. "No, I'm not Farren." Jackson said quietly after he quickly looked around the docks. "My name's Jackson."

The boy Jackson saved gasped. "You're the boy who saved my sis and I yesterday!"

Leavan gasped as well and jumped to her feet to point at him. "Yeah! See, I told you guys we were telling the truth!" She cried.

"You said the boy had a white tail though..." One of the older boys looked doubtful. "Not that he was gray colored."

"He did..." Terven sounded confused as he gave Jackson a perplexed look, "and he wasn't gray yesterday."

84

"Oh, come on, you two must've knocked your heads on something when you fell off the boat." The oldest girl shook her head. "You really shouldn't make up stories like that."

"They didn't really make up anything." Jackson let his color spell break as he swam over to the dock.

All the kids gaped when the spell broke, and they saw him splash the surface of the water with his tail.

"You-you have a TAIL!?" The youngest girl squeed.

The two older boys and the oldest girl suddenly exchanged guarded looks before they swiftly stood, pulling the younger kids behind them protectively.

"How do we know you aren't a siren?" The oldest boy asked Jackson suspiciously.

Jackson paused. "I... I don't know. How do you prove you aren't a siren?"

The oldest boy came and held out his hand. "A siren won't touch a human and look you directly in the eye at the same time."

The oldest girl came forward and held out her hand as well, while the second oldest boy held the younger kids behind him.

Jackson looked up at the outstretched hands thoughtfully for a moment before sighing. "Ok, give me just a second." He brought up his hands and forced a column of water up from under him, raising himself high enough to be eye level with the other kids. The kids all jumped back nervously when Jackson held his hands out to shake theirs, but after a second the two older kids both came forward and shook his hands, looking him in the eye as they did.

"I wanna shake his hand too!" Donner pushed his way forward and shook Jackson's hand despite the second oldest boy's protests.

"What are you?" The youngest girl asked shyly while the other kids moved in closer. "Are you a merman?"

Jackson giggled and moved forward to sit on the edge of the dock, letting the column of water drop back into the sea. "No, I'm a kid, just like you guys. I just have a tail instead of legs."

"Where did you come from?" One of the older boys questioned, "and why haven't we seen you before?"

"My friends and I got dragged here by the whirlpools a little bit ago." Jackson answered.

Leavan was dancing around. "Wait until I tell Mom and Dad, they won't believe you actually exist!!"

"Wait!" Jackson held out his hand. "Uh... could you not tell the adults just yet?"

"Why shouldn't we tell them about you." The oldest girl put her hands on her hips and gave him a suspicious look. "Are you hiding something?"

Jackson bit his lip, suddenly regretting his split-second decision to reveal himself. "Yes... and... no." He said lamely.

"What are you hiding then?" One of the boys said as he crossed his arms.

Jackson had to think for a moment. "My existence for one thing, you guys are some of the first people who have ever seen me like this, and second, I'd rather not have your parents think I'm some scary monster and attack my friends and I again like they did yesterday."

"Wait, that was you the guards attacked yesterday?" Terven asked, his eyes widening.

"Yeah, I think they thought my white skin belonged to the Shattered One and they attacked me when I was exploring around the harbor..." Jackson winced.

"The Shattered One?" Leavan asked, tilting her head questioningly. "Who's that?"

"That's what the ocean creatures here call the monster that your clans have been fighting against since you got here." Jackson said. "The one who can turn people to stone."

"How do you know about that creature if you just got here?" The oldest girl pointed out suspiciously.

"Yeah, and who are your friends?" Donner scowled. "How do we know they aren't the monster?"

Instead of answering, Jackson leaned over and called. "Daychaser! Could you jump out of the water for me really quick?"

"What are you kelp-crazy? Get back down here! Spinescale and I have been frozen stiff since you suddenly swam towards them." Daychaser called, his voice tight with shock.

"They won't hurt you, come on." Jackson pressed. "Please, they won't believe me if you don't."

"If Startide were here she'd have a fit." Daychaser grumbled before he came shooting forward and jumped out of the water with a disgruntled squee.

"You're friends with a dolphin??" Leavan asked excitedly. "Can I pet him?"

"Leavan no, that's a seawolf!" The oldest boy hurriedly grabbed her hand when she scrambled towards the edge, "and you shouldn't go into the water with wild animals."

"He's not wild, Bennor, he's Jackson's friend." Leavan said stubbornly and gave Jackson a pleading look. "Can I get in the water and pet him?"

Jackson looked at the older kids uncertainly and was met with tiny and nervous shakes of their heads. "Um... Maybe later Leavan." When she stuck out her lip in a pout, he caught her eye and gave a small smile. "Maybe another day, ok? It's getting dark and it's hard to see where you're going in the water at night."

Leavan went quiet for a moment before she nodded. "Ok…" She said quietly.

The older kids relaxed, and the oldest girl mouthed a quick "thank you" to Jackson before the eldest boy—who had short dark brown hair, brown eyes and a lean leggy frame—introduced himself. "I'm Bennor, and this is my younger brother Donner and my little sister Danna." He pointed to Donner and the youngest girl.

"I'm Henri." The second oldest boy, who had light brown hair, green eyes, and a thicker build than Bennor, added. "And this is my sister Kayla and our younger twin siblings Terven and Leaven. Our Dad is the chief of our tribe."

"It's nice to meet you guys." Jackson paused when Daychaser let out an urgent series of clicks, barks, and chirps. "Uh… I think I had better go. Daychaser is sounding like he wants to talk about something."

"Wait." Henri pressed. "You can't just go running off like that, we gotta figure out what to tell the adults! They won't believe us if you aren't here."

Jackson gave him a hurt look. "I'm not letting the adults see me. They've attacked me once already, and after seeing you guys get all nervous when you thought I was a siren I doubt the adults wouldn't see me as a threat either."

"But why did you let us see you?" Leavan asked with a frown. "If you don't want to be seen?"

Jackson bit his lip. "You guys just reminded me of my cousins and my family…" He looked out over the darkening sky sadly. "We used to watch the sunset together too, before they…" He shook his head when he choked up a bit and took a deep breath. "I can't stop you from telling your parents. I wouldn't blame you if you did…" He shrugged. "I likely would too, if I was in your shoes."

"You don't have a family anymore?" Danna asked as some tears formed in her big hazel eyes.

Jackson looked out over the rolling waves. "We... all have family. It's just sometimes our families go where we can no longer be with them." He felt a tear run down his cheek and wiped it off as Daychaser jumped out of the water to check on him again. "I'd better go, maybe I'll see you guys again."

"Wait." Terven and Leavan said, making Jackson pause before he could slip off the dock.

Leavan pointed down the coast. "We often play in a little lagoon down the coast that way."

"Yeah, you should come by one of the afternoons we're there." Terven continued.

Jackson nodded. "If I see you guys there, I might stop by and say hi. Bye now." He shoved himself off the dock and splashed into the water, hurrying after Daychaser and Spinescale as they swam off into the night.

Once they were out of earshot, Daychaser made a relieved sounding howl while Spinescale leveled Jackson with a dumbfounded look. "Um hello, we were trying to not be seen. What were you thinking?"

Jackson just shrugged uncomfortably. "Sorry... I... I don't really know what I was thinking." He rubbed the back of his neck uneasily. "I think they just really reminded me of my family and... yeah..."

"Oh..." Spinescale's intense gaze softened, though she had a strange look in her eyes. "I don't know if I understand the family bit, snakes only really know our siblings, not our parents." She looked behind them. "It would be hard to not see my siblings once in a while though, especially Deepbite."

Daychaser gave a conflicted quark, although he looked like he understood why Jackson did what he did. "I just hope you showing yourself to the humans won't be a problem for us…"

"I hope not, but if the adults find out about me, I doubt it will go well." Jackson sighed, his shoulders sagging dejectedly. "After seeing how guarded the kids were, I'm sure the adults are even more wary. Especially if there are sirens in these waters."

The group travelled quietly for awhile before Daychaser spoke up.

"I'm not familiar with sirens… what're they?" Daychaser asked, "and why're they such a problem?"

"Sirens are humanoid creatures that live in warmer oceans." Jackson explained as they headed back to the lagoon where Startide was waiting. "They're described as looking part human, part fish or dolphin with dark gray skin, and strange looking faces."

"Well, the description did fit you a bit." Spinescale gave Jackson a quick look over. "At least when your skin was gray."

"I think that's where the similarity ends." Jackson said thoughtfully. "From what I've heard about sirens, they have odd looking wings as well as arms, and they can cause mirages, leading people or sailors into dangerous waters that few ever return from. One of the books I read said they are vicious creatures that hunt other creatures in packs, using a strange mix of water and shadow magic to bring them down."

"If they're so dangerous, why did the boy ask you to look him in the eye and shake his hand?" Daychaser looked dumbfounded.

"I think that a sirens mirage magic fails if you touch them…?" Jackson said uncertainly. "I don't know what the whole looking me in the eye bit was about, but maybe siren eyes look different than human eyes somehow?"

"Huh, creepy sounding creatures." Daychaser replied.

"I know a small group of sirens live around one of the islands further south of us." Spinescale mused. "Although, I've never seen or heard of one here."

"Perhaps the humans ran into them after they arrived." Daychaser offered while they entered the lagoon. "It could explain why the kids were so worried."

"It would make sense, I guess." Jackson agreed. "But if there really are sirens here, I'm pretty sure the kids will have a pretty hard time convincing the adults I'm real..."

"Which is why they wanted you to stick around." Spinescale finished. "Because they probably knew they would need proof."

"YAWN! Who needs proof of what?" Startide asked when she came over. "Did I miss something?"

"You could say that." Daychaser said in an amused tone.

"You know our parents won't believe us, Bennor." Tervan said while they wandered back to the village. "Even though our Dad saw Jackson, he still doesn't completely believe me and sis. Only your Grandpa Toceth seemed to really believe what we said."

"Then maybe Grandpa Toceth should be the one we tell." Kayla commented thoughtfully as she tied her long brown-red hair into a ponytail. "He would be more willing to listen to us then the other clan leaders..." She got a wry look on her face as she glanced at one of the soldiers with her pastel green eyes. "And he'd be less likely to freak out about it."

"I feel like we gotta tell someone," Henri agreed, his voice full of concern. "Someone needs to know what's going on, and that the monster didn't come by yesterday after all."

"Then let's go tell my grandparents right now." Bennor began running down the dirt road into the medium sized town the kids called home. "Come on! They should be home this time of night."

"Bennor, wait for us!" Kalya grabbed Leavan's hand as she and the other kids tore after the long-legged boy.

The kids rushed through the streets of town, the large glowing lantern-lights dancing in the gentle evening breeze while they slowed in front of a large dark brown wooden house. Some old red and purple robes fluttered on a clothesline stretched across the front porch as the kids stepped up the walkway. When the kids came up and wiped their feet on a large horsehair welcome mat a long viper, that was stretched out along the clothesline, lifted its piercing gaze to watch. Donner jumped up to peek in the front window and pointed excitedly when a candle flickered inside the house, casting strange shadows around the room as someone moved around inside.

"Grandpa? Grandma?" Bennor knocked lightly on the door. "Are you up?"

"Just a second." The kids heard a grunt as someone got up from their chair before there was the thunk of a large book being sat on a table. A moment later, a tall, wiry, white haired, and friendly looking old man opened the door. The man's eyebrows rose in surprise when he noticed the small group of kids congregated on his step. "Well hello Bennor, Henri, Kayla, what could you kids all need at this hour?"

"Is there trouble with the clans again?" A sweet looking old lady asked as she peered out of the kitchen, her curly white hair tied into a messy bun while she wiped soapy water off her hands. Behind her a long tatzelwurm, a creature with a long powerful serpentine body but the forelimbs and head of a cat, opened an eye curiously.

"Uh well…" Kayla, Bennor, and Henri exchanged a worried look as another tatzelwurm—who was resting on a sturdy shelf—glanced over at them.

"We were down at the docks and saw something that was kinda um…" Bennor looked over his shoulder uneasily when some of the other villagers wandered past with a couple venstorns.

Grandpa Toceth's eyes widened ever so slightly, and he gently motioned for the kids to come in. "Why don't you all come in and sit down? You guys can tell me all about it after Grandma grabs us a snack."

The kids all crowded through the doorway into the large house, nervously sitting down in Grandpa Toceth's study while Grandma Zelli rummaged around in the kitchen. After a few moments, Grandma Zelli came into the room with a plate loaded to the brim with sweet crackers and a few glasses of milk. She placed the plate down on a small table while Grandpa Toceth lit a few candles as Donner and Danna each hungrily grabbed a glass of milk and a couple sweet crackers.

"Now, what is it that you wanted to tell us?" Grandpa asked kindly as the first tatzelwurm slithered over, coiling around his chair.

The older kids all gave each other worried looks before Henri spoke up, his voice quiet. "You might not believe us…"

Grandpa folded his hands and thoughtfully sat back in his chair while Grandma leaned forward worriedly. "Now Henri, you kids have always been perfectly honest with us." She said kindly. "Come now, what's troubling you?"

"We saw the boy again at the docks tonight! The one that saved me and Leavan yesterday." Terven blurted out and quickly began telling the story, with the other kids adding their bits and pieces to the tale. The old couple, and the tatzelwurms, listened intently as the kids told them about what had happened, and waited until the children finished before they asked any questions.

"Bennor, both you and Kayla shook the boy's hand?" Grandpa Toceth asked, looking at them with the piercing gaze he used to make sure people were telling the truth.

"Yes, and Donner did too." Bennor said confidently, sitting up straighter in his seat, "and Jackson sat on the dock and talked to us for a few minutes, so we know he was really there."

"I don't know if I've ever heard of such a thing." Grandma Zelli seemed awestruck. "A human with the tail of a sea creature?"

"Hm…" Grandpa Toceth slowly lifted himself from his chair and wandered over to a large bookshelf that took up the entire back wall before he started fingering through the books. "I've only heard of such a thing in legend, a race of magical water magi." He pulled out a very old book and quickly wiped a bit of dust off the cover before he flipped it open. "Long before the Steelserpent War they were a powerful nation that was said to rule the seas." He stopped about halfway through the book and flipped it around to show the children one of the pages. "Did he look something like this?"

The page had a large picture of a man, human on top but dolphin below, who was wearing strange apparel and wielding a long staff. Behind the man a dolphin hovered protectively around a woman and a child who were wearing similarly styled clothes and jewelry.

"COOL!" Donner jumped forward and leaned his hands on the table, nearly spilling his milk. "He looks a lot like Jackson!"

"Yes, but Jackson's tail was different." Leavan noted thoughtfully while Kayla steadied Donner's glass, "and his clothes didn't look that strange."

"Do you think Jackson is one of them?" Kayla asked while the tatzelwurms moved around to try and look at the picture.

"He very well could be." Grandpa Toceth slowly sat down in his chair and picked up the large book he'd been reading earlier, thumbing through it slowly. "After I saw your young friend save Leavan and Terven yesterday, I began searching through my library for any mention of humans who were part ocean creature." He reached over and adjusted the lamp so he could read better. "I found mention of them in a couple old books I have about the Steelserpent War. There wasn't any mention of what this race of water magi called themselves, but it does say they were a very powerful people before they mysteriously vanished when the war ended."

"So, you believe us?" Danna asked shyly. "You don't think we just saw a siren or something?"

Grandpa and Grandma exchanged a concerned look before nodding.

"We believe you dear." Grandma patted Danna's hand comfortingly. "And I'm relieved Bennor and Kayla had the presence of mind to make sure the boy wasn't a siren. We have enough trouble with the monster and all these storms, we certainly don't need to add sirens to the mix."

"You mentioned the boy said he was attacked at the docks yesterday?" Grandpa asked.

The kids nodded.

"Then I'd better go get some people on watch, if Jackson was the one they attacked yesterday, that means the monster could still show up." The old man quickly shot up from his chair and grabbed a long tan and purple staff. "What did you say the boy called that thing again?"

"The skittered one?" Donner said uncertainly as the tatzelwurms slipped after Grandpa Toceth.

"Not skittered you silly, he called it the Shattered One." Kayla corrected, ruffling Donner's hair.

Grandpa hmphed. "It's a fitting name, matches the beast perfectly. Now all you wait here, I'll be back in a bit." With that he ran out the door into the town.

CHAPTER EIGHT

MYSTERIES AND MORNINGSHELL

Jackson was awoken early the next morning when a small tidal wave crashed over him, sweeping him off the sandbank and into the water with a splash. "HEY! WHAT THE—!?"

"FINALLY, I thought we'd never wake you up." Spinescale snipped while Jackson struggled to get his bearings. "Deepbite and I have been trying to wake you for the last ten human minutes!"

"I told you it would take more than some poking and prodding." Startide smirked. "I should use that trick more often if we end up stuck here for a while."

"Now that you're up, there is someone here to talk to us." Daychaser grinned while Jackson rubbed the sleep out of his eyes and looked around.

When a large hawksbill sea turtle came swimming over, Jackson stumbled over his words in apology. "S-sorry I didn't know you'd be here this early. Are you Morningshell?"

"That I am, and do not fret, I came much earlier, than you might expect." The turtle said in her old, slightly rough, voice. "I desired to know if the tale of a lightborn in our waters was indeed true. Now what do you wish for me to tell too you? I have much to tell, for much I've seen, beyond the ocean blue, and the land so green."

"We were hoping you knew of a way to escape from here?" Startide asked kindly. "We urgently need to get Jackson to the Starkelp Strand."

"I heard the message on the waves, that the oceans had seen far better days." Morningshell began soberly. "There is only one way to leave our shores, and it's now the way we all abhor." She paused, as if gathering her thoughts. "In times past the canyon was the way to flee, before the Shattered One's anger churned our sea. The magic of the canyons is a fickle one, but could once be traveled when the moon's light was redone." Her eyes darkened sadly. "Alas, when the human's ships drove through, the canyon's magic they did skew. Since that time the magic strays, and the Shattered One's cries fill our days."

"Does she always talk in rhyme?" Jackson heard Daychaser whisper to Deepbite, who gave a tired sigh.

"No, not always, but most of the time, yes." He whispered back. "Yes, she sure does."

"The magic is straying from the canyons?" Jackson asked in alarm, "but doesn't it petrify whomever it touches?"

"Indeed, the magic of the canyons is a frightening thing, and death and stone is what it brings. Since the humans made their fateful trip, the magic grows and extends its grip. I fear it will soon reach our dear shores, until they are at last no more." Morningshell said sadly. "Unless you can find a way to set things straight, here you shall stay til your lives grow late."

"How could we set things straight?" Jackson asked, feeling a bit lost. "I know nothing about dealing with magic that's gone whirlpool."

"It was told to me by elders now long gone, that secrets lay in the ruins of the ocean's song. Secrets of a race long past, and who the magic of the canyons cast." Morningshell pointed with her fin to the northeast. "Hidden amongst the smallest of isles, an ancient city used to smile. The answers you need, that were once known, may well be hidden, within her stone."

"Do you know where the city is located?" Startide asked, not looking troubled by the turtle's strange way of speaking.

Morningshell shook her head. "I only know it lies northeast, between the smallest isles peaks. It was hidden many long years ago, when battles and blood our seas did show."

Jackson bit his cheek, anxiously wishing that Morningshell would talk normally. "What do you guys think?" He asked Daychaser and Startide.

"It sounds like our best bet." Daychaser mused, glancing over to the sea snakes. "Maybe we can find someone who knows where to find the city."

"The eastern side of the island is too deep for coral reefs." Deepbite said quickly. "Our kind rarely travel that way. There are some tiny islands over there though, and the seafloor is ridden with deep cracks. Although there are a lot of sharks…"

"Mm, why didn't you mention that sooner?" Startide licked her lips. "That might make up for the lack of trout in these warmer waters."

"I've been meaning to ask, but where in the currents did you pick up a taste for sharks?" Daychaser asked, giving Startide a wry look. "Aren't your pod fish specialists?"

Startide's eyes twinkled. "One year we had an abundance of dishonored sharks that kept interfering with our hunts or trying to attack the calves. One thing led to another, and it seemed like such a waste to let all that meat just sink to the bottom."

"Oh… well that makes sense." Daychaser said, while Deepbite and Spinescale gave Startide a dumbfounded look.

"You like eating sharks?" Spinescale asked, her eyes gleaming in interest.

"But of course." Startide said mischievously. "As long as they don't take a chunk out of you."

"I, and every other human I know, will pass on eating shark, thank you." Jackson commented. "Uh… but could we focus on the task at hand?"

"Sorry." Startide replied.

"Right," Daychaser turned to Morningshell. "Thank you for your help Morningshell." He said with a respectful dip of his head. "We'll try to search around the eastern side of the island for the lost city; at least unless we can figure something else out."

Morningshell rose in the water slightly. "I am grateful to help in some small way, perhaps I will visit again some other day. In the meantime, ask the sharks, they might know where your search should start." She bowed before she calmly swam away.

"Thanks again!" Jackson called while she vanished from view.

"Well let's get to searching." Daychaser proclaimed, swimming around the group quickly. "You two coming along?" He asked Spinescale and Deepbite.

"I'll tag along, I've always wanted to see what lies beyond the shallower waters of the reef." Spinescale said excitedly before she glanced at her brother. "What about you Deepbite?"

"I'll pass, I have some other things I need to take care of." Deepbite said and began to move off, "but I'll keep an earhole open, I'll meet up with you all later."

Jackson and his friends spent the rest of their day searching around the east side of the island for any clues about the lost city. The group split into two teams after they had a quick break for lunch, with Startide and Spinescale leaving to search the deeper waters, while Jackson and Daychaser stayed in the shallower waters close to shore.

Jackson once again found he needed to turn his skin a medium gray so the sight of his white tail wouldn't send the local creatures into a panic. As he and Daychaser investigated around the shallows, they ran into lots of sharks who, unfortunately, didn't know much about the lost city.

"Sorry fellas but I just don't know what a lost city would even look like, and I doubt any of my kin would either." A large female hammerhead shark said when they asked. "I remember the elders of my kind saying the city was hidden out by the tiny islands that are surrounded by deeper waters. You could try asking some of our other open ocean cousins, they see a lot of strange things on their travels over deeper seas."

"I'd be careful around them though." A small gray reef shark with white tipped fins called from his hiding spot inside a small cave. He peeked out, giving the hammerhead a wary look. "Those shark species who live in more open waters can be an unpredictable bunch. It comes from living in waters where food isn't as easy to come by. I doubt you have much to fear from them Jackson, but your friends might not be so lucky."

On the second day of searching, Jackson and his friends decided to try asking some of the open ocean sharks for help, but found they weren't very... cooperative.

"Like I care about something that's made of stone." One grumbled before swimming off.

"Ya sure I can't eat the sea snake? I just finished a long trip and haven't had a bite to eat in ages." Another one had pressed hungrily, avoiding any questions about the lost city before Startide finally had enough and drove it off, much to Spinescale's relief.

"If I did know, why would I tell you lot?" A long, grumpy brown shark with white fin tips growled later while he and his friends circled Jackson and his friends threateningly. "If ya didn't have the Sonaeko with ya, we'd consider y'all a meal if there were more of us."

At that, Startide's eyes had flashed angrily before she let out a threatening noise and charged the circling sharks, making them scatter. As she drove them off, Jackson's shoulders slumped and he let out a weary sigh. *Spells, this isn't going so good...*

Daychaser let out a sigh of his own. "Onto asking another open ocean shark I guess..."

CHAPTER NINE
THE SHATTERED ONE

This is getting ridiculous!" Startide grumbled at the end of the third day of searching. The open ocean sharks and other creatures they'd managed to find hadn't proved helpful, and their own efforts to find the lost city hadn't gone much better. "I have half a mind to start actually hunting the sharks here, just to teach them a lesson."

"While I'd normally love the idea, right now I don't think that'd be for the best. You need the creatures around here to trust you, not fear you." Spinescale pointed out, "and getting on the open ocean sharks' bad side wouldn't do us any good. Besides, there are bigger sharks here that we don't want to anger because you were eating their cousins."

"Still, they sure aren't very friendly." Daychaser was frustrated. "Some of them seem to be trying to pick a fight. The dolphinkin I've met have been much more amiable."

"Maybe we should take a break tomorrow?" Jackson suggested a bit nervously. "I think we could all use a break from searching..."

Startide and Daychaser both hesitated a minute.

"I mean, it sounds tempting..." Startide said slowly. "We were in such a rush before, I didn't get the chance to ask the black dolphin pods here about their customs and culture." Her eyes lit up at the mention of customs and culture. "Their dialects here are so different from back home, and I could tell they had different hunting techniques and sang different songs. Maybe they would know something about the lost city as well, dolphinkin always keep a deep vocal record."

"While you're doing that, I'd just like to find something decent to eat…" Daychaser grumbled. "Since they don't even have side eyes in these waters for some reason. Shouldn't've gotten my hopes up for fish that taste like what we have back home."

Jackson and Startide locked gazes and rolled their eyes.

"Daychaser, why don't I show you some of the reef fish Deepbite and I enjoy?" Spinescale offered. "Perhaps you'd like them better than some of the other fish you've been eating."

"Speaking of which, where does Deepbite vanish too all the time? We don't see much of him." Startide was perplexed. "I thought he'd be helping us look for the city."

Spinescale puffed in amusement. "Nah, he's not one to travel in unfamiliar waters, he prefers the safety of the reef and the feel of land under his scales." She laughed. "If it wasn't for his mischievous streak, I'd wonder how we're related, but to answer your question…" She glanced at the waves washing against the shore. "He and his buddies like to go spying on the humans, he's been utterly fascinated with them since they got here." She shivered a bit, "and unlike yours truly, it doesn't bother him if he's caught and held once in a while." She sighed. "If these humans weren't so respectful and kind to us snakes, I'd be worried about him."

"That's venom clans for you." Jackson yawned tiredly, although he smiled a bit. "They utterly love venomous species. Most of the clans I used to know always had some type of venomous animal living with them…" He frowned in thought. "Actually, with how curious Deepbite and the other snakes are, I'm surprised they haven't tried to make you familiars yet."

"A guy tried after the humans landed on the island…" Spinescale's voice was sad. "The familiar spell affected the poor snake so badly, they've never tried again since." Spinescale winced. "The young man felt horrible, and it took Slictoc three weeks before he could slither in a straight line again."

"Ooooo…" Jackson cringed before he went quiet. "I wonder if the spell went wrong because your species are tied to water magic as well as venom?"

"What would that have to do with—!?"

Spinescale was interrupted when a bone-chilling sound shivered through the water.

"What was that?" Daychaser wildly sounded the dark water before the sound returned, making their skin crawl.

"The Shattered One!" Spinescale squeaked in alarm.

They crowded together nervously when the blood-freezing cry made the water tremble while Jackson felt a strong pulse of magic shoot by them. "It sounds like a cross between someone screaming while grinding metal together." He shivered.

"What in the seas is metal?" Daychaser asked.

"Never mind that, we have to get out of here!" Startide urgently whispered when the wind suddenly picked up, making small waves splash above them. "We don't want him to turn us into stone and add us to his trophy reef."

"But where is the sound coming from?" Jackson asked.

"I'll bet he's heading to the village…" Spinescale nervously looked up at the darkening sky. "The sound is from that direction. I hope Deepbite and the others aren't hanging around the docks tonight."

"THE DOCKS!" Jackson exclaimed and shot towards the surface! "This is the time of night when the kids are hanging out there!" He cried, flying out of the waves to see which way the docks were. He splashed back under the surface and charged towards the harbor. "I gotta go warn them, they said the village hasn't been putting out the guards to watch for the Shattered One since they thought I was the monster the other day."

"Are you crazy?" Startide protested as she tried to catch up to Jackson. "What if he catches us?"

"Then we will be petrified for a good cause." Daychaser offered Jackson his dorsal fin. "Grab my fin, it'll be faster."

"We're all completely mad." Startide joined them. "If we survive this, not a word to my grandpodmother, got it?"

"You all go without me!" Spinescale called. "I'll slow you down, the Shattered One might catch up to us if you wait for me."

"Be careful." Startide called back while they dashed towards the town.

"Right back at-cha!" Spinescale replied.

Jackson hung tight to Daychaser's fin while the water behind them seemed to boil and bubble as another wave of magic surged past. "Hurry!" Jackson whispered when another cry rang out. "There's no telling what type of magic does that!"

"We're almost there, I can sound some of the boats." Startide panted as the dark forms of the ships came into sight.

"Change your colors, just in case there is someone on watch." Daychaser hurriedly suggested.

Jackson quickly changed his skin to a darker gray than he was before as he let go of Daychaser and quickly darted under a large ship. "There they are." Jackson pointed.

"Haven't they noticed the wind?" Startide questioned while Jackson quickly checked the harbor for any adults.

"Apparently not." Jackson said, his blood pumping faster once another surge of magic shot through him, making his skin crawl. "They probably don't know enough about magic to sense the pulses the Shattered One is sending off." He rushed over to the end of the dock and poked his head out of the water and whispered loudly.

"HENRI! BENNOR! YOU GUYS!!"

"Who's there?" Bennor looked around nervously until Leavan pointed down to Jackson.

"It's Jackson!" She said excitedly.

"You came back?" Donner exclaimed as he leaned over the dock for a better look.

"Why didn't you come to the lagoon to see us before?" Terven asked but Jackson waved his hand.

"There isn't time, the monster will be here any second! You have to get out of here NOW!" Jackson tried to keep the panic from making his voice crack when a very strong burst of magical energy shot through the harbor.

"How do you know it's comi—?!" Danna froze when a heart pounding shriek rang across the waves and Jackson cringed when another stronger burst of magic seemed to attack his skin.

"RUN!" Jackson yelled as the water began to whip around the dock. "I'll try to distract him, GET OUT OF HERE!"

"Go, GO!!" Henri and Kayla shouted, grabbing their younger siblings' hands and fleeing down the docks as Daychaser and Startide came swooping over. Jackson latched onto Startide's dorsal fin before she flipped about and charged out of the harbor as Jackson heard the kids screaming for help while one of them found an alarm bell and began ringing it wildly.

Jackson held on for dear life as they swooped out of the harbor, only for them to slam to a stop when something suddenly swooped to block their path!

"The Shattered One!" Startide squeaked.

They all yelped, jumping back as the strange creature opened its glowing eyes. It's dull smokey-gray humanoid crystal body was riddled with a webbing of glowing orange cracks. The cracks ran across its chest and right arm and then spread up over the right side of its face. It opened and closed its one good hand while its long shark-like tail swayed back and forth as its empty eyes flashed a frightening shade of orange.

The creature suddenly noticed Jackson and reared back, pointing at him as it screamed! Jackson choked when the soft corals and seaweed below them were immediately blasted into stone while the wind lashed the monster's cries around with the waves!

"SWIM FOR IT!!!" Startide shouted, yanking Jackson alongside her as they dashed eastward! The Shattered One's screams suddenly turned terrifyingly livid and shrill, and Jackson glanced back to see it crash its hands together, forming a bright blue ball of energy that crackled with power.

"NO!" Jackson yelled, releasing his hold on Startide's fin before flipping around and throwing his hands together!

"SKKKKIRRRRRIYIYIYIYIIIIIIIIIII!" The Shattered One screamed as it blasted a dark blue beam of magic towards them while a bright light flew from Jackson's hands as he slashed the water in front of him!

BOOM!

Jackson recoiled from the deafening explosion when the blast erupted against his shield, sending sprays of water shooting in all directions while Startide and Daychaser whipped about!

As the water crashed back into the sea Jackson froze while the Shattered One stopped, staring at him with its glowing orange mouth agape. Jackson glanced down to see his color spell had broken, and he groaned when the glow of the Shattered One's eyes dimmed slightly.

"Honpenoalbel" The creature said in the quietest voice Jackson had heard it speak and the boy looked up in surprise, meeting the creature's gaze as they stared at each other.

The moment ended when Startide barreled over, grabbed Jackson in her mouth, and took off with Daychaser hot on her tail! The Shattered One screamed again and raged forwards, churning the water around it and firing magical attacks after Jackson and his friends as they fled!

"CLOSE YOUR EYES!" Daychaser yelled to Jackson when he and Startide suddenly dove into the dark depth below them! Jackson pinched his eyes closed while the cries of rage grew further and further away as Daychaser and Startide quickly left the monster behind once it lost sight of them in the darker depths. Jackson kept his eyes tightly closed while the minutes slowly ticked by. He heard Startide signal Daychaser to change course many times while they rushed through the darkness of night. Jackson only dared to open his eyes once Daychaser tapped his shoulder when they came up to the surface for a quick breath.

As Startide and Daychaser caught their breath, Jackson looked around curiously until he gave Startide a long look and tapped her snout. "Uh, Startide. Thanks and everything, but I think you can let go of me now."

She blinked before giving him a sheepish look. "Sorry..." She opened her mouth just enough for Jackson to swim free and he moved up to grab hold of her fin. The three friends took a long detour towards the lagoon as they tried to avoid the path the monster might take back to the canyons. Their detour took them half the night, and Jackson was exhausted by the time they finally reached the lagoon where Spinescale and Deepbite were anxiously waiting for them.

"There you are." Deepbite made a relieved sounding puff. "What happened? Spinescale lost track of you after she was forced to hide in the jungle when the Shattered One came back to the docks."

"Oh my currents!" Startide gave Spinescale a horrified look. "Are you ok?"

Spinescale's attempt to shrug off the scare failed when her voice cracked from fear. "I-I'm fine..." She took a deep breath as her wings trembled slightly. "Though a few of the humans aren't. After I got into the trees, I saw a man get petrified during the Shattered One's attack, a few others got hit too as they drove it off..." She shook her head. "What happened to you guys?"

"We were able to warn the kids before the Shattered One found us and attacked." Daychaser shivered a bit. "Thankfully, Jackson was able to block its attack and save us before we got away. I'd hate to think of what would've happened to us if his shield had broke."

"You were lucky." Deepbite added glumly. "Not all the creatures or people along these shores have been."

Everyone was quiet for a few moments before Jackson spoke. "Did the Shattered One drag the petrified man away?"

Spinescale looked rather embarrassed. "Honestly Jackson, I kinda lost my cool when the man turned to stone. The moment I saw they were starting to drive the monster off, I made a run for it, so I didn't see what happened to the man he petrified."

Jackson sighed and glanced sadly out of the lagoon. "I wonder why the Shattered One attacks the humans so much? And why would he even bother to drag the petrified bodies away to his canyon in the first place?"

Spinescale shuddered. "Beats me, perhaps he thinks humans are better suited to decorating his lair."

"Still…" Jackson mumbled. "I have a hard time believing he'd risk getting hurt or killed just to add to his trophy case…"

"Well, whatever the reason, we have to stay clear of him from now on!" Startide said firmly. "I vote we get a bite to eat and take a breather tomorrow like Jackson suggested." She let out a weary sounding squee. "After tonight I could almost sleep like Jackson does."

"Yeah right, no sea creature can sleep that deep!" Spinescale quipped, making the others laugh when Jackson blushed in embarrassment.

A short time later, Jackson tiredly pulled himself ashore to sleep while everyone went their separate ways for the night. He grinned slightly to himself when he heard Daychaser protest Startide's plan to go see the black dolphin pods immediately, instead of getting a bite to eat first. He gave Spinescale and Deepbite a weak wave when they slithered ashore and headed up the rocks inland, looking to stop at a small stream nearby for a drink.

When Jackson awoke late the next morning he stretched with a loud yawn before rolling off the sandbank into the water of the lagoon. He was a bit perplexed when he found himself completely alone, but decided he might as well have breakfast while he waited for the others. After quickly inhaling a few fronds of seaweed and cooking a tiny frozen fish, he pulled himself ashore to relax in the warm morning sun awhile.

Jackson's mind wandered while he lay on the soft sand for a while before he suddenly sat up. *I wonder if the Book of the Sonaeko would know anything about the lost city or the Shattered One?*

Jackson tucked his tail under him as he summoned the book and began flipping through the pages while he searched for anything about the Lost Jewels or lost cities. After flipping through a very long chapter on the culture of different water golems, he sighed and gave the book a pleading look. "By chance do you have any information about a Sonaekian city around the Lost Reefs? Err, I mean the Lost Jewels?"

The book promptly snapped closed before a faint glow coursed across its pages. When the glow subsided, the book fell open to a chapter titled "The Jewel Island Sanctuary."

When Jackson noticed the title of the chapter he sighed in relief. "Thank you, that makes this so much easier."

"Why didn't you just ask in the first place?" Spinescale questioned as she slid along the cliff behind Jackson.

"AH!" Jackson jumped. "Spinescale!? How long have you been there?" He demanded.

"I got here right when you made that book pop out of your hand." Her eyes twinkled while she slithered down the last of the cliff, causing a shower of dust before she landed on the sand with a thunk. "You were so focused on those squiggly things in the book you didn't hear me."

"Oh…" Jackson replied.

Spinescale wound her way over to inspect the book in Jackson's lap. "You mind telling me why didn't you just ask the book about the lost city in the first place? I take it, it found something for you now?"

"The Book of the Sonaeko won't show me everything it knows." Jackson slowly turned a page. "Oceaono suggested I read through what it offers to show me first, before I ask to see something specific."

"Huh, seems strange, but whatever." She looked over the open page. "What are all the scribbles?"

"These are words that have been written on the page." Jackson tapped the page lightly with his finger. "People or creatures who know how to read can... uh, well read, the words in books and other things to learn different stuff. For example..." He pointed to a picture on the second page. "The writing below this picture tells me that this is the entrance of the lost city." He leaned in for a closer look. "Apparently the lost city was once called the Jewel Island Sanctuary. It was a remote city that was inhabited by the Sonaeko and their allies."

"Hm... never seen anything that looks like that, but it's a good lead." Spinescale said as she inspected the picture. "If you could show that picture to some of the sharks or other ocean animals, they might be able to help us find it."

"I hope so..." Jackson sighed. "Wish the open ocean sharks were more willing to help though."

"Many shallow-water creatures quickly learn that open ocean predators can be a bit unpredictable." Spinescale puffed in annoyance. "In the deep open seas there isn't a lot of food, and it's first come first served." She rolled her eyes. "Doesn't make some of those animals very cooperative or friendly."

"Still... we ran into some open ocean creatures before we ended up here and the dolphinkin were nice enough, so were some of the sharks." Jackson commented while he broke off a chunk of rock from the cliff with his magic.

Spinescale shrugged her wings. "I've met some nasty dolphins in my day, but they're usually more social than most sharks." She watched closely when Jackson started etching a copy of the picture of the Jewel Island Sanctuary entrance onto the chuck of stone. "Jackson, there's something I think I'd better tell you."

"What's that?" Jackson looked up from his work.

"I didn't mention it before, but when the Shattered One attacked the humans last night, he did something that could be a problem." She had a serious look in her eyes. "He threw three crystals in front of him when the first few humans fired their attacks, and after a second the crystals began glowing like crazy before they morphed into glowing being-like things that looked somewhat like you."

"ME!?" Jackson nearly dropped the stone. "He made copies of me out of crystal?"

"No... not really." She said slowly. "They were glowing white, and their bodies and tails looked a lot like yours, although they had no eyes or mouth..." She hissed thoughtfully. "They seemed to protect the Shattered One while he tried to get to town."

Jackson looked down at the sand thoughtfully for a moment. "Did the creatures disappear after he left?"

"I don't know, I wasn't there to see the end of the fight." She coiled up on the warm sand. "They were still there fighting when I fled though."

Jackson let out a drawn-out and stressed breath. "Great, I thought I only had to worry about the people here thinking I was a siren..." He was quiet for a minute. "I wonder if it would be best for me to stay away from the harbor completely...?"

"That's why I wanted to tell you." She said, "after I saw those things, I was worried maybe the humans would think you were somehow connected to the Shattered One and go after you too."

Jackson nodded. "Thanks for telling me..." With a sigh he leaned back on the sand, looking up at the clouds for a moment. "I think, I'll have to think about it a bit." He said before leaning forward and resumed etching the picture.

A warm ocean breeze gently lifted Jackson's hair off his forehead while he finished his sketch, and he glanced over to check on Spinescale. The snake's eyes had unfocused while she rested, and her wings moved slightly with each long, calm breath she took. Jackson reached over and grabbed his bag, teleporting the stone tablet inside before he quietly slipped into the water.

Spinescale lifted her head and gave him a questioning look when he surfaced for a moment.

"I'm going to go see if I can find the lagoon the other kids told me about." Jackson explained when he saw her confused expression.

She gave him a dry look. "So much for thinking about not showing your face to the humans… you were supposed to rest today. Or at least I thought you were."

Jackson shrugged sheepishly. "I… I know, but my mind won't stop spinning, and I feel like I could talk to the kids if I ran into them."

She gave him a long, slightly skeptical look. "Alright, whatever. I'll let the others know where you've swam off too. I'm sure they'll be thrilled to hear your 'resting up today.'" Spinescale's sarcastic tone was at odds with the mischievous twinkle in her eyes.

Jackson leveled Spinescale with a suspicious glance when she laid back down on the sand. "Whaddaya know that I don't?"

"Nothing, whatever could give you that impression?" She replied all too innocently and slid her head partly under her coils.

"Uuuuh-huh." Jackson crossed his arms over his chest. "Maybe the fact that your eyes are sparkling and you're hiding your head so I can't see if you're smirking or not."

"JACKSON!!!"

"GAHH!!" Jackson yelled when Daychaser tackled him from behind, sending them tumbling into the lagoon as Spinescale burst out laughing.

"Haha, we got you!" Spinescale's laughter made her uncoil and she rolled around wildly on the sand while she giggled.

"What in the spells!" Jackson gasped. "Daychaser?! Were you hiding somewhere in the lagoon the whole time?"

Daychaser snickered. "Maybe, we're not revealing our secrets."

"I'll have to use my magic to search through the lagoon tomorrow." Jackson grumbled good naturally. He jokingly glared at Spinescale who was flipped over on her back and wreathing around as she laughed.

"You should've seen your face!!!" She crowed. "Ahahahah, that was priceless! I wish Deepbite and Startide would've been here to see that."

"I doubt they would've appreciated it as much as we did." Daychaser grinned.

"Where are they anyway?" Jackson asked. "I was kinda surprised when I woke up to find myself all alone in the lagoon."

"Startide's still in a deep discussion with the elders of the black dolphin pods about cultures and customs." Daychaser rolled his eyes and flared out his fins in exasperation. "They've been at it long before dawn, and they showed no signs of stopping when I finally managed to get away for a snack. On my way back through the reef I ran into Spinescale and Deepbite. We talked for awhile before Deepbite left to go join some large reef fish who were hunting along the reef, he said something about them trapping the fish where he could catch them better."

"We love to hunt with those guys." Spinescale stretched out on the sand with a sigh. "Those big fish always chase the smaller fish into crevasses and cracks where we can corner them. Any fish that escapes from us snakes usually get caught by the larger fish, it's a wonderful way to get a meal." She opened her mouth wide in a yawn. "Now if you'll excuse me, I'm going to take a nap. A girl needs her beauty sleep you know."

Daychaser and Jackson gave each other a disbelieving look at Spinescale's mention of beauty sleep, but wisely kept silent.

"Well, I was just heading out anyway…" Jackson inched his way towards the exit.

"I'm coming along with you." Daychaser said. "A whole pod of creatures would have my hide if you got yourself in trouble on my watch."

"Well, hurry up or I'll leave you behind." Jackson joked before he rushed out of the lagoon.

"You leave me behind? Give me a break!" Daychaser laughed, making a show of dashing past Jackson which sent the boy flipping around in the water when he darted by.

"HEY, no fair!" Jackson cried and charged after Daychaser with a laugh.

CHAPTER TEN
THE HUNTRESS

Jackson and Daychaser happily chased each other down the shoreline towards the village as the sun rose overhead. Their joyful romp ended with a quick stop so Jackson could use his color change spell to camouflage himself before they reached the harbor.

While they snuck under the gently swaying ships, Jackson's breath caught when he saw most of the dock had been shattered apart the night before. While some men sawed off broken or poison scarred pieces of wood from what remained of the docks, other groups of people on small boats rowed around the harbor and cleared away the debris.

Jackson turned his skin nearly black when they noticed the small multitude of men and women standing watch on the five immense ships that were anchored some ways from the main dock. Jackson and Daychaser quickly dove deeper before they could be spotted and skirted around the harbor as inconspicuously as possible.

After they had silently left the harbor far behind, Jackson had just noticed a small group of stingrays swimming past when Daychaser suddenly paused and began sounding heavily.

"What's wrong?" Jackson swam over worriedly.

"There's a huge amount of splashing over there." Daychaser pointed with his snout towards the deep offshore waters. "I can't make out what it is though, it's too far."

"Should we go check it out?" Jackson nervously eyed the darker waters and gulped when a large school of fish swirled through them.

"I... it probably wouldn't be a good idea. That much thrashing is going to attract the attention of every predator around here..." Daychaser was uneasy, "and I heard there are lightning speed sharks around here."

"Lightning speed?" Jackson gave Daychaser a confused look. "What are those, are they magical?"

"No, at least, none I know about." Daychaser's ears pinned back against his head nervously. "For ocean goers, the term 'lightning speed' usually means a creature that swims really, really fast. Those fish you called swordfish are often called lightning fish for their speed, but there are types of sharks that can swim fast enough to catch those fish." He growled softly. "They're what I'm worried about. They move so fast even I couldn't get away from one if we were attacked."

"You aren't normally worried about sharks though..." Jackson pointed out. "We rarely run into truly bad ones."

"I know." Daychaser sighed. "It's just that the deep ocean creatures here have been so moody..."

Jackson's mouth twisted thoughtfully. "True, but do you think whatever's thrashing about might need help?"

Daychaser gave a rueful growl. "Probably... but if it's too dangerous, we're gonna clear out. I'd feel better if we had Startide along, but your magic is usually enough protection." He crept forward through the water slowly, sounding carefully while he and Jackson went towards the thrashing.

The two friends kept close once the water below them dropped off into deeper depths; Daychaser continued to sound the water heavily while Jackson kept an eye on the water behind and below them. After a few minutes Daychaser slowed when a dark shape coursed into view ahead of them.

"Sharks." Daychaser whispered. "Quite a few of them." He lifted his head for a better look. "They're circling a boat."

"Why? Is someone throwing fish they don't want back into the water?" Jackson squinted while he tried to make out how big the boat was.

"No?" Daychaser moved slightly closer. "I think there are some sharks in that net they have hooked to the side of the boat. That's where the thrashing is coming from."

"You think we can get in closer? I can guard us with my magic if I need to." Jackson tilted his head, watching thoughtfully when a ten-foot-long shark coasted into view a little way away.

Daychaser thought a moment before he agreed. "Ok, but let's be careful, stay behind me and guard my back."

Jackson's spells wove around his hands while they inched closer. Around ten sharks watched them with a sort of cold curiosity as they circled the two friends and the boat. Once Jackson got close enough to see what was in the nets, he was met by the sight of two sharks, each about ten feet long. The larger brown one angrily slapped the hull of the ship with its white tipped tail while its long, white-tipped pectoral fins struggled against the netting. A second, slightly shorter, but more powerful looking, silver-blue shark thrashed his long-streamlined form angrily as he latched onto the nets with his teeth before both sharks spotted Jackson and Daychaser.

"Come ta watch the end of us have ya dolphins?" The brown one snarled. "Hate to disappoint ya, but I'm breakin out of this net and then I'll show ya what for."

"That isn't a dolphin ya old fool, it's the seawolf, and the other is the lightborn in disguise." The silver shark eyed Jackson with its sharp black eyes. "Doubt they're here to watch us, more likely wantin to offer us help."

The brown shark's gills flared as he twisted around and clamped down onto the net with his teeth. "I ain't bein disgraced by some Sonaeko helpin me. I'd be the laughin stock of my shiver." He snapped towards Jackson and Daychaser. "I can free myself, thank ya, and before the Huntress comes to end me for ma folly."

The silver shark huffed in agreement while he bit down into the net holding him and thrashed about.

Jackson and Daychaser exchanged surprised looks. *The Huntress?*

"Since when is accepting someone's help considered a disgrace?" Jackson whispered, "and who's this Huntress?"

"Beats me, must be an open ocean shark thing: and I have no clue what they mean by the Huntress." Daychaser whispered back while they watched the two sharks lash the water.

After a couple of moments, Daychaser leaned over and asked in a hushed voice. "They aren't getting through that net, are they?"

Jackson shook his head. "The venom people don't fish often, but they make really strong nets treated with some strange stuff that makes them super tuff." He frowned. "They're not breaking free on their own."

"But if we help them, I have a feeling we could be in trouble..." Daychaser warily eyed the other sharks who were still circling them. "If it's their custom to not accept help, the others might attack us for helping them."

Jackson raised a brow as an idea popped into his head. "Only if they knew about it…" He whispered very quietly. "Let's stick around, I have an idea."

When the other sharks started moving in closer, Daychaser gave Jackson a questioning look and the two friends moved under the boat nervously. As the minutes ticked by, the surrounding sharks grew bolder and darted in closer once netted sharks began to tire.

Suddenly the surrounding sharks dove towards Jackson and Daychaser, making Daychaser flare out his fins defensively! The sharks turned away at the last moment and Jackson lowered his hands when a deep chant echoed through the water.

More and more sharks began slicing through the water, making the chant grow in volume as the other sharks joined in. As the chant suddenly hit a climax, Jackson and Daychaser jumped when the sharks almost shouted as a huge shark—that was well over twenty-five feet long, and had dark grey skin with a scattering of light colored stripes and a white underbelly—suddenly slipped out of the darkness. The chant abruptly died while the immense shark shrewdly eyed the boat and the two captured sharks as she slid towards them.

A royal white… Jackson's eyes widened while Daychaser anxiously surfaced next to the boat for a breath before he rushed back next to Jackson. Jackson bit his lip once the royal white took notice of them and cruised ever nearer.

"Beautiful day is it not? Lightborn, and friend." She said lazily while she wound around Jackson and Daychaser, a small school of suckerfish clinging to her belly. "My boys were just calling me for a supposed meal of fools. It's not often one, such as I, can hunt such easy prey."

"Good day Huntress." Daychaser said calmly while the nervous fire of fear danced in his eyes. "I wasn't aware any of your kind dwelt in these secluded seas."

The Huntress chuckled slowly. "Some stubborn old sharks decided to stay when others fled many generations ago." She responded. "I must say, I never expected that such delicious morsels like yourselves would come into these deeper waters. You've been largely hiding in the shallows since you arrived." Her mouth opened in a frightening show of teeth. "MUCH to the disappointment of us big open sea sharks, we often enjoy a challenging hunt you know."

Jackson shivered when the Huntress eyed them like a cockatrice eyes a cricket. As she swung back around, he somehow caught her gaze and held it, looking deep into her eyes. The Huntress's eyes flashed with interest while Jackson stared into her eyes, failing to see the darkness of dishonor. *I wonder...* He thought before she suddenly dashed towards them, causing Daychaser to flare out his fins and growl defensively!

The shark laughed. "I love taunting you seawolves, your kind never get used to something my size hunting you, or so I'm told..." She got a sly look in her eyes. "I must say it's been awhile since I've had something like you for dinner... I'd say it's **long** overdue."

Daychaser snarled when the other sharks swirled madly around them, blocking their escape routes. Jackson held his hands at the ready while Daychaser made a series of threatening sounds, bared his teeth, and hunched his back as some of the other sharks taunted them with false strikes.

Jackson and Daychaser steeled themselves while the smaller sharks made quick agitated dashes towards them, only to suddenly scatter when the Huntress lunged towards Jackson, her jaws agape!

SNAP!!

Jackson's jaw tightened while he stared into the Huntress's snout, her teeth just inches from his face. She pulled back slightly, but he held his ground while she stared at him, waiting for a reaction.

Everyone was quiet as Jackson let out a short breath, tightened his fists, and held himself tall.

The Huntress's body abruptly began to vibrate before she started laughing and moved away, an impressed gleam in her eyes.

"Back off boys, these two here are good ones. Tell me lightborn, did you know I was testing you?" She questioned as the other sharks backed off.

"I wasn't completely sure." Jackson's voice quivered a bit from the fright, "but your eyes weren't dark with dishonor."

"And yet, I'm sure you know that isn't always a true judge of a creature's intent." She grinned. "I like you young lightborn, you got guts." She went over and nudged the two sharks who were in the nets. "Now what to do about these two... they had such potential before they stupidly took the humans bait. I'd almost ask you to release them..."

She made a show of looking them over with the smallest bit of disdain. "It would shame them for their folly, and I do hate to see them go in such a pathetic manner." She seemed to ponder for a moment. "As it is, I may just eat them. It'll put them out of their misery if they can't break free."

Her comment caused the two sharks to violently renew their battle for freedom, and she seemed to sniff as her fin cut through the surface. "Thought you two had more fight in you."

Jackson suddenly felt a powerful surge of magic above them and dove forward! "HUNTRESS LOOK OUT!!" He shouted! The Huntress's eyes widened when a black glow fired into the water towards her before Jackson used his magic to shove her away!

Daychaser let out an alarmed howl and dove away when a huge barrage of dark arrows shot into the water, causing the surrounding sharks to scatter! Jackson flipped around and blasted away a long black, hooked harpoon before it could get close to him and the

Huntress, who quickly shook off her surprise and shoved Jackson deeper before a long spear was fired into the water, a dark billowing cloud of poison flying from its handle!

Jackson and the Huntress turned to watch as someone angrily sliced the water with a long black sword. Jackson noticed the cloud of poison working its way towards the two thrashing trapped sharks and frowned thoughtfully. He squinted when the sharks' bit into the nets again and, as inconspicuously as he could, he used his light magic to cut the nets along where the sharks were biting.

There was the tiniest of flickers when the ropes were cut and he heard the brown shark grunt in triumph as he wiggled out of the net, spat the piece of net out of his mouth, and dashed away! The silver shark charged free a second later, throwing his chunk of net into the water before he met Jackson's eyes, stretched his jaws, and then took off into the deep at breakneck speed.

"You!"

Jackson turned as the Huntress closed in on him.

"You just shoved me out of the blue!" Her voice was angry, and Jackson gulped while Daychaser rushed up next to him protectively. "Me, the Huntress, the one who rules these waters and all the sharks within it! You shoved me and—!"

Jackson braced himself as she opened her mouth wide.

"You saved my hide." She finished, her voice softening just a touch while she glanced over to see the spear and harpoon being dragged back towards the boat by long cords. "How did you know?"

Jackson shivered slightly at the Huntress's flashing eyes and prayed he wouldn't suffer for saving her as he quietly answered.

"I've been able to sense the forming of spells since I was little." Jackson gave the boat a leery look, "and shadow magic has a particular feel to it."

"Shadow magic? I thought these humans where venom people." Daychaser commented, looking startled.

"They are…" Jackson looked back at the boat with a perplexed look, "and yet that was definitely shadow magic."

"I could've been killed without your actions." The Huntress gave Jackson a long look. "I'm in your debt."

"You mean you aren't going to attack me for helping you?" Jackson couldn't stop the question before it burst from his mouth.

The Huntress blinked before she chuckled. "Lightborn, you know little of us offshore sharks. It is considered a disgrace for a shark to accept help when he has brought upon himself his own trouble…" She glanced in the direction the freed sharks fled, "but, for someone to aid or defend a shark who has done no folly, is considered very generous."

Jackson relaxed. "Thank goodness, I was afraid I'd offended you Great Huntress."

She laughed. "Hah, don't worry young lightborn, I'm far from angry with you, this has been the most eventful day I've had in **ages**. Although if that sorry lug in the boat ever enters the water well…" She yawned, showing off her rows of sharp teeth. "I will enjoy having him as an entrée."

"Perhaps the person on the boat was just frightened by all the sharks?" Daychaser suggested uncertainly.

"No…" Jackson looked back at the boat. "That was planned, no-one would have that many spells and enchantments ready to fire just because they were worried about sharks." He shook his head. "The enchantment on that harpoon felt strong enough that it would take a lone person weeks of preparation to cast."

"That person is hunting sharks?" Daychaser was dumbfounded. "You've gotta be kidding?"

Jackson looked over at the Huntress. "Has this happened before?"

"Not that I know of..." The Huntress's eyes were flashing dangerously. "But after this, no shark will ever get close to these boats again, and any human who falls overboard out here better watch their back!"

"I doubt the other humans even know about this..." Jackson bit his lip as he thought. "The only reason I can think of for hunting a shark of your size would be for your teeth..."

"Scuse me, my teeth?" The Huntress gave Jackson a dubious look. "Did you breathe some of that poison after those attacks hit the water?"

"There are a couple of shadow enchantments that require shark teeth..." Jackson seemed lost in thought. "Other large teeth can be used too, but they need to be big and very sharp." He shook his head, "but those spells are despised by nearly every person I know of, so why would someone be doing this?"

"What do the spells do?" Daychaser asked.

"They're power spells, used to boost another spell, make it stronger." Jackson frowned. "There's also a spell that fuses the teeth into a weapon, but I've only heard of people using it when they're desperate for a weapon. That spell nearly always backcasts, and it's often fatal."

"Either way, that human will pay!" The Huntress said lividly before she shot to the surface and breached, flying high above the waves before crashing back into the sea.

"I know his face. If I ever see him again, he'll face my wrath!" She swam past Jackson and Daychaser. "If you ever need a helping fin, ask the offshore sharks for Slaycer. Good day lightborn and seawolf." She promptly swam off into the deep and Jackson noticed

Daychaser relax for the first time since they had come out to investigate the boat.

"Thank currents they're gone!" Daychaser breathed once the sharks vanished. "You've got no idea how many sharks were swimming around watching us after the Huntress arrived. I swear there were more than three dozen, if not more. My great-aunt would have completely flipped if she'd been here."

"I'd suggest we don't tell her about it." Jackson grinned. "She finally started to warm up to Sandfang and the other sandtyr before we left."

"Yeah, I think I'll leave this story for Mom and the others." Daychaser shuddered. "Can we please go find that lagoon now? I swear I'm going to have nightmares after that."

"And here I thought you weren't afraid of sharks." Jackson joked while they swam to shore.

"I'm not afraid of shark species that don't hunt dolphins or seawolves. None of the species we just faced fell into that category." Daychaser responded somewhat tartly.

"I guess now checking in on a few human kids won't seem so dangerous?" Jackson smirked teasingly.

Daychaser snorted. "I doubt it, you and humans always seem to add up to trouble." Daychaser gave a wry smile. "Let's not count our sea turtles before they hatch."

Jackson shrugged sheepishly. "Guess I can't argue with that…"

"Nope. If you did, you'd either be lying or daft." Daychaser laughed.

CHAPTER ELEVEN

BLADE

The two friends searched along the coastline until around midafternoon. At that point, they finally gave up on finding the lagoon the kids had talked about and headed back to their own lagoon. When they returned, they found the lagoon empty, save for a large octopus hunting amongst the rocks.

Daychaser decided to scrounge around for a quick snack while Jackson went ashore to read the rest of the information the book offered about the Jewel Island Sanctuary. As Jackson quietly studied, Daychaser finished his quick hunt and started practicing his spinning and flips.

"Find anything interesting?" Daychaser called after a few more minutes.

"Oh, have I!"

Startide crooned enthusiastically as she swooped into the lagoon. "Daychaser, you left before you could learn about all the fascinating customs of the black dolphin pods here! They have so many unique songs and hunting techniques, their calving seasons are different here and—"

"Ugh make it stop!" Spinescale interrupted loudly as she slipped around Startide and stuck her head out to the water to give

Jackson a pleading look. "PLEASE tell me you've found out more about the Sanctuary! If I hear about one more black dolphin custom, I think I'll burst."

Jackson chuckled quietly at Spinescale's exasperated expression. "Well, I've learned a few things. It sounds like the Jewel Island Sanctuary is much larger than we thought. Part of it was even above the surface, which means we don't need to bother checking those underwater outcroppings we thought could hide a city inside."

He flipped back a page. "Also, before the Great Petrifying, there was a guardian that was in charge of protecting and caring for the sanctuary. The book says his name was, Koiwae, and he's some type of animal called a billowfin…" Jackson lifted a brow curiously, wondering what a billowfin was. "It sounds like he's magically connected to the sanctuary somehow, so if we find the sanctuary, hopefully we'll find Koiwae." He tapped a page with his finger. "And as Spinescale already knows, there's the picture of the Sanctuary entrance that I copied down so we can show it to other creatures."

"Sounds like ya could use a guy who knows these waters like the back of his tail." A silver-blue shark suddenly flew into the lagoon, making everyone whip around in surprise.

"What in the currents! Who're you?" Startide exclaimed.

"Name's Lashblade. Believe I already know your friends." The shark inclined his pointed snout towards Daychaser and Jackson.

"Wait a minute, aren't you one of the sharks from earlier?" Jackson curiously slipped into the water. "One of the ones who escaped from the net?"

"Huh yeah. I was fortunate I was able to *escape*, don't fancy getting myself killed by the Huntress or that shadow dude." The Shark locked eyes with Jackson as he said the word, "escape," putting the slightest emphasis on the word.

"Nice I somehow broke free when no one was lookin." He gave Jackson a long look. "If someone helped me escape, I would've been disgraced."

Jackson's skin turned cold while he gulped and exchanged a worried look with Daychaser.

Startide sensed the tension building and moved in front of Jackson protectively.

"Huh, none of that oroca." Lashblade gave her a dry look. "I'm not'a threat to any of ya." He gave Jackson and Daychaser a meaningful look. "So long as we all have an understandin that everycreature knows 'I' escaped from that shadow bloke."

Jackson let out the breath he was holding as Daychaser relaxed. "Understood Lashblade." Jackson answered.

The shark visibly relaxed. "Great, and call me Blade. Only my old ma calls me Lashblade, seems weird comin from anyone else."

"It's nice to meet you, Blade." Daychaser dipped his snout. "I'm Daychaser, and this is Startide, Spinescale, and Jackson."

"Did I miss something?" Startide looked between Jackson and Daychaser. "You've met?"

"Sorta, we'll fill you in later." Daychaser gave her a nudge.

"So why're you here again?" Spinescale asked, a dubious expression on her snout. "You don't seem the type to be coming into the shallows, Blade."

"Word's been travelin through the open ocean sharks that y'all are lookin for the lost city." Blade replied nonchalantly. "I know some sharks who might know how to help, although some identification might be useful." He dipped his head sideways to Jackson.

"What's the catch?" Spinescale asked tartly, still slightly suspicious.

"Since we have an understandin, there's not catch." Blade gave Jackson another look, "but I'll need ya to bring that picture thing y'all were talkin about. Might help."

Jackson pulled the stone slab out of his bag. "Do you think those sharks you talked about will be able to recognize this?"

Blade swam past and glanced at the copy. "Huh, if they've seen it, they will. I gotta track them down today, but since one of them owes me a favor, it shouldn't be too hard to get them to own up and help out. Y'all know where the Point of Sunderin is?"

"I do, although I've only been there once." Spinescale answered.

"Cool, meet there tomorrow afternoon, right after the sun starts sinkin from the surface of the sky. Should have some help for ya then. If I don't, I'll bring y'all along for a quick trip. Later snacks." Blade slashed his tail and vanished out of the lagoon in a blue-silver blur.

"Can someone please tell me what's going on?" Startide pleaded.

"I've got a feeling we should'a gone with Jackson and Daychaser today." Spinescale gave Jackson a quick look, "and what was that about an understanding?"

"That's something that's staying between us and Blade." Jackson gave an apologetic smirk, "but we'll fill you in on the rest of it."

Spinescale shook her head. "Ok, well why don't you fill us in while I show you guys how to get to the Point of Sundering? Deepbite wanted my help with spying on the humans tomorrow, and I don't know when I'll be back." She motioned southward with her left wing. "Come on, it's not too terribly far from the harbor."

CHAPTER TWELVE
THE MIRROR'S SECRET

While the group traveled towards the harbor, Daychaser and Jackson filled their friends in on their morning, though they left out Jackson's part in freeing Blade. Once they reached the point of the peninsula just up the coast from the harbor, they went straight, following the peninsula's point towards the shallow seabed that stretched far beyond the island.

"Was this Huntress around my size?" Startide asked when Spinescale slowed her pace.

"She was definitely bigger than you..." Daychaser replied, "but you aren't quite done growing yet, right? Your grandpodmother was a good dolphin length longer than you are."

"I hope I'm not done growing..." Startide flicked her fins thoughtfully, "but I'm not sure. My mom wasn't the largest female in our pod, I've heard my dad was a giant though."

"We're here." Spinescale spun around and fanned out her wings dramatically. "The Point of Sundering, in all its glory."

"Uh... How can you tell?" Jackson glanced around them.

"Look down." Spinescale pointed to the seafloor with her right wing.

"Woooaaah." Daychaser and the others gasped at the sight of a deep crater in the seafloor beneath them. Immense long cracks spread out from the crater's center, branching into a huge web of canyons.

"If you can't tell why it's called the Point of Sundering…" Spinescale's eyes sparkled mischievously. "I think I'd better bite you, you know, just to make sure you're not dead."

Jackson closed his mouth, which had been hanging open in shock. "W-what on Mythos caused this?" He finally asked while his eyes followed the lines of cracks.

"Morningshell's always claimed the Point of Sundering was created during a ancient war, so unless the seafloor decided to sneeze itself apart, I'd say magic is the likely culprit." Spinescale joked.

"How deep is the crater?" Jackson regarded the dark hole with a guarded expression.

"Deep, very deep." Spinescale said forebodingly.

"Actually, it's not that deep." Startide said after she'd sounded the crater. "I can sound the bottom."

"Way to ruin my scary comment…" Spinescale grumbled, making Daychaser chortle.

"There's something strange in there…" Startide said, ignoring Spinescale's grumbling, "and it's messing with my sounding."

"Your sounding is more powerful than mine, I can't sound a thing down there." Daychaser frowned. "Is it very big?"

"No?" Startide said uncertainly. "I don't think so… Again, it's interfering with my sounding. Not big enough for an ophiotaurus though. Thankfully."

"Toxic! Then let's go check it out?" Spinescale sounded excited.

Jackson felt a shiver go down his spine. *Why does something interesting have to be in the bottom of a deep dark crater?* He moved back a few strokes. "Um, I'll stay up here and keep watch while you guys investigate, or maybe I'll head back to the shallows."

"Oh, come on, don't be a minnow." Spinescale quipped. "You stood up to the Shattered One: what's wrong with a dark little crater?"

"The dark part." Jackson gulped, looking nervously into the crater's gaping maw.

Startide nudged Spinescale with her snout before the snake could respond. "We'll explain on the way. You going to be ok up here alone for a bit Jackson?"

Jackson nodded. "Yeah, I'll be fine. I'll just wander towards the shore where I can see around me a bit better. You guys just be careful down there."

"Don't worry about us, we'll be fine." Daychaser said confidently. "There isn't anything big down there, so there's nothing to worry about."

Jackson gave Daychaser a dubious look. "Just a strange unidentified something that interferes with sounding calls."

Spinescale sighed. "Great serpents. We get it. Everyone be careful, there could be something dangerous, and no one die. Let's go!" She began swimming down towards the crater. "Or I'm going without you all."

"Wait up." Daychaser said as he and Startide took off after Spinescale. "See you soon Jackson." He called back.

"Bye…" Jackson sighed while he watched his friends vanish into the depths of the crater. *Guess I might as well head back to shallower water…* He slowly flipped around and swam towards the shallows, casting many a glance behind him while he wished he dared follow his friends. *Wish the ocean didn't get so dark.*

The surface of the sea rose and fell above him gently as the shoreline came into view up ahead. When he noticed something strange floating on the surface a little ways away Jackson slowed uncertainly. Instinctively, he changed his color to a muted gray and dove a bit deeper before he inched his way over to investigate. Whatever he was looking at didn't move when he got closer, and his eyes widened once he noticed it was a furry little fish.

A stuffed toy? Out here? He reached up and grabbed the stuffed animal, sending a small plume of bubbles from its soft fluff when he pulled it below the surface. *What's a stuffed fish doing way out here...?* Jackson thought while bubbles continued to escape from the once dry fur. As the fish became waterlogged, he broke through the surface to look around. *If it was still somewhat dry when I found it, it can't have been in the water for too long."*

He glanced around a few moments until he heard voices carrying over the water to his left and he slowly slipped towards them. Soon he noticed a small boat up ahead of him and he submerged, cautiously closing the gap between himself and the boat.

"Don't worry Danna, I'm sure it's around here somewhere."

Jackson paused when he heard Bennor's voice while the boy tried to comfort his sister.

"I've already looked everywhere Ben, I can't find it!" Danna's little eyes were beginning to brim with tears. "It must've fell off the boat, but I'm afraid to wake Grandpa..."

"What's going on?" Kayla came over worriedly. "Danna? Are you ok?"

"She lost the stuffed fish our mom made for her." Bennor said rubbing the back of his neck uncertainly. "She doesn't know where it ended up."

"Oh no, have you checked under the supplies?" Kayla immediately began searching around the small boat while the other kids came over to see what the fuss was about.

"Sssh! Kayla, be careful you might wake our Grandpa and your great Uncle." Leavan whispered. "They're so tired they haven't even touched their fishing gear."

"Dealing with the monster's last attack wore everyone out." Henri said sadly. "Especially, Dad and your Grandpa. They've been doing everything they can to comfort Aunt Katrina and her kids since their dad was petrified and carried off by the monster."

A few tears escaped Danna's eyes and Kayla gave her a quick hug. "Aunt Katrina will be ok Danna, don't worry." She brushed her hair comfortingly. "Let's look for your toy, I'm sure if we all look around, we can find it. It should be here somewhere."

Jackson's heart dropped when he heard Danna whimper dejectedly and slipped up to the surface next to the boat. "Lose something?" He asked as his head broke out of the water, and he held out the soaking wet toy.

The kids flipped around and gawked at him before Danna squealed and ran over to grab the stuffed toy from his outstretched hand. "You found my fish!" She clasped the toy to her heart. "Thank you, Jackson!!"

"Where did you find it?" Bennor asked as Danna hugged the water out of the fish.

Jackson pointed in the direction he came from. "I found it over there, it must've fallen off the boat."

"Oh, thank you, thank you!" Danna danced around. "Thanks mister Jackson."

"We all need to thank you for warning us of the monster." Kayla said kindly as she and the other kids crowded around. "You saved us."

Jackson blushed. "I just did what anyone would do…" He shrugged. "I'm really sorry to hear about your uncle though."

"Yeah…" Henri took a deep breath. "He got petrified by the monster before it dragged him away when the mages started to drive it off…" He said solemnly. "Nobody dares to try and get him back; it was the same way with the other men the monster's dragged off."

"Where does that stupid monster take them anyway?" Donner interjected. "If I could go there, I'd give him a lickin he'd never forget!"

"Donner, even the highly trained mages in the clans have a difficult time driving him off, you wouldn't stand a chance." Bennor chastened.

"He's right, Donner." Jackson said before the boy could retort. "Even if you went where the Shattered One leaves the stone bodies, you'd probably get petrified too. There's dangerous magic in the canyons where the monster lives that petrifies anyone who gets too close."

"You know where the Shatter One takes people?" Donner asked, his eyes wide.

Jackson shook his head. "Not really, I've just heard about it from the ocean animals." He shrugged. "They all say the Shattered One takes petrified creatures into the canyons, I don't know why though."

"We should tell Dad, maybe he could send a search party to look there!" Terven said excitedly. "If they could find Uncle Steven, maybe they could bring him back and revive him."

Jackson groaned, hating to burst the other kid's bubble. "Didn't you hear me say the magic in the canyons petrifies those who get too close? A search party would probably get petrified before they could do anything."

Jackson felt his spirits drop when Terven's shoulders slumped.

"Well you're not helpful." Donner grumbled. "Kill joy."

"Donner he's only warning us of the danger, he's not trying to be depressing." Kayla chastened, though she looked crestfallen too.

"Is there any way we could get our uncle back?" Leavan asked Jackson quietly.

"I don't know." Jackson's head drooped. "I'm pretty sure he's not dead, only petrified. The problem isn't finding him, it's trying to survive the place he's been taken to." He shrugged hopelessly.

"It's just weird the monster keeps coming back and heads straight for the storage building." Kayla said sadly. "He's attacked it the last few times."

"The storage building?" Jackson's head flung up.

"Yeah, it's a big building the clans built not long after we landed here." Henri said. "Before it was built, the monster always attacked the town and tried to break into people's houses."

"Especially mister Defsli's house, the monster nearly always attacked him before the storage room was built." Kayla added.

"WHO?!" Jackson blurted before he quickly covered his mouth, giving the two sleeping men a worried look. "What was that name you said?" He asked urgently.

The kids all exchanged confused looks.

"Mister Defsli." Bennor gave him a confused look. "Why, do you know him?"

"What's his first name?" Jackson asked stiffly as blood began pounding in his ears.

"It's Dillox, Dillox Defsli." Kayla answered. "He had a brother named Defilin, but he went down with the ship that sunk when we first got here."

Despite himself Jackson felt his features harden in anger and had to take a couple deep breaths. "Is this Dillox… a shadow user by chance?"

"Yes…" Bennor said slowly. "Why?"

Jackson bit his lip and glanced to his right, trying not to glower angrily. "I… might've ran into him since I got here. Are there any other shadow users in your clans?"

"No, he's the only one, he isn't very friendly though." Terven rolled his eyes. "He mostly keeps to himself and is always sneaking around doing something."

"Sounds like him." Jackson muttered under his breath.

"Huh?" Leavan and Kayla asked.

"Uh, nothing." Jackson said. "I guess it was him I ran into earlier, he was trying to hunt some big sharks."

"He what?" Terven face turned red in anger. "Why would he do that!? The sharks don't hurt anything. They're so cool!"

"You sure it was Mister Defsli you saw?" Donner looked really upset too.

"I'm sure, unless you know anyone else who can cast high level shadow enchantments on weapons or cast a shadow arrow spell." Jackson said, struggling to keep his voice calm.

"Why would he be hunting sharks? They aren't good eating, and we have plenty of food." Bennor was perplexed.

"All I could think of is he wanted their teeth for a power spell. There're some shadow spells that require shark teeth, but they're only used by… less than honorable individuals." Jackson tried to keep bitterness out of his tone and failed miserably, earning him suspicious looks from the older kids.

"Do you know Mister Dillox?" Danna suddenly inquired.

Jackson was quiet for a few moments when Daychaser's questioning squee rang out over the waves and he almost sighed in relief. "Oh, there are my friends!" He said a little too quickly as he turned to look for Daychaser and the others.

He was saved from further questions when Daychaser jumped clear of the water and clicked-razzed.

"Uh, I gotta go, maybe see you guys later." Jackson dove away with a splash, darting over to Daychaser and Spinescale as they circled the small boat from a safe distance.

The kids watched Jackson rush off in confused silence before a deep voice said. "This boy keeps getting more and more interesting, now doesn't he?" The kids yelped as Grandpa Toceth lifted the brim of his hat, which had been draped over his eyes.

"You heard all of that?" Leavan asked in surprise.

"Of course, I'm a very light sleeper young lady. I woke up the minute you kid's all gasped when Jackson showed up, can't say the same for your great uncle though Henri." He slipped his hat back on his head and gazed thoughtfully in the direction where Jackson had gone. "Hm, I would've liked to hear about how Jackson knows Dillox; the boy seems to have something against him."

"Jackson's friends with the ocean creatures." Terven suggested. "Maybe he's just mad because he saw Dillox hunting his friends?"

Grandpa Toceth shook his head. "No, there was something beyond that. Jackson went on high alert the minute he heard the name Defsli." He rubbed his chin. "He wouldn't have known Dillox's name if he'd just run into Dillox when he was hunting sharks. Jackson knew Dillox's name before you even told him, and I'd wager he knew Dillox's brother's name to."

"But, how could he? He lives in the ocean?" Leavan asked.

"I don't know my dear girl, but this boy keeps getting more and more mysterious." Toceth leaned forward, "but listen. I don't want any of you to ask Dillox about this. I've never liked the man nor trusted him, and if he does somehow know this boy…" He glanced over as the other man on the boat snored loudly. "Jackson could be in danger if Dillox finds out." He looked at each of the kids in turn, giving Donner a particularly stern look. "Not a word to Dillox. Ok?"

The kids all nodded.

"Maybe all ocean creatures hate Dillox, he always complains about how the monster always goes after him when it comes ashore." Henri said.

"You'll want to see what we found, Jackson. It looks magical." Daychaser said when Jackson swam over.

Jackson managed to give Daychaser a tight-lipped nod as he rushed past them to where Startide was swimming a bit further off. Daychaser and Spinescale exchanged a shocked look before they hurried after him.

"What's got your scales flared?" Spinescale asked, giving him a searching look.

"I'll… I'll explain later. What was it you guys found?" Jackson tried forcing himself to relax, although his voice was still tight.

"We thought we'd have a hard time explaining what it was, so we brought it back with us." Daychaser said. "We think it's some human thing, Startide has it."

They were quite a ways away from the boat when Startide came over to meet them. Jackson could tell she was keeping a sound on the boat by the way she kept tilting her head up and down slightly. When they drew near, Startide opened her mouth and stuck out her huge tongue to show a dark purple mirror around the size of a grown man's hand. The lens glistened in the light and the rusting iron encircling it showed a series of dark black symbols enchanted into the metal.

"SPIT THAT OUT NOW!" Jackson yelped and flew backwards at the sight, his hands glowing briefly before he stopped himself from blasting the mirror with a light spell! The scene made his friend jump in surprise, and Startide promptly dropped the mirror.

"What's the matter?" Daychaser swooped down to snatch up the mirror before it could fall to the seafloor and gave Jackson a confused look. "Isn't it just a human thing?"

"That's a messenger mirror!" Jackson backed up even more, "and please tell me it hasn't flashed or pulsed with magic since you found it."

"Ooookaayyy... Did those humans cast a spell on you or something?" Spinescale gave Jackson a once over. "You're sure acting weird."

"Please just drop it, or have Startide put it in her mouth, or better yet bite it in half." Jackson said in a hushed voice as he kept inching away.

Daychaser and Startide exchanged a look before he tossed the mirror towards her. "Don't bite it." He said before she gently closed her jaws around it.

"Why is a mirror scaring you so bad?" Startide asked.

"It's not just a mirror." Jackson said quietly. "It's a messenger mirror, and if those symbols are what I think they are, it's connected to some very bad people."

"The people who attacked your family?" Daychaser's eyes widened in understanding.

Jackson nodded.

"We heard a voice coming from it asking for someone named Dillox…" Startide said, "before the mirror suddenly went almost black."

If Jackson had been on land his mouth would've gone dry in fright. "Did the voice say who was speaking?"

"No, it just asked if Dillox was there a couple of times before it went dark and then returned to its normal color." Startide said. "Do you really want me to bite it in half? I'm not sure if my teeth are strong enough for that."

"This is really bad." Jackson mumbled anxiously. "If Dillox is trying to contact them, they could find their way here."

"Who the venom are you talking about?" Spinescale asked. "Can someone please tell me what's going on before I bite something."

"In the outside world there's a war going on between the humans." Daychaser said. "Jackson's family was being hunted by an evil group of people called the Toxicshade who wanted to kill them. Jackson is the only one who's left…"

"My family were trapped in stone for protection." Jackson explained quietly. "That's part of why I started this journey, I'm trying to learn the spell I need to free them."

"Wait, ya mean ya are only on this journey to help yourself?" Everyone turned when Blade came darting through the water, gazing suspiciously at Jackson.

"Blade? Where did you come from?" Daychaser asked in surprise.

"I was coming by this way searchin for an old friend o' mine when I heard ya'll talkin." He looked over at Jackson with a disapproving look. "You're on this journey just to help yourself?"

Jackson shook his head. "What? No, not really." He paused as he gathered his thoughts. "The whole reason I'm even on this journey is because I offered to help Oceaono and the other medians free the Sonaeko. This whole thing might've started with me searching for help for my family, but it's become more than that, it was never all about me."

Blade's disapproving look faded. "Cool, glad to hear it. Was worried I'd misjudged ya." He indicated his head towards Startide. "Now why's this mirror things so bad again?"

"A few years before my family was attacked by the Toxicshade, my grandpa helped warn some large venom clans we were friends with about a plot the Toxicshade Emperor devised to destroy them." Jackson looked back towards the boat that had begun heading towards shore as some pieces of a very complicated puzzle fell into place. "They were the Spherefang Clans, they had been subjected to the Toxicshade Empire about a year before, but still refused to help the empire." Jackson looked down at the seafloor while he thought. "The emperor was so furious that he decided to try and secretly wipe them out, but they were able to escape because of my grandpa's warning."

He scowled. "But later we found out a couple spies had fled with them and were giving away information on where they planned to flee. Somehow, their ships vanished before the Toxicshade could attack." Jackson's jaw tightened. "But not before one of the spies, who used to be my dad's friend, found out we were the ones who warned the clans and told his superiors."

"And that man is here?" Daychaser click-barked in alarm.

Jackson nodded, looking over at Blade who was circling the group. "He's the shadow user that caught Blade and that other shark, and who was trying to kill the Huntress. Dillox Defsli."

"The dude who almost killed me is the same kelp-head who tried to kill ya and your family?" Blade's voice took on a dangerous edge. "This whole thing's just got personal."

Jackson let out a tight breath. "And if this mirror is what I think it is, Dillox was probably using it to speak to his superiors and lead the Toxicshade here so they can eradicate the Spherefang's like they originally planned to."

"Ok, now your reaction to the mirror doesn't seem so insane." Spinescale tucked her wings back against her sides.

"Uh, thanks…" Jackson responded uncertainly.

"Then… should I break the mirror?" Startide asked. "Or at least spit it out? It's getting hard not to swallow it."

Jackson bit his cheek nervously and rallied his courage. "No… I… I guess I better take a look at it." He begrudgingly held out his hand while Startide stuck out her tongue and extended the mirror towards him.

Jackson hesitantly reached over and picked up the mirror, taking a deep breath before he began looking it over. He shivered when he saw the stark black symbols of the Toxicshade and took a deep breath. *Ok, almost every messenger mirror I know of has a history crystal…* He thought as he turned it around. *There!* He gently touched a clear crystal that had some strange purple mist swirling around inside of it. Cautiously, he reached into the mirror and felt around the crystal with some shadow magic. He searched around with his magic carefully while he tried to find any enchantments affecting the crystal. After a few minutes he only detected a couple shadow enchantments and huffed.

"He's gotten lazy with his protective spells." Jackson smirked.

"Come again?" Blade asked, making Jackson aware his friends had crowded around him to watch what he was doing.

Jackson quickly checked to make sure the mirror wasn't functioning before he spoke. "Dillox only used shadow enchantments to protect this little history crystal connected to the mirror." He pointed to the small gem. "I guess he was only worried about one of the Spherefangs finding the crystal; they wouldn't be able to break his shadow enchantments in a way that would keep the crystal's memory intact."

"Since when do crystals have memoires?" Blade muttered while Jackson closed his eyes and gingerly forced his own shadow magic into the mirror, mixing it in with the enchantments. He slowly formed his magic into a ring around the crystal before he abruptly switched to light magic, causing a loud clinking sound as the crystal popped off the mirror.

"What'd you do?" Startide asked when Jackson sighed in relief and picked up the crystal.

"I broke the enchantments that were protecting the history crystal." Jackson held the crystal up to the sunlight. "Shadow enchantments are weak to light magic, so I simply made sure there weren't any hidden surprises before I nullified them. I didn't want the history contained in the crystal to get destroyed when the spells broke, or for me to get zapped with something nasty."

"Why didn't he have anythin to protect it from light magic?" Blade asked, looking unimpressed. "Kinda stupid to not protect it from somethin its weak against."

"I'd bet he never expected someone who can use light magic to find this..." Jackson scowled darkly. "Years ago, the Toxicshade set a bounty on anyone who had knowledge of light magic. They tried to wipe them out since they posed too much of a threat to the empire. As it was, most light users fled to the other nations years ago for protection." He said sadly, using his magic to make the crystal glow a faint purple as the mist within began to swirl.

"Commander, this is Defsli. Can you hear me?"

Everyone quieted when Dillox's voice came from the crystal.

"This is scorspent spy Defsli, can anyone hear me?"

Jackson tensed when another voice answered in a demanding tone.

"This is Commander Slavson. Where have you been Defsli? You better have news for me. We've heard nothing from you since your message about the Growingstar Tribe."

"Oh, I have news Commander, news I'm sure you'll love to hear."

"...I'm listening."

"I'm with the Spherefang Clans who are trapped on some hidden islands with no way to escape and—"

"They shouldn't even still be alive! You were supposed to have set off the shadow holes if we weren't able to make our move in time."

"The ship that had our men and equipment on was destroyed by some crazy monster, so I wasn't able to proceed as we had planned. I haven't had the resources to damage the clans from within, but I've found a way to set off a beacon you can use to find us."

There was a long pause. "You better be telling the truth Defsli; why haven't you contacted us before this? It's literally been years."

"Again, the ship with all my supplies was sunk and is in treacherous waters. I was finally able to get the supplies I needed to repair the mirror when a storm washed some stuff ashore last month."

"You keep mentioning these treacherous waters, will they be a problem for our ships if we come?"

"I have that covered, you and your men will be perfectly fine. I can start setting off the beacon every fourth night from now."

"Fine, we'll send our ships out soon. You still have the right spells memorized?"

"Of course, I wouldn't of been able to contact you without them."

"Sass me DIllox and we'll mow you down with the Spherefangs! I'll contact you in a couple weeks to get more information. The mirror on our end is nearly out of power."

"Then I'll speak to you then."

Jackson waited while the mist stilled for a moment before it began swirling around again.

"Dillox, this is Commander Slavson, our ships will reach the Whirlwind Isles in a matter of days. Where do we go from here?"

"Head southeast towards the whirlpools, the island the clans are hiding on is somewhere around them. I'll keep activating the beacon to give your ships an idea of where we are."

"Have you figured out a way for our ships to get safe passage through the treacherous waters?"

"I have a plan, don't worry. You'll soon have the Spherefang's in your grasp, and a new hidden island base to tell the Emperor about when you're done."

"I'd better, Commander Slavson out."

Jackson stared incredulously at the crystal. "What on Mythos does Dillox mean when he says he'd take care of the treacherous waters? There's no way he could control the magic in the canyons or the Shattered One."

Startide shrugged. "Search me, perhaps he thinks the Shattered One is what caused the ships to sink? He might be assuming he'll only have to draw the Shattered One away long enough for the ships to get through."

149

"But how does he plan to lure the Shattered One away?" Spinescale got a snarky look in her eyes. "I doubt he'd do so himself, it's not like he's usually around during the fights when the Shattered One is attacking the town."

"The kids mentioned that when the Shattered One first started attacking the village that it tried breaking into people's houses." Jackson said thoughtfully, "but ever since the clans built the storage building, it's headed there each time."

"Did they say anything else?" Daychaser inquired.

"Actually, yeah, they said that the Shattered One often tried to attack Dillox for some reason." Jackson mused, "but they didn't know why."

"You think Dillox has something the Shattered One wants?" Spinescale suggested.

"Doubt it, how would he have gotten it? I think that anyone with a bite of sense can just tell he's a nasty dude." Blade quipped.

"Perhaps we're missing something?" Daychaser quarked.

"Maybe Deepbite or his friends will know? They spend a lot more time spying on the humans than I do." Spinescale offered. "I'll go find him and see if he can help us figure out what's going on."

There is definitely something strange going on... Jackson thought.

CHAPTER THIRTEEN
THE LOST CITY

The following morning Jackson, Daychaser, and Startide were wandering over to the Point of Sundering to meet Blade when Deepbite and Spinescale suddenly came rushing over.

"Thank venom! I was afraid we missed you and would have to swim to the meeting place on our own." Spinescale gave a tired gasp.

"You haven't tried to go ashore, have you, Jackson?" Deepbite interjected worriedly.

"No…" Jackson said hesitantly.

"Good, because you'd be incredibly stupid to try right now." Deepbite said, his gaze serious. "Ever since the Shattered One attacked the other night, almost all the clans have been in an uproar. Some of the men are even planning an attack on the crystal beings and the Shattered One at the canyon."

"Are those crystal beings he created still around?" Daychaser asked in alarm.

Deepbite flicked out his tongue. "No, but the humans think a couple might be. The first one was destroyed in the fight before it vanished back into the Shattered One. The second got damaged and made it under the dock before it disintegrated, and the last one

151

escaped, but was seen floating through the harbor later. Though from what I heard from the seabirds, it dissolved and vanished too."

"Great..." Startide said dryly, "and by any chance is a man named Dillox the one planning the attack on the Shattered One?"

"I... don't know the names of the people, but the man planning the attack is the shadow user." Deepbite said uncertainly.

Jackson groaned. "That's Dillox."

"Do you know when they're planning their attack?" Daychaser asked.

"About four days from now." Deepbite answered. "The man you call Dillox seemed to think that would be the best time for some reason."

"Sounds like we were right..." Startide sighed. "Dillox assumes that if they distract the Shattered One, the Toxicshade ships could get through." She glanced over at Jackson and Daychaser. "Does that mean what I think it means?"

"That the Toxicshade are way too close." Daychaser said in a concerned voice. "We really gotta figure out what to do, there's more than just us at stake now."

Jackson flipped around when thunder rumbled across the sky. "You think a storm would work? Sounds like one is brewing."

"It should buy us some time." Spinescale followed Jackson's gaze. "Storms seem to hover over the canyons awhile before they hit the islands: but just the fact that one is brewing might make the clans hesitate with their plans to attack."

"It might drive back the Toxicshade ships to." Daychaser added while more thunder rumbled.

"Either way, we've got a couple more days before anything happens." Startide's expression was serious, but thoughtful. "Today let's focus our energy on finding the Jewel Island Sanctuary. If we find it, maybe we can get some help." She suggested. "We should also hurry, or we're going to be late for our meeting with Blade and the other sharks."

"And we really shouldn't keep Blade waiting…" Daychaser said. "Let's get the meeting over with and go from there, we'll take one bite at a time."

Jackson glanced longingly over his shoulder towards shore while the group swam off. *But who's going to warn the Spherefangs of the Toxicshade? My family almost died protecting them…* He bit his lip as he tried to catch up to the others.

Daychaser seemed to sense something was off and looked back at Jackson and slowed. "What's up?"

"I'm just worried about the Spherefangs." Jackson said as they reached deeper waters. "I feel like I need to warn them, if I don't and the Toxicshade get through…" He left his sentence unfinished.

"My grandpodmother always said; 'You can't take care of everything at once…'" Startide commented from up ahead. "Or you'll get nothing done."

"We have time to figure something out." Spinescale encouraged, "and if we find this Sanctuary, maybe that sanctuary guardian you mentioned can help us find a way to help the humans."

Jackson nodded. "Ok, I'm just worried…"

"Aren't we all." Deepbite smiled wryly.

Jackson and his friends reached the Point of Sundering just before noon and found Blade and three other sharks lazily circling the deep crater. Blade was the first to notice them and glided over with thoughtful flicks of his tail. "Glad to see you lot are on time. Took a bite to get these sharks here."

"Oh knock it Blade! We ain't that hard to convince." One brown shark with white fin-tips said as he swam within earshot.

"Speak for yourself. I heard there was a whale carcass around Emerald Reefs, would've been the best meal I've had in weeks."

Another solid dark brown shark grumbled. "Only reason I'm here is because the lightborn is involved."

"Blade here says ya'll need a bit o help finding something." A female blue shark came swimming closer. "Something around these parts."

"We're searching for the lost city that used to be around here somewhere." Daychaser explained. "Morningshell indicated it was somewhere around the smaller islets on this side of the main island."

"Haven't seen a city, can I go now?" The dark brown shark grunted.

"They ain't done asking ya questions." Blade snapped impatiently, "and if there's actually a whale carcass, there'll be plenty left over for you."

"In the Book of the Sonaeko I found a picture to the entrance of the city." Jackson pulled out the tablet he etched the picture on. "We were wondering if you might recognize it, or know of anyone that would?" He held the tablet out for them to see.

The female shark was the first to swim by and look at the sketch before the two male sharks took their turn. The three sharks grumbled thoughtfully to each other as they spun around in a circle.

"I think I've seen something like this." The female blue shark said after a minute. "What do you guys think?" She glanced over at the other sharks.

"Yep, I saw somethin like it, few years back; there was a good schoolin of bait fish near it." The darker male said.

"That's right!" The female shark's eyes lit up. "I remember now, I know exactly where it was."

"Could you show us the way?" Spinescale asked.

"Shouldn't be too much trouble." The lighter male said. "It's around an islet not too far from here."

"Suit yourselves. Now that I've done my bit, I'm off to enjoy a meal." The dark male promptly swam off into the deep and Blade glowered at him.

"Forget about him Blade." The female shark said dryly. "If he'd rather fill his belly than help the Sonaeko, he can answer to the Huntress when she finds out later."

Blade still grumbled angrily through his gills while the other sharks led everyone away from the Point of Sundering. The sharks nonchalantly guided the group in the direction of a bunch of smaller islets that Jackson and his friends had begun searching around a few days ago.

No one said much while the group was taken towards the larger islets. Their guides seemed to be in no great rush, and casually swam over the deeper waters towards the isles. As the group drew near, their guides calmly glided downward along the outward slopes of the isle, towards a section where a large rockslide had swept down part of the slope. The two sharks nosed around a couple minutes before the male made a smug sounding humph and pushed a large rock with his snout.

"The entryway's behind here." He looked up at the others. "Rockslide covered this spot a couple months ago during a storm."

"You sure this is the place?" Blade asked.

"Yep, look over here." The blue shark pointed at the edge of the rockslide where she'd been searching around.

Everyone hurried over to see the edge of a large circular door peeking through the rubble.

"It matches Jackson's drawing almost perfectly." Spinescale looked from the corner to the etching on the stone slab. "That is, what little pattern I can see matches."

"No wonder we couldn't find it." Startide said. "I never would've thought to look behind here."

"Take awhile to clear the rubble enough for you to get to the door." The male shark pointed out.

"Maybe not…" Jackson smiled thoughtfully. "Everyone swim back."

"Be careful you don't damage the door." Deepbite twisted around with Spinescale as they gave Jackson some space.

"I'll be careful." Jackson replied.

"Why we movin back?" Blade asked. "No offense, but Jackson's no whale."

"He has a few tricks up his fins." Daychaser gave a smug smirk.

Jackson went over to tap a few rocks and a large boulder experimentally before he nodded to himself and backed away. He took a deep breath and clasped his hands together above his head while they began to glow before he reared back and slammed them into the boulder! Bright pulses of magic rippled from his hands through the rocks, which began to tremble and crack loudly as the stones crumbled apart and spilled down the slopes around him.

"You guys mind helping me move these so I can keep digging?" Jackson turned, finding the shark's mouths hanging open wider than normal while Daychaser and Startide struggled to keep from laughing. Spinescale, on the other fin, was howling with mirth as she twisted around in the water while Deepbite gave Jackson an impressed look.

"Told ya he had a trick or two up his fins." Daychaser finally couldn't hold it in anymore and started laughing while he swam forward to push away some of the smaller rocks and stones.

"That's… that's some trick." Blade said after a moment.

"Oh, we've seen better." Startide's eyes danced with amusement as she helped Daychaser shove a piece of the boulder down the slope. "Now are you three going to keep staring, or are you going to help us move some of this away so Jackson can continue his trickery?"

Blade firmly shook away his surprise and swam over to start shoving some rocks away. His movements seemed to snap the other two sharks out of their shock, and they quickly came over to help as well.

As the group worked, Jackson noticed that the sharks often took big chunks of rocks in their mouths before dumping their load down the slopes. Jackson was certain he saw a couple of the shark's white teeth go tumbling away with their loads, and noticed Startide and Daychaser were careful to not damage their own teeth as they shoved things around with their snouts, fins, and tails.

They spent most of the afternoon digging out the entrance as Jackson used different types of earth spells to help loosen and remove the rubble, or to stabilize other areas so the slope wouldn't collapse again.

As the day wore on, Jackson figured out how to create small currents of water to sweep away large amounts of gravel and small debris. Spinescale nearly gave him a heart attack when he accidentally swept her away in a current, which made her let out an ear-splitting shriek as she swirled down the slope. Jackson anxiously darted down after her, but his attempts to apologize were quickly curtailed when a wide-eyed Spinescale excitedly demanded another ride!

The sun was hanging low against the surface of the sea when the last of the rubble was cleared away and Jackson sighed in relief as he moved back to look at the immense circular door. He took a deep breath while he tried to keep his body from trembling with exhaustion and folded his arms tightly to keep them from noticeably shaking.

"It's beautiful." Startide said. "Those designs are absolutely gorgeous."

She's right. Jackson thought.

There was a single large island engraved in the middle of the door with a seven-pointed star sitting in the center. Two large circles encased the star, from which trails of magic had been etched, spreading from the main island to six other islands surrounding the one in the center. Each of the islands carried a distinct symbol in its center and a multitude of different ocean creatures, ships, and Sonaekians, were drawn swimming in the waters around the islands.

"How we get it open?" Blade went and bumped the door with his snout. "Looks pretty solid."

"I don't think we open it alone..." Jackson ran his hand along the beautiful engravings. "I read that a guardian named Koiwae oversees the Sanctuary. I think he's gotta open it." He put his hand on the orb in the middle of the door, carefully reaching out into the orb with his water magic. His spell abruptly ended when he was hit by a dizzy spell from the strain of using so much magic in one day. He shook his head a bit and took a moment to breathe and gather a bit of energy before starting again.

"Hello? Is anyone there?" Jackson asked, sending his thoughts magically swirling into the orb. *"My name is Jackson, Oceaono and the Medians have asked for my help, but my friends and I are lost and could really use some help."* His features tightened while he searched for any signs of the guardian.

Suddenly a warm magical glow reached out to gently connect with Jackson's own magic and an older, wise male voice reached his mind. *"It has been many years since I've heard those names, or much of anything at all. Thank you for freeing me from my stasis young lightborn. I, Koiwae, will be but a moment."*

Jackson's hand dropped down as magic flooded through the door, causing the engravings to shine with magical light while the orb glistened brightly. He backed away when light spiraled out from the orb, gradually forming into the six-foot-long body of a glowing white-blue fish, who blinked slowly while he glanced around. The fish regarded Jackson with wise, thoughtful eyes as his form solidified, though his long liquid-like fins continued to fade away at the tips.

Koiwae drifted past Jackson to intently inspect the boy's friends, who were watching the magical fish in awe. Startide barely moved when the large fish gracefully glided around her, looking deep into her eyes. Koiwae seemed to smile at her before swimming alongside Daychaser while the seawolf watched curiously, returning Koiwae's gaze with a respectful dip of his head. Koiwae returned the dip and coursed over Deepbite and Spinescale, both of whom watched him uncertainly before the fish swept over to the sharks.

Blade's eyes were slightly wider than usual, but he only gave Koiwae a cool, slightly interested look, while the other two shark's gills and fins were flared in surprise. Jackson swore he saw a mischievous look flash across Koiwae's eyes before the fish suddenly shrunk to the size of Jackson's fist and darted into Blade's slightly open mouth to inspect his teeth.

Blade let out a curt yell of surprise and his eyes spun around wildly, as if he was trying to see what the guardian was doing inside his mouth. After a minute, Koiwae's form dissolved, flowing out of the shark's gills before reforming to his original size as he swam back over to Jackson. Koiwae gave Jackson a quick wink before he vanished into the door with a low chuckle.

Koiwae's sage voice rang from the orb. "Welcome lightborn and friends. You are free to enter the Jewel Island Sanctuary."

There was a loud grinding sound when the door suddenly shifted and rolled into the mountainside. The sound of rushing water greeted Jackson's ears when a gentle, but strong, current started flowing into the sanctuary, carrying Jackson and the others through the entrance and down a large, long hallway.

Jackson looked around in wonder as glowing white sunlight stones illuminated the hallways that were decorated with scenes from the everyday lives of the Sonaeko. Jackson's eyes widened when the pictures on the walls moved as they passed, acting out the different scenes.

Jackson smiled when they passed one of a bunch of children and ocean creatures romping through tall kelp beds while they played games and chased each other. It was followed by one of adult Sonaeko growing coral gardens and tending to underwater forests of some strange plants Jackson didn't recognize. Another mural showed Sonaekians and their friends and families gathering together for dinner and dancing. As they drifted down the hallway they passed moving images of Sonaekians: hunting fish with dolphins and sharks, building strange circular homes, harvesting kelp, raising krill and other small creatures, practicing magic, and training with different ocean creatures.

One particular scene stood out to Jackson as they neared the end of the hallway; a young man with a tail like his stood tall in the water while an older man handed some strange item to him before the two bowed to one another. Jackson looked back to watch the living picture as the current carried him away, but the sight was quickly forgotten when he turned and saw they were being swept into an immense cavern.

Jackson gasped quietly and looked around the utterly massive dome shaped cavern in wonder, while a huge sunlight stone gleamed from its place in the middle of the ceiling. The light from the stone glistened off the waves that were gently lapping against the semicircular tract of land running along the edge of the cavern. A pair of strange looking birds let out long cries as they skimmed the waves, casting small shadows over Jackson and his friends when they passed.

The ceiling was crisscrossed with strange patterns and runes that faded out to show stunning images of beautiful sunset. Jackson saw a small town along the left side of the cavern where white Sonaekian buildings and homes–that were trimmed with gold, silver and blue designs–sparkled next to a small shining white and blue palace and a large academy. The town was lined with semicircles of coral gardens which were surrounded by expansive fields of seagrass that waved gently in the current. *It's so beautiful...* Jackson sighed before Startide suddenly groaned.

"Oh no..." She exclaimed, sadly swimming up beside Jackson.

"What?" Jackson asked, quickly following her gaze before his heart cracked!

Far to their right, the seafloor sloped upwards to form a semicircular amphitheater where a brightly glowing orb flashed from atop a tall pillar at the back of the semicircle. Jackson's chest tightened when the light from the orb cast a myriad of shadows across the petrified forms of thousands of Sonaekians and ocean creatures. The multitude was so great, that many of the stone forms had spilled out of the amphitheater and coated the grounds around it.

"I... I've never seen the effects of the Great Petrifying like this before." Daychaser said in a hushed voice.

"We have." The female blue shark said. "Around the edges of the canyons and one other place not far from there."

"Though there aren't nearly this many bodies." The male shark added with a disheartened flick of his fins.

"Are... are they all dead?" Spinescale quietly hissed in horror.

"No, only frozen in stone: awaiting the day someone will awaken them from their slumber." Startide said.

Jackson hastily backed away as tears stung his eyes. "Oh Mom… You were right…" He whispered.

"You ok Jackson?" Blade looked over with a slightly concerned expression as everyone turned to look.

"I'm… No. No, I'm not…" He tore his eyes away and rubbed them as a sob threatened to escape his throat.

"You're family?" Startide asked tenderly as she and Daychaser came over and leaned into his shoulders comfortingly.

Jackson nodded. "They're trapped the same way they are." He said quietly, glancing over his shoulder at the petrified multitudes. "Although at least my family had a choice." He shivered. "These people didn't." He looked down at the seafloor below. "Mom forbid me from going to see them after they were petrified, she said it would break my heart…" He glanced over to the sobering scene and bit his lip when tears came floating out of his eyes. "It did…"

"There is much heartache in this cavern my young friend." Koiwae said sadly as he appeared in front of Jackson and the others. "These…" The fish swept one of his billowing fins over the petrified throng. "Truly did not choose their fate." He looked closer at Jackson. "Forgive me, but I'm afraid I do not know which family you come from, young lightborn." He swirled around him. "Did some of the royal family escape the Petrifying all those years ago?"

"Didn't you hear the message on the currents the Medians sent out?" Startide asked in surprise while Jackson's eyes widened at the mention of the royal family.

"Of course I did young oroca, but the Medians did not say where the newly awakened Sonaeko had come from." Koiwae replied gently. "I merely wish to know why, after two hundred years, a Sonaeko has finally returned to the seas. For—while I have heard much of what has gone on in these sheltered waters since my imprisonment—I have not heard anything about what has happened outside these islands since the Lost Ones."

Jackson looked down in surprise when his hands started glowing brightly, he quickly held them out as the Star of the Sea flashed into view and started dancing around Koiwae.

The Star shot back over to Jackson. "Do you mind if we show Koiwae, and later the medians, your journey and how it began Jackson?" A familiar voice asked as the star floated around him.

"Huh?" Jackson asked.

"Might we show Koiwae your journey?" The voice asked. "At least the parts that should be shared."

"I… I guess..." Jackson said with the slightest bit of reservation.

The star swept over to Koiwae before a bright light flew from its core to engulf Koiwae in an orb of light. Jackson watched in stunned silence while the light seemed to swirl around Koiwae for a time before it suddenly grew even brighter and began gathering into the Star. When all the light had returned, the Star blinked before quickly vanishing into Jackson's hands.

"By the star-currents." Koiwae said quietly. "I'm… I'm afraid I don't know what to say…" He looked over at Jackson. "You truly know almost nothing of your heritage?"

Jackson shook his head while he tried to toss away his shock and rubbed the side of his head in wonder. "Uh... no? I know I had ancestors who were water users on my grandfather's side, but beyond that no. There's only myths and legends about the Sonaeko now-days. Most people barely know anything about them, other than they existed at one point."

Koiwae looked deeply troubled. "The Stars of the Sea were always strange in when they would intervene."

Jackson thought that was a weird response, but any questions he would've asked died when Koiwae continued.

"We must reach out to the median's immediately; they surely fear you might've perished by now." He swam off towards the orb atop the tall pillar in the amphitheater but turned when Jackson hesitated to follow.

"Jackson," Koiwae's voice was understanding. "I'm sorry. I know it's hard to see those trapped in stone, but the conference beacon in the amphitheater is the best way to contact Oceaono and the others."

Jackson nodded weakly and bit his cheek before he tentatively moved forward with his friends while they followed Koiwae. As they drew near the assembly of stone figures surrounding the pillar, Startide and the other air breathers quickly swam up to the surface for a breath.

"What were these creatures doing here?" Startide asked once she had returned and noticed the stone figure of an oroca shielding a young calf and a small Sonaekian child.

"These creatures had gathered to lend their energy to help cast a powerful spell that would heal and calm the ancient beasts and return them to their homes." Koiwae answered. "Almost every Sonaeko had been gathered to help with the spell." He paused next to the stone form of a young teenage girl who was wearing a beautiful, but fragile looking, crown on her head and a long, elegantly flowing dress who was petrified in the act of shielding a young child.

"I was so caught up in helping power the spell, I was unaware of what happened: but I heard my dear pupil, Princess Ocemalia Suncrest, gasp something about betrayal before the spell miscast." He looked up at the orb. "After that, the world went dark for a time while the spell continued to miscast, petrifying nearly everything it touched."

He shook his head as if shaking away the memories. "Jackson, would you please put your hand on the orb? Try to call out to Oceaono like you did to me. I will aid you."

Jackson nodded and he swam forward to place his hand on the orb. *"Hello Oceaono? Can you hear me? It's Jackson."*

"Please answer our summons crystal Median." Koiwae's voice called out with Jackson's.

Not a moment later a warm glow answered and the shining miniature form of Oceaono flashed into view next to the orb, quickly followed by the other medians.

"JACKSON!" Oceaono cried out in relief. "You're ok? You're alive!" He flew over and looked Jackson over. "What in the great seas happened? We've been trying to reach you, but have felt nothing."

"Calm yourself Oceaono." Koiwae said. "The lad is fine, as are his brave group of friends." He smiled at Startide, Daychaser, and the others.

"We were chased into the whirlpools by dishonored." Startide began. "The Star of the Sea saved us from the whirlpools, and we ended up here, at the Lost Jewels."

"Ah," Seanel said as she swam over. "That would explain why we couldn't reach you or the Star of the Sea. Are any of you hurt?" She looked the others over before her eyes lingered on Jackson. "Jackson, you seem weaker than when we last saw you, have you been overworking yourself?"

Jackson's face colored in embarrassment. "No, yes... maybe... I just used a bit too much magic when we were clearing away the entrance to the Sanctuary. I should be fine."

"You must learn to pace yourself, young man." Sharval said. "It will do no good to tire yourself out, there will be much we must ask of you in the near future, and you must have your strength."

"I know but…" Jackson started to say before Docion cut him off.

"Sharval is right, and we have much we must teach you. You should learn to rely on your friends, such is the way of the dolphin." Docion added.

Jackson gave his friends a pleading look.

"We wouldn't've let Jackson overwork himself if we had known he was." Startide said firmly, sounding like a worried older sister as she gave Jackson a serious stare.

Not the help I was looking for… Jackson thought, his mouth twisting in frown.

"I'm sure you wouldn't have." Seanel said gently, "but while we were worried about you, I'm sure there wasn't any reason for you to take a bit longer to unblock the entrance."

"Actually, that's where ya lot are wrong." Blade cut in. "Ya don't know what's been goin on here and what's about to happen." He gave Jackson a curt nod. "Jackson's got a lot more on his fins then I think ya realize."

"Preposterous." Falganous grumbled. "We know way more of what he has to deal with than you would."

"Wait." Oceaono held up a hand for quiet. "What do you mean?"

Jackson looked down at his hands which began to glow again. "Um…"

Koiwae noticed Jackson's hands and chuckled, drawing the attention of the medians. "I believe young Jackson has the way to answer that. Don't you Jackson?"

Jackson held out his right hand as the Star of the Sea peeked out and began glowing brightly. Bright blue beams of energy shot from its core, stopping directly in front of each median before they reached out to it and were engulfed in light.

When the Star of the Sea vanished once again Oceaono blinked a couple of times. "Oh whirlpools, you get involved in many a current, don't you Jackson?"

"It looks like I misunderstood." Seanel said. "Forgive me Jackson, I had no idea this was going on."

"It's ok." Jackson said, relieved he wasn't in trouble anymore.

"Koiwae, do you know anything about this Shattered One?" Docion asked.

"I'm afraid I know very little. I didn't recognize him when the Star showed him to me." Koiwae said ruefully. "I was either caught up with other things or trapped within the sanctuary when the magic in the canyons was trapped there."

"I think I know him." Oceaono face tightened in thought while he thrummed his crystal fingers on his thigh. "I think that may be Lorgeo. He was one of the ones who helped stabilize the whirlpools right before the spell miscast."

"Excuse me?" Spinescale asked. "You're saying you **know** the Shattered One?"

Oceaono nodded. "I believe this Shattered One may be Lorgeo, an elder of my kind." Oceaono seemed concerned. "He was known for his skill with magical artifacts and weapons, and I know he and his son were sent to help stabilize the whirlpools around the Jewel Isles in the aftermath of a horrible battle."

"I do believe you're right." Seanel agreed, letting out a concerned bellow, "but something terrible must've happened for him to have shattered like that."

"Wait, are you saying the Shattered One is a good guy?" Startide asked in disbelief, "but he's been petrifying creatures and dragging them off to the canyons for years, and he attacked us!"

"I wonder…" Oceaono started pacing. "The phrase he said to Jackson after he noticed he was a lightborn was a strange one…"

"I don't speak shattered well, but there was something about it that seemed like a plea." Koiwae said.

"Are you saying he was asking for help?" Daychaser seemed dubious. "Couldn't he have asked for it instead of attacking us?"

"Wait a minute," Jackson moved forward and addressed Oceaono. "Do you know what that spell was that he fired at us?"

"Yes, good point Jackson." Oceaono snapped his fingers as he paced. "That was some kind of vortex spell. It would've trapped you in a swirling vortex until he broke the spell. Koiwae." Oceaono turned to the billowfin guardian. "Do you have any chio crystals by chance?"

"I have a small stash of them in my special storage chamber." Koiwae answered before he turned away. "Are you thinking Lorgeo is in need of help?"

"Do you think Lorgeo is still in his right mind?" Fulrion interjected. "After he's been stuck in the canyons with the rogue magic all these centuries?"

"Rogue magic can't cause you to go insane Fulrion." Docion said, "but I do remember that Lorgeo was always a bit... peculiar."

Oceaono held up his hand again for quiet. "Lorgeo's words were a request, or plea, but we won't be able to truly understand him until he's healed."

"Wait, you mean the Shattered One wasn't always shattered?" Spinescale asked.

"Of course not." Oceaono waved a hand as Koiwae dissolved away. "He is the same species as I; when we are under intense pain, or strain, our bodies shatter and crack. Once that's happened our words become twisted, and our magic becomes hard to keep under control."

"But why would he be petrifying people and creatures and dragging them to the canyons?" Startide still didn't seem convinced.

"Perhaps he knows something we do not." Sharval said, "but we won't know unless we find a way to ask him."

"I'm not so sure about this…" Startide looked nervous. "You sure that it's safe to get anywhere near the Shattered One? Maybe Daychaser and I should go investigate first."

Oceaono shook his head. "I appreciate your concern Startide, but after you swam off with Jackson when Lorgeo was trying to speak to him, I doubt he'd be happy to see you again."

"You are only to go with Jackson to the outskirts of the canyon. He will have to speak to Lorgeo alone." Seanel said firmly. "Jackson's connection to earth magic will help him withstand the magic of the canyons. The rest of you would quickly be overwhelmed and petrified."

"Even so." Koiwae appeared once again with an assortment of items floating around him. "Jackson, I want you to wear this, and for currents sake don't get too close to Lorgeo." Koiwae shook a strange looking vest that was being carried behind him. "By now Lorgeo's body has been saturated with the magic infecting those canyons; he could accidently petrify you with his touch." A small number of glass-like crystals swirled above Koiwae's head as he came up to Jackson.

"Put this on." Koiwae said, while floating the vest in front of Jackson. "It's made of special material that deadens the effect of magic around it, it should help protect you."

"Won't it affect my own spells though?" Jackson asked uncertainly while he undid the clips and slipped the vest over his shirt.

"Probably, but it's more important that you are kept safe from the rogue magic of the canyons." Koiwae said, "and there's something else I think you should have on you."

"What's that?" Jackson asked as he clipped the vest on.

"The small blue raindrop shaped crystal your grandpa left you." Koiwae said with a knowing smile.

Jackson froze, looking over to Koiwae with a surprised blink. "How'd you know about that?"

"The Start of the Sea made a point of showing me." Koiwae smiled. "Bring the crystal out if you'd please."

Jackson teleported the blue crystal out of his bag and held it out to Koiwae, who used his magic to twirl the crystal around him as it started to glow.

"An ocean's tear." Sharval commented, looking impressed.

"What's an ocean's tear?" Spinescale asked while they watched Koiwae twirl the crystal back over to Jackson.

"A special crystal that gathers power from the magic of the seas that can be used by mages and magical creatures." Koiwae said, placing the crystal back in Jackson's outstretched hand and looking him in the eye. "Think of it as the water version of a nature's emerald."

Jackson's eyes widened and he nodded before he took the moonstone out of his armband and inserted the ocean's tear.

"If you need a magical boost to help you fight off the magic in the canyons, use the magic from the tear." Koiwae suggested.

"But get out of there immediately if Lorgeo turns out to be unreasonable, or if the canyon's magic becomes too strong." Seanel's eyes were serious. "We can't risk you getting harmed, or worse."

"Try giving these to Lorgeo." Oceaono took one of the crystals Koiwae had brought. "If he begins to absorb them, you'll have nothing to fear from him." His brow creased in worry. "However, if they begin to shatter, do everything in your power to get away from him as fast as possible, and don't let him touch you."

"What does it mean if the crystals shatter?" Daychaser clicked in confusion.

"You don't want to know." Oceaono said forebodingly.

"Huh, that's comforting." Spinescale hissed sarcastically.

"Daychaser and Blade." Oceaono pointed to them. "You will accompany Jackson to the canyons tonight. It will be easier to see Lorgeo in the dark, and you'll be better able to notice any rogue magic too. Daychaser, I'd like Jackson to ride along with you while Blade swims lookout." He glanced over to Blade. "We're trusting you to make sure it's safe, you know these waters better than the rest of us."

Blade flicked his fins in affirmation and Oceaono turned to the snakes.

"Spinescale and Deepbite, would you be willing to do a bit of snooping around the Spherefang's buildings; particularly that storage building and the residence of this Dillox character? I have a hunch as to why Lorgeo might be attacking the village, but I want more information before I say what it is."

"Love to." Deepbite's eyes sparkled in anticipation. "We're normally snooping around there anyways."

"Excellent." Oceaono inquiringly looked to Startide. "Would you please escort Deepbite and Spinescale back to shore and then return here?"

"Yes, of course." Startide said, "and I'll be back as quickly as I can."

Oceaono nodded, a small smile crossing his lips. "Thank you."

"I would ask a favor of you two if I may?" Sharval moved towards the other two sharks. "Could you find this Huntress I've been hearing about? I'd like to have a word with her."

The sharks exchanged a quick, slightly surprised look.

"The Huntress travels all around these islands, it could take a bit of time to find her." The female blue shark answered, looking a bit worried.

"But we could find her pretty quick if we ask around…" The male shark interjected. "Who should we say is asking for her?"

"Sharval." Sharval said calmly. "The median of the sharks."

The two sharks fanned out their fins in surprise when Sharval mentioned her name, while Blade just "raised a brow."

"Of-of course. We will head out to find her right away, wise one." The male stuttered after a moment.

"You have my thanks." Sharval said, before the two sharks whipped around and charged out of the Sanctuary at top speed: leaving Jackson wondering why Sharval garnered such a reaction.

"You must leave before the day grows any later." Seanel's calm voice brough Jackson's attention back to the matter at hand. "And Jackson, once you leave Daychaser and Blade keep focused on finding Lorgeo and don't touch anything in the canyons."

"Ok." Jackson nodded as he was given the crystals.

"Let's go." Blade said while Jackson slipped the gems into his bag.

"See you soon." Koiwae said. "Be careful now."

"We will." Daychaser called before Jackson could answer, while he and Blade rushed Jackson towards the exit.

CHAPTER FOURTEEN

THE CANYONS

With Daychaser ahead and Blade a few tail-strokes behind, Jackson swam silently through the long hallways towards the doorway. Once they exited the sanctuary, Daychaser slowed so Jackson could grab his dorsal fin while the seawolf looked over at Blade. "Do you know the way to the canyons?"

"Sure, how fast can ya go?" A smug look flashed across Blade's eyes.

"Not as fast as you." Daychaser smirked confidently, "but if you set the pace, I'll keep up."

"Hah, sounds almost like a challenge, seawolf." Blade shot off into the dark water and Daychaser tore after him while Jackson rolled his eyes in exasperation.

Daychaser kept close on Blade's tail as they raced off while Jackson anxiously clutched Daychaser's fin. "You guys, it's not a contest!" Jackson called, only for the rushing water to sweep the words away.

"Course it ain't, ya'd both lose!" Blade shouted from up ahead.

Jackson looked skyward and rolled his eyes again. As he was dragged along for a wild ride while Daychaser and Blade raced, Jackson just tried to hold tightly to Daychaser's dorsal fin as they shot under the waves.

Like he often did after dark, Jackson lost track of time as they traveled beneath the night sky while clouds gathered in the distance. After a time, Daychaser squeed for them to slow down and they slackened their pace enough Jackson could release his death-grip on the seawolf's dorsal fin. Blade continued to lead them confidently through the dark water while the stars twinkled above them until he finally started swimming in a lazy circle.

"Canyon's straight ahead." Blade said.

"How can you tell?" Jackson peered around in the dark uncertainly.

"Look, you'll see it." Blade pointed straight ahead with his snout.

Jackson strained his eyes and stared before a ripple of light bloomed through the water a little ways away. After a few moments, more ripples of energy followed, the colors changing from gray, brown, blue, orange, and—strangely enough—an off-tan. "Is that the magic of the canyons?" He asked.

"Yep, strange stuff. Used to always stay in the canyons but lately…" Blade motioned to an area off to their left, where the magic energy suddenly spread out through the water in strange lighting-like patterns. "Stay away from those."

Jackson carefully swam forward: the magical glow of the canyons flashing brighter and brighter ahead of him. As the distance between him and the canyons shortened, he noticed the pulsating glow of magic seemed to be hitting some sort of invisible barrier. Cautiously he came up to the unseen barrier and gingerly reached his hand out to touch it. The edges of his hand glistened with the unseen energy, and he took a deep breath and pushed his hand through.

That's some barrier. There was a bright glow around his wrist where it stuck through the barrier and Jackson's mouth twisted in a frown while the magic contained behind the barrier strained to penetrate his skin. Thankfully, it was fairly easy to fight off the effects of the magic, and he pushed himself carefully through the barrier and was greeted by a beautiful, yet sobering, sight.

The canyons were aglow with magic as currents of softly glowing energy weaved about through the water. The magical glow cast strange shadows on the seafloor, while magic energy danced around the small multitude of stone creatures and ships at the bottom of the canyons. Forgetting Seanel's warning to stay focused, Jackson drifted down towards the human bodies. He swam through the petrified forms for a moment while he sadly looked at the faces and clothes of the stone figures. He suddenly recognized one man from an old picture his dad had shown him years before and sneered softly, unaware of something moving in the water behind him.

It took an immense amount of self-control to refrain from blasting the stone form of Dillox's brother in the face. Jackson took a calming breath before turning away, and looked right into the glowing eyes of the Shattered One!

"GAH!!" Jackson cried and bolted backwards, only to come face to face with the crystal beings the Shattered One was able to make! The Shattered One let out one of his shivering cries and the crystal beings held out their arms to block Jackson's escape, giving him little choice but to turn around and look at the Shattered One once again.

The Shattered One eyed him shrewdly for a minute before he bent over and touched the sand on the seafloor below. The sand suddenly turned to the darker color of stone and a loud cracking sound echoed through the canyons. Jackson shuddered as the Shattered One straightened and slowly drew closer.

"Um, Lorgeo?"

The Shattered One froze, hesitating as the glow in its eyes died down a bit.

"Uh, Oceaono and Koiwae sent me to give you these." It took more effort than usual for Jackson to teleport the crystals out of his bag. He held the crystals out, keenly hoping the creature he was addressing was indeed Lorgeo.

"Rgelihofay." The Shattered One said quietly and Jackson felt the water around his hands begin to move, swirling the crystals above him. A slightly glowing current of water carried the crystals over to the Shattered One who clasped them in his hands and closed his eyes.

A bright light spread from the crystals over the Shattered One's hands, reaching across the cracks riddling his body and quickly traveling over his head. Jackson watched in awe as the shattered pieces of Lorgeo's body slowly fused back together while the color of his body changed from a dull gray to a shimmering dark metallic blue. Gray crystals suddenly sprouted from the top of Lorgeo's head, forming a sort of silver crystal crown and hair before the glow died away and the crystals in his hands vanished.

"Aaah." Lorgeo's voice was old and gravely. "That feels so much better." He opened his eyes, which were still orange but no longer empty. "Make sure to give Oceaono and Koiwae my thanks, lightborn. It is wonderful to be free of pain after all these years."

"I will." Jackson automatically held out his hand. "I'm Jackson, I'm helping Oceaono and the medians find a way to free the Sonaeko Nation from the Great Petrifying."

"You wouldn't want to shake my hand boy." Lorgeo said. "I've been around the magic of this canyon for far too long. You may be keeping the magic from affecting you right now, but if I touched you, you'd be in serious trouble."

Jackson quickly pulled his hand back.

"I suppose you have a few questions." Lorgeo said.

Jackson nodded. "Yeah, what happened to you? And why…" Jackson looked around the canyons curiously. "Are you here out of all places?"

"Well boy." Lorgeo rubbed his head thoughtfully. "Many decades ago, not long before the Great Petrifying. I came here with my son to help contain the whirlpools that had formed after a large number of damaged magical Sonaekian weapons were thrown into the sea by the Ironmamba."

He gave a small scowl. "They hoped the rogue magic the weapons released would destroy these pristine seas. My team and I succeeded in our efforts to contain the whirlpools, and made this canyon a safe passageway for our people." He glanced over his shoulder. "It was here where I went to work stabilizing the magic, using some magical artifacts and spells of my own creation to prevent the whirlpools from growing."

He looked off towards the sanctuary longingly. "All was going well until the great spell miscast. I was in the canyons when it happened and somehow my connection to the spells and artifacts in the canyon saved me from being petrified like my son and comrades." He looked down sadly at a group of stone figures Jackson hadn't noticed before.

"However, when I realized that the rogue magic from the miscast spell was fusing with the spells and artifacts we used to stabilize the magic here, I used almost every drop of energy I had to prevent everything we'd done from falling apart…" He put a hand to his face as if remembering the feeling of it cracking, "and I shattered from the strain. Despite my efforts, some of the artifacts still became corrupted from the rogue magic and started casting small spells similar to the magic of the Great Petrifying." He let out a terse sigh. "It was only after a few months that I was able to find out how to contain the corrupted magic within this canyon, and I've been here ever since." He looked around the empty canyon. "I needed to remain here to keep the spells stable."

"But when I first saw you, you were heading towards the island." Jackson said.

Lorgeo's face darkened. "Yes, those coal-dusted venom clans." His eyes slitted. "A group of men stole something from this canyon that was helping keep things stable. All but one of the men and the ship they were on fell victim to my attacks, and the magic of the canyon did the rest." He grumbled angrily. "Course the one man who had the items I needed made it onto another ship and escaped."

"Why didn't you go after him?" Jackson asked.

"Two reasons boy," Lorgeo held up two fingers. "One, the ship he escaped to had children on board. Two, with the items he took gone, I had to turn my focus on keeping the magic from breaking free. If the magic had made it into the weapons at the bottom of the whirlpools it would've been a complete disaster! The magic could've infused with the damaged artifacts and caused the whirlpools to go completely berserk."

Lorgeo shook his head. "I've gone ashore as often as I dare to search for the items, but since I was unable to speak, I couldn't explain what was happening to the humans and had to fight back when they attacked me. To add to the problem, my body is infused with the magic of this canyon and each time I left I had a hard time keeping it under control."

Jackson was silent for a minute. "But why do you bring the stone people and creatures back here?"

"To protect them." Lorgeo's face was tight with guilt as he looked towards the stone figures a little ways away. "The magic here is highly unstable, I've been worried it might kill those that were petrified by it, so I bring them here." He waved his hand over the groups of creatures and people. "Here they are under its effect continuously and remain alive, at least for now..." Lorgeo cast a dark glance towards shore. "Might not be for long though at this rate..."

Jackson followed Lorgeo's gaze and frowned worriedly. "I guess that makes sense." He sighed as he looked around the canyon. "I take it you couldn't make another item to help keep things stable here?"

"If I could have, boy, I would've long ago." Lorgeo's voice was tight with strain and worry, "but that piece was specially made and enchanted at the capital, and I don't have the resources here to remake it."

He paused when a rumble of thunder rolled above them. "Boy, if Oceaono and the others are here, you better tell them to get as far away from this place as they can. I'm already struggling to keep the magic contained, and if I don't get those pieces or something similar here soon..." He paused as another blast of thunder shook the sky. "The magic here will escape, and it won't go calmly." His tone was grave. "It could petrify everything within a thousand whale lengths and cause a storm the likes of which you've never seen."

Jackson gulped while more lighting cracked above them. "Uh, could you show me what the pieces you're missing looked like? Maybe I could sneak ashore and find it for you."

Lorgeo's shoulders sagged in relief. "I was hoping you'd make that offer. Come here, I'll show you what you need to look for." He hurriedly escorted Jackson to the surface where a strange object was floating on the waves. "The two pieces are part of a single unit, and I'll need them both to get things stable here."

"It looks like a four-pointed star." Jackson said, looking at the faintly glowing green object. "With a lot of water-based enchantments, right?"

"Correct, and here in the middle of the top is the second piece." Lorgeo pointed to the spot where a black pearl sat snuggly in the middle of a spiral casing. "Both pieces must be intact for me to complete the pattern I have that strengthened the spells, keeping this place under control, one piece won't be enough to help for long."

They both stopped when a strange humming sound coincided with the magic in the water increasing in speed and brightness. Jackson gasped as he was suddenly blasted by a wave of energy that slammed into his body and threw him back.

"Leave NOW!" Lorgeo barely stopped himself from pushing Jackson while the boy straightened up, struggling to fight the magic away. "Go, GO! The next wave will be even stronger than that one."

Jackson hurried towards the place where he came in. "There's something I need to warn you about before I go though." He gasped.

"Then make it quick, we don't have all day." Lorgeo's tone was tense.

"The man who stole the items from you is planning to attack you here in a few days. He's trying to distract you so the bad men he works for can come through the canyon and kill the people here. I wouldn't be surprised if he or the men he works for will try to steal some of the other pieces you have here."

Lorgeo eyes flashed. "Just what I need, I appreciate the warning. Now get out of here, and if you get the items, call for me and drop them right outside the barrier. I have no clue how the magic in the canyon will be behaving at that point."

Jackson nodded and darted through the barrier just as another loud humming sound began.

CHAPTER FIFTEEN
THE STOLEN STAR

T his is bad." Koiwae said after Jackson had returned with the news, and the Star of the Sea filled everyone in.

"I can't believe we didn't sense this." Fulrion snipped. "It should've been blatantly obvious."

"We can't blame ourselves for not knowing about the magic in the canyons." Docion said. "Our power has faded with time."

"How long until Startide and the snakes get back?" Daychaser asked.

"They should be back anytime." Seanel was pacing slowly in slow half circles.

"I was right." Oceaono muttered to himself. "I had a feeling that Dillox must've done something to cause Lorgeo to act the way he did."

"Pity he didn't know his stealin could destroy every creature within thousands of whale lengths." Blade quipped.

"If he'd known, he would've just tried to go back through the canyon and escape." Jackson pointed out with a scowl. "The Toxicshade don't care about what destruction they cause, just so long as it benefits them."

"They sound like the Ironmamba all over again." Sharval said tightly.

"Are you telling me that I and every-other creature here are doomed because of that fool who tried to kill me?" The Huntress snapped, her eyes ablaze.

Jackson had been surprised to see the Huntress already here speaking with Sharval when he, Daychaser, and Blade had returned. He was even more surprised at how quickly Sharval had caught her up on everything.

"Basically." Falganous snapped in his usual ornery way.

"We're back!" Everyone turned as Spinescale, Startide, and Deepbite came hurrying into the cavern.

"I hope you have good news." Oceaono said grimly. "Because we do not."

"Well I don't know if it's good, but we found Dillox playing around in the back of the Storage room with some strange looking trinkets." Deepbite said. "One of them was a deep purple orb and the other looked like a four-pointed star."

"That's it!" Jackson exclaimed!

"What's it?" Spinescale asked.

"We'll explain later, did you see where he keeps them?" Oceaono interjected.

"He put the star in a chest he hid under a large crate. The orb is one I've seen the mages in the clans use when they need a bit of umph for powerful spells." Deepbite said.

"Did the star have a black pearl in the top?" Jackson asked.

"We didn't get a good enough look; we really didn't want him to see us." Spinescale looked perplexed.

"We need you to take Jackson there immediately." Koiwae said. "We must get that star before things fall apart beyond repair."

Spinescale and Deepbite looked at each other in alarm.

"Why are we the ones that keep missing the important events?" Startide got an annoyed look in her eyes. "First the whole thing with Blade and now thi—"

"There isn't time, we can explain on the way!" Daychaser said, shoving Startide urgently. "We need to hurry."

Jackson suggested the snakes wrap around his backpack for the trip before the group swooped out of the sanctuary and headed towards shore. The journey was a quick one, but instead of going to the harbor, Startide led them further down the shoreline.

"Follow us." Deepbite said as he and Spinescale untangled themselves from Jackson's pack. "We'll enter into town a back way where they don't have guards posted."

"Lemme go change really quick." Jackson said, vanishing into his bag where he found a dark brown shirt to replace the light tan one he'd been wearing, though he figured his dark green shorts and dark brown overshirt were camouflaged enough. As he came back out of the bag Jackson turned his skin a dark gray, so his face, arms, and lower legs didn't give him away.

Jackson clambered ashore after the two snakes, quickly drying himself off so his legs would return. Once he could walk, he quietly followed the sibling serpents through the undergrowth as they crept into the torchlit town. The snakes led him down an alley between a couple of large houses and Jackson ducked down while he snuck under the windows, praying he wouldn't wake anyone.

They slipped around a small store before coming to a very large building with some magically glowing gems lighting the entrance.

"That's the storage building." Spinescale hissed.

"Wait here. I'll go make sure Dillox isn't close by." Deepbite said, slithering off quickly.

While they waited, Jackson leaned over and tapped Spinescale on her long scaly back. "If someone sees me and I have to run, don't try to follow me; they shouldn't suspect you of anything."

"Got it, I'll tell Deepbite." Spinescale darted over to her brother when he came slithering over, speaking quietly with him as they returned to where Jackson was waiting.

"Follow me, Dillox is tinkering with the star right now." Deepbite said. "Maybe we can swipe it before he puts it back in that locked box."

Jackson scurried after the snakes while they slipped quietly through the door. He paused for a second to look around before he softly shut the door behind him. A small lamp at the far end of the building provided the only visible light amongst the tall rows of wooden crates, barrels, and boxes that were stacked higher than he was. Large bundles of produce hung from the ceiling where they were safe from rodents, and Jackson could smell a faint scent of dried fruit from somewhere.

As Spinescale and Deepbite led him through the maze, Jackson carefully watched his every step. His bare feet made it easier to step quietly and he focused on placing one foot in front of the other while avoiding the slithering forms of the serpents. After a few minutes of careful creeping, the snakes twisted to the right and slipped down a short aisle between the large boxes and crates.

Jackson squeezed after them, crouching low when the snakes stopped and pointed with their heads through a big crack between the crates. He peered through the crack and immediately glared at the bent over form of Dillox: who was hunched over the star with a bar and hammer, trying to break it apart.

Jackson could hear Dillox cursing under his breath before he threw the hammer in Jackson's direction where it smashed into a crate and stuck! Jackson and the snakes glanced at each other nervously while Dillox angrily tossed the star into the corner where it clinked into the wall. The star landed close to where Jackson was hiding and he held back a relieved sigh when he saw that it looked whole, although he couldn't tell if the pearl was in the top.

"Should've heard from the Commander by now!"

Jackson stiffened when Dillox grumbled loudly to himself. "Used the Orb of the Basilisk to set out the beacon, and they should've gotten my message." He marched over to a large, medium-purple orb and pulled something out of his pocket which he placed against it.

The orb flashed in a seemingly angry way before a dark line formed, starting from a point at the base of the orb and stretching up to touch the black crystal Dillox was pressing against the orb. The magic in the orb seemed to fight back against the dark line and Jackson heard Dillox curse the orb when the dark line was suddenly torn apart.

While Dillox was occupied with trying to get the line to reform, Jackson looked over at the star and smiled. Now was his chance. He concentrated on the star as best he could before it vanished into his bag without a sound.

He tapped Spinescale and Deepbite's tails and they nodded at him before they all turned and started making their way up the aisle. A sudden angry shout from Dillox made them freeze before the man hustled over to where he threw the star and began digging around. After a minute of him searching there was a tense moment of silence.

Everything was quiet.

Too quiet.

"I know you're in here, and whoever you are, you better return my star." Dillox sneered. "Or I'll blast you apart."

Jackson looked down at a few small bags of nuts and carefully grabbed one before he threw it as high and far as he could in the opposite direction. The amount of noise it made when it crashed into something startled him and Dillox charged after it.

Jackson quickly crept out of the alley and was rushing past the orb when someone snarled and lunged towards him! He yelped when he was shoved backward, smashing into the orb which rocked precariously before falling off its pedestal! Jackson threw himself to the side, catching the orb in his arms just before it could smash into the ground!

Jackson rolled across the floor with the orb in his arms before he anxiously looked up and saw Dillox's hardened features glaring daggers at him. "Thought you could distract me and get away could ya? Well to bad I—!"

Jackson realized Dillox was staring at Jackson's gray hands and legs and the man paled slightly. "The monster? But how? the guards were—"

Jackson noticed some of the wooden barrels held clean water—probably used for drinking—and quickly made the water explode from them and crash over Dillox! Dillox let out an angry shout as the water smashed him onto the ground while Jackson scrambled to his feet and began running! He turned when he felt the beginnings of a shadow spell and saw Dillox jump to his feet with his hands aglow! Just as Dillox spotted him, Jackson quickly collected the puddle of water off the floor and used it to knock an empty barrel off its shelf before his magic flung it over the man's head!

Jackson dashed through the storage building while Dillox continued to scream lividly for help. As the shouts of men sounded from outside, Jackson saw the door up ahead and braced himself! He turned, using his shoulder to smash it open, knocking back a group of three men who stumbled to the ground while he charged past.

"DON'T JUST STAND THERE YOU FOOLS!" He heard Dillox scream. "The monster's disguised itself and stole something of mine and the Orb of the Basilisk!"

Jackson looked down at the orb he had clutched tightly to his chest and winced. He'd completely forgotten he still had it. "I'm so sorry! I'll return you later." He whispered as he fled down the street while more men, women, and creatures came running over!

Jackson felt the flow of magic behind him and out of the corner of his eye saw one of the men's swords shining brightly as he reached back to swing! Jackson quickly jumped into the air while earth magic swirled around his legs before he smashed his feet back onto the ground as the man swung!

A thin dirt wall flew into the air behind him before a long purple blade of energy smashed into it, sending a plume of dust exploding across the street while Jackson darted into a small alley that he was fairly certain led to the docks. He skidded around the corner and jumped to the side when he came face to face with Terven, Leavan, Herni, and Kalya who dropped what they were carrying and stared at him in shock while he raced past.

"Jackson?" Leavan said.

"I'll explain later, and I promise I'll return the orb. I had to stop Dillox." Jackson called quickly as he raced down the docks!

While his feet quickly thumped against the smooth wood of the docks, Jackson readied himself when he heard the whizz of arrows, the hiss of angry venstorns, and the unnerving sound of a venom-fang spell. Not wanting to give away his light magic, he reached out and pulled water from the harbor, spinning it around him as he ran! He broke out in a cold sweat when arrows flicked into his barrier of water before long purple-white fangs of the venomfang spell crashed into the vortex spinning around him!

The thunder of feet sounded behind him as he reached the end of the broken pier, took a deep breath, and flew off the dock into the water just before another barrage of arrows and venom spells sailed over him! Jackson only waited long enough for his feet to change into a tail before he dove as deep as he dared and fled from the harbor, teleporting the orb into his bag where he couldn't lose it. As he soared over deeper waters, he found it ironic that he felt relief at not seeing the ocean floor below him while he continued diving slightly deeper and further out to sea.

"Did you get it?"

"AAAAH!" Jackson about jumped out of his skin when Blade charged into view next to him.

"Blade!" Jackson gasped. "You scared the magic out of me!" He took a deep breath. "and yeah, I think so. I got the star, but I don't know if the pearl is still in it." Jackson looked away in embarrassment. "aaand I might've unintentionally taken more than just the star…"

Blade got a sly look in his eye. "Ya didn't strike me as a thief."

"Huh, what! No. I'm not!" Jackson protested. "I took something else by accident! And I'm going to return it as soon as…" He looked nervously back to shore. "As soon as it's safe."

"Uh-huh" Blade said smugly. "Sure ya are. Ya sound guiltier than a shark in a feedin frenzy."

Jackson gave him a glare before he finally sighed. "Where are the others?"

"They're meetin us back at the sanctuary."

CHAPTER SIXTEEN

THE STORM

Jackson wanted to smack the smug look out of Blade's eyes while they hurried back to the sanctuary. The shark goaded him almost the whole way, and Jackson did his best to ignore him as he tried to figure out how he was going to explain this to Oceaono and the others.

As it turned out the Star of the Sea—which had been making an unusual amount of appearances lately—showed the medians and Koiwae the whole event before Jackson could get a word out.

"You could've dropped the orb." Fulrion commented dryly when the glow faded away.

"I was scared…" Jackson said lamely, "and you can't just drop something like that."

"We'll worry about that later." Koiwae said. "Jackson, bring out the star. I want to make sure that it's not damaged before we send it to Lorgeo."

Jackson procured the star from his bag before it was whisked from his hands by a small current of water and carried it over to Koiwae. After a brief inspection he looked over to Oceaono. "The pearl is gone."

Everyone in the cavern groaned.

"Then where is it?" Docion asked.

"The one person who knows, is probably turning the entirety of the venom clans against us." Seanel sighed. "Perhaps we can somehow enchant an item that could replace the pearl?"

"We won't know until we ask Lorgeo." Oceaono's voice was strained as Koiwae brought over a small crystal that he held up next to the star. "Blade, please take these over to Lorgeo; just call out his name and say you are delivering some items for Oceaono. Leave the items on the seafloor and back away when he comes, just make sure he gets them." Oceaono handed Blade the star and a strangely shaped crystal.

"What's the crystal for?" Blade asked before taking both items gingerly in his mouth.

"You'll see, just get it there as quickly as you can." Oceaono answered.

"Got it." Blade said around the stuff before he charged out of the cavern.

"Jackson..." Koiwae was giving him a suspicious look. "Can you turn around a second?"

Jackson raised a brow in question but did as he was asked. He felt something tap against his clothes before he felt a quick jab and a yank.

"Got it." Koiwae said and Jackson turned around to see a dark black barb floating next to the billowfin guardian. "And I believe you are quite lucky this didn't penetrate your skin."

Falganous came over and inspected the barb. "It's part of a tracking arrow, the shaft must've broken off after it hit."

"Does this mean Dillox knows where Jackson is right now?" Seanel sounded worried.

"Of course not, the venom and shadow nations magic wasn't nearly strong enough for that type of thing." Falganous said dismissively. "This type of arrow is connected to a compass-like contraption that will point to where the barb is. If we go drop the barb off in the ocean somewhere, then Dillox will be looking for a shrimp in a kelp forest."

"I know just the place." The Huntress said smugly. "May I?"

"Be our guest." Sharval said before the Huntress took the barb between her teeth.

The shark chuckled enthusiastically while she swam off without a backward glance, soaring quickly out of the sanctuary.

"Should I be worried about how excited the Huntress is about that?" Startide asked.

"No, I wouldn't expect anything less." Docion smirked. "She didn't become the top shark around here by playing nice."

After a few minutes, Jackson was left alone while the medians spoke with Koiwae and his friend while everyone waited for Blade. Jackson quietly went off to the side as the others talked and silently brought out the Orb of the Basilisk and flipped it over to look at the bottom curiously.

Carefully running his hand along the orb's smooth crystal, Jackson searched around until he found a small domed black bead that had been stuck to the orb's base. Jackson hmphed quietly and started fiddling with the bead, unaware that Koiwae and Oceaono were quietly watching over his shoulder.

Jackson tisked in annoyance when he couldn't find a simple way to remove the button, and carefully used his magic to reach out to the orb. Years ago, his grandpa taught him that the oldest and most powerful of magical items were nearly always alive, and were to be treated with respect. Jackson intended to do just that.

"Do you know how to remove the little button the shadow user stuck to you, powerful one?" Jackson thought to the orb. *"I want to get it off you so he can't try to use you to hurt the people you're allies with."*

The energy within the orb swirled around in response to Jackson's question and slowly formed into letters.

"Light." Jackson whispered looking up to the sunlight stone above. *"Light magic?"* He asked. *"My light magic won't hurt you then?"*

Jackson felt a warm feeling from the orb in response.

Carefully he started a light spell, trying his hardest to keep his light magic from hitting the orb while he formed the tiniest beam he could muster and directed it onto the button. As the beam hit the button there was a faint cracking sound once the button split. Jackson abruptly stopped when the orb began to flicker violently, and he quickly shielded his eyes as the orb flashed. Only once the flashing stopped, did Jackson dare to peek through his fingers at the orb. He sighed in relief when the orb seemed fine, and the button had started sinking towards the bottom.

"You have a way with magical items." Koiwae said from behind Jackson.

"Huh?" Jackson turned to see Koiwae and Oceaono watching him intently. "H-have you been watching me this whole time?" Jackson asked, a bit surprised.

"Jackson." Oceaono smiled. "We can sense the presence of powerful magical items; we knew the minute you brought it out of your bag."

Koiwae swam down and picked up the now cracked button and looked it over. "Falganous." He called. "Would you mind looking at this, I'm not very familiar with the devices used by shadow users."

The dragonturtle median swam over with his usual scowl and seemed to glare at the button as he inspected it. "Not sure on the details, but it seems to be enchanted in such a way as to absorb the magic of whatever it's touching."

Jackson's eyes widened. *He can tell that much by just looking at it?*

"After what the star showed us, I'm guessing that shadow user was using it to siphon the energy from the orb to power some of his own shadow spells." Falganous grumbled. "Or maybe make the orb retaliate and send off powerful waves of magic."

"The beacon he was talking about!" Jackson exclaimed.

Falganous looked over at Jackson. "Very likely. The orb is a very powerful venom artifact and wouldn't take kindly to having other types of magic being used on it. Often such artifacts respond by lashing out with an intense amount of magic energy as they try to disable or destroy whatever is threatening them."

"Koiwae, Oceaono? Can you hear me?" Everyone paused when the form of Lorgeo appeared next to the communication crystal.

"We hear you, I take it you have figured out one of the reasons I sent you the crystal." Koiwae said.

Lorgeo sighed. "Unfortunately. I take it we have no idea where the pearl is at this point?"

"The only one who would know is our enemy." Seanel said.

"I need that pearl, I can't get the magic here stable without it..." Lorgeo was beginning to sound desperate. "If the containment barriers fail, every living thing around here is as good a stone, maybe dead."

"Can you direct the magic another way for the time being?" Falganous inquired. "Am I right to assume that some of the devices that were corrupted were weather related?"

Lorgeo seemed conflicted. "I hadn't seriously considered that option… it could be dangerous. The storm that much magic would conjure could be enormous."

"Worse than if the barriers were to burst?" Falganous pressed.

"No…" A resigned look literally flashed across Lorgeo's face. "But the damage it would cause could be immense, but it would buy us some time."

"Perhaps you could release the magic slowly, maybe making the storm last for longer instead of unleashing a hurricane like it might if you did all at once." Oceaono suggested.

"I don't know how much control I will have once the magic finds an outlet. It could release all at once. Might even make it rain rocks." Lorgeo still seemed hesitant.

"What is the main thing bothering you Lorgeo?" Koiwae looked concerned.

Lorgeo exhaled very slowly. "I've never released magic from here before, I never needed to before the star-pearl unit was stolen. I had things setup so the magic was cleansed and siphoned off to help with keeping the whirlpools stable. I'm worried that if I try to channel the magic out of here, everything will fall apart and the magic of the whirlpools and the canyons will go rogue."

"I understand your concern, but at this point we don't have much choice." Falganous said, making Jackson's jaw drop in shock. He never thought he'd see the ornery dragonturtle median be even remotely understanding.

Oceaono noticed Jackson's expression and quietly cleared his throat, although his eyes twinkled ever so slightly in amusement. Jackson shut his mouth and looked away before Falganous noticed him staring.

"Alright, I'll try it, but be ready to move if things go whirlpool." Lorgeo said.

The whole cavern seemed to hold its breath while Lorgeo's form glowed slightly for awhile. Everyone tensed when the silence was shattered by the noise of lightning hitting the water and the ominous roll of thunder.

"Are you keeping control of it?" Falganous asked.

"Yes, barely." Lorgeo's voice was strained.

"Don't shatter yourself again, we can't afford to lose you." Seanel said.

"Don't plan on it."

Jackson wasn't sure how Lorgeo's crystal features could tighten but they did.

"Jackson!" Blade came flying into the cavern. "Ya need to come see this. There's a human boat out there and they're bout to get hit by a huge storm that came rollin in out of nowhere."

Jackson bolted for the exit but was stopped by Koiwae.

"You should stay here, if Lorgeo loses control of the magic, you could be petrified."

Jackson gave Koiwae a stubborn look as Oceaono came over. "Koiwae is right, there is protection in the sanctuary, the walls would absorb much of the magic if it goes rogue."

Blade shook his head. "I know you lot are worried about Jackson, but I only saw some kids aboard that ship."

Jackson paled as Koiwae and Oceaono eyes widened in horror.

"Are you sure?" Seanel had been listening in too.

"I even breached to make sure that toothless mage wasn't aboard. It's just the kids Jackson's met." Blade said curtly. "You gonna let him come help them or not?"

"We'll all go." Daychaser said.

Oceaono looked extremely conflicted and opened and closed his hands. "Blade if any of you hear a loud explosion, bring Jackson back here immediately. If Jackson gets petrified, then we'll all be trapped."

"Got it, grab on." Blade came over and Jackson reached out and grabbed his fin. "It isn't that far away, the wind was blowin them this direction when I came back."

Blade swam so fast Jackson felt like his face would be permanently scarred from the water smashing across it! As they hit open water Jackson heard thunder boom above them again and again while Blade torpedoed out of sight of Startide and Daychaser.

Blade dove when the surface of the sea began to be thrashed by the wind and Jackson prayed they weren't too late to help his friends. The surface waters started to churn around them when Jackson felt, more than heard, Blade grunt before he made a sharp turn and nearly threw Jackson off.

Jackson only faintly registered the shadow of a small boat up ahead before Blade came to a halt. The sudden stop tossed Jackson forward towards the small skiff and he quickly dodged out of the way when the boat spun over him!

"Go look to see if anyone has fallen off!" Jackson yelled over the rushing waves as he darted to the surface.

Jackson's chest tightened with fear at the sight of the small fishing boat twirling around in the surf while the storm continued to grow. He jumped free of the water and saw the kids he'd befriended huddled together in the middle of the boat, hugging each other tightly and completely soaked to the skin.

As the rain began falling in sheets Jackson dove back under the water, flipped around, and went barreling up to the surface as fast as he dared. He slightly turned his face away when he flew clear from the water, bracing himself before he crashed into the middle of the boat next to the kids with a loud smash!

"OWOwowowow!!!" Jackson groaned as he lifted himself up to see the kids staring incredulously at him.

"Jackson!!" Leaven came crawling over, followed by the other kids who were all shaking and scared.

"You found us!" Terven said.

"My friend Blade did and brought me here. What on Mythos are you guys doing out here all alone?" Jackson asked as he slipped over to them.

"We were looking for you. Dillox was organizing men to come hunt for you." Henri said while he tried to shelter his sister from the rain. "He said he shot you with something that would lead him to you, he's planning to kill you!"

"We wanted to warn you before they started following you, so we snuck out when no one was looking." Kayla said.

Jackson felt warmed in his heart as the kids came closer. "Guys I…" He looked up when lightning streaked across the sky. "Thank you, but this storm is only going to get worse… is there anyway to get you back to shore?"

Bennor shook his head, looking terrified. "We lost our oars awhile back, and we hit something right before you got here and were starting to take on water just before you arrived."

Jackson looked around frantically for something, anything. *The waves are already getting too big, even with Startide's help we couldn't push it to shore.* Jackson saw his hands were faintly glowing again and looked down at them. Tendrils of blue light spread from his fingers and reached out to each of the kids and touched them. Jackson' eyes widened in understanding once a bright blue fish formed near his hand.

"You have water magic in you…" Jackson breathed.

"What?!" Henri looked flabbergasted. "What are you talking about? We're from the venom clans."

Jackson just stared at the kids as an idea formed in his head. "I have an idea, but you'll all have to trust me, and let me use a spell on you if this is going to work."

Kayla hugged her younger siblings tightly when they heard a loud crack as some of the wood in the boat splintered and more water began flooding in. "Can't you just make the storm stop?" She whimpered.

"Or even call an army of ocean creatures to take us back to shore?" Donner asked while Bennor clasped him and Danna closer when a wave crashed into the skiff.

"I don't think they could keep you above water, this is only the first part of this storm." Jackson was having to yell to be heard. "This isn't a normal storm, it's being caused by magic, and it's only going to get worse!"

Jackson didn't think the other kids could look anymore terrified, but they did.

The older kids had a wordless exchange before Bennor and Henri nodded to each other, and Kayla nervously shook her head up and down.

"What do you need us to do?" Henri asked.

Jackson let out the breath he'd been unconsciously holding while another wave spun the ship. "I need you all to hold onto each other and me." He slipped over and held out his hands as more water began to fill the boat. "Once we're in the water don't let go."

Bennor, Kayla, and Henri all reached out and grabbed Jackson's hand as they gripped their younger siblings tightly.

"Ready?" Jackson called.

"Just go!" Kayla yelled and the whole group jumped off the sinking boat and into the swirling water. Jackson nearly lost hold of his new friends when they were thrust around by the storm's wrath, and drawing on every bit of water magic he could, he cast the spell!

He heard Daychaser and Startide call in the water around them when his friends were enveloped in blue energy. The group twirled lower under the waves until the magic cleared and Jackson let out a cheer.

"It's ok! You can breathe now!" Jackson yelled.

Leavan and Terven were the first to open their eyes, and Leaven squealed in excitement, making all the other kids' eyes pop open. "I can breathe underwater!" She cried, letting go of her siblings and spinning around. "I can breathe!!"

"Cool!" Terven was only a second behind his sister as he paddled forward.

"What? What did you do?" Henri asked incredulously.

"I cast a spell that allows land goers to breathe underwater." Jackson grinned in relief. "I'm so relieved it worked..."

"THIS. IS. AWESOME!!" Donner shouted as he rushed past his older brother Bennor.

"I never thought I'd see this." Daychaser said when he came swimming over with Startide and all the kids fell silent.

"Did—did it just talk?" Leavan squeaked.

"Looks like we got more humans to keep track of." Blade said as he came swimming over.

The kids' eyes all widened, and Blade gave them a suspicious glance.

"What, never heard a shark talk before?" He asked.

"N-no." Terven said. "You... all can talk?"

"Of course, they can." Jackson said. "These are my friends, Daychaser, Blade, and Startide." He pointed to each creature in turn.

"I think we better get back to the sanctuary island..." Startide said, giving the kids legs a ponderous look. "It's only going to get rougher out here."

"Follow us." Daychaser squeed. "We know a place that will be safe from the storm."

Jackson helped the other kids swim over to his creature friends, who let the children grab onto their dorsal fins. The group slowly made their way towards the Jewel Island Sanctuary, moving a bit deeper in the water while the waves crashed up above.

"What did you mean when you said this storm was caused by magic?" Kayla asked after a couple minutes of hard swimming.

"Well…" Jackson stopped as he thought about how he should answer. "You know the pass your clans sailed through to get here?"

"Yeah?" Henri answered. "What about it?"

"That pass isn't just the home to the Shattered One…" Jackson began. "It's where he's been trapping a huge amount of harmful magic for the last two centuries so it wouldn't spread and hurt others. He didn't used to be the Shattered One before, but because of his efforts to contain the magic it made him that way."

"Wait, are you saying the monster isn't a bad creature?" Bennor's face was contorted in disbelief. "You can't be serious."

"Let him finish." Blade grumbled.

"But the Shattered One has been attacking our clans for almost a decade now." Leavan said. "And he took our Uncle to."

"Let Jackson finish what he's trying to say." Startide echoed Blade. "You might change your mind a bit."

Jackson nodded his thanks to Startide and Blade. "When your clans came through the pass all those years ago, Dillox and his men stole something from the Shattered One. That's why he attacked one of the ships while you were sailing through. The item Dillox stole helped the Shattered One control and contain the magic of the canyon, and with it gone, the harmful magic began to escape."

Jackson turned to look at the other kids. "Remember when you told me that the Shattered One seemed to seek out Dillox when he attacked? And the storage building?"

"Yeah… it was kinda weird." Donner said.

"It's because he knew Dillox had the items he needed to keep the magic in the canyon in balance." Jackson said. "He was trying to get them back so the magic wouldn't escape and destroy everything."

"And he didn't intend to turn anyone to stone either." Daychaser added. "Over the years the harmful magic of the canyon has bonded with him, which means he unintentionally can petrify anyone he touches."

"And since the magic of the canyons is unstable, he was afraid that if the spell wore off it could kill those people that he accidently petrified, so he took them back to where the spell would be renewed." Startide finished.

The kids were all quiet for a minute.

"But what does that have to do with the storm?" Henri asked.

"The reason I snuck into your town was to try and retrieve the item Dillox stole. I didn't mean to take the orb that was… unintended." Jackson blushed in embarrassment. "I got part of the item back, but Dillox had removed a piece that the Shattered One needed if he was going to be able to keep the magic contained."

"What was missing?" Danna asked.

"Large black pearl that had lots of enchantments on it." Blade said. "We don't know where the guy hid it."

"Since the Shattered One can't contain the magic in the canyons he's channeling it into the storm to prevent the magic from escaping." Startide said. "Although that might not work very well if he loses control, in which case, the magic in the canyons could escape in a big explosion and turn everything around here to stone."

"Everything? You mean everything, everything?" Terven asked, looking pale.

Jackson and his creature friends nodded.

"So, this whole time the monster was trying to protect us?" Danna's eyes were wide.

"Yep, but y'all didn't know what Dillox did, so ya wouldn'ta known." Blade said.

"That's not all he's done…" Daychaser grumbled.

"Hold up!" Startide suddenly slowed to a stop.

"What's wrong?" Kayla asked as she and the other kids peered around anxiously.

"There's a large ship that is heading towards the isle we were going to shelter at." Startide said, sounding the water heavily.

"That must be our father's." Henri sounded guilty. "They must've noticed we took one of the boats and left without telling anyone."

"Can you take us there? I'm sure our parents are really worried…" Bennor said. "We didn't think we'd get caught in the storm."

"You sure it's one of your ships?" Blade asked. "Might be a Toxicshade vessel."

"WHAT?!" All the older kids cried out in alarm.

"How do you know about the Toxicshade?" Bennor demanded.

"Jackson found out that's who this Dillox dude is working for. We found a mirror the guy dropped into the sea and heard him speakin to one of their commanders." Blade said.

The older kids all exchanged panicked looks.

"We have to tell our Dad." Kayla's voice was shaky. "If the Toxicshade find us, we're doomed."

"Then let's go make sure that ship is one of yours, not one of the Toxicshade's." Startide said, changing her course and moving at a slightly faster pace.

The older kids' faces were tense with fear as the group closed in on the vessel which seemed to be moored next alongside a small dock Jackson hadn't seen before.

"It's the Viper." Bennor breathed in relief.

"Which means Dad and your grandpa are here." Henri relaxed a bit.

"Take us to shore, they're probably sheltering in the building they use for storing emergency supplies." Kayla said, pointing up ahead.

"There's a small boat stopped here too…" Daychaser commented while they swam into the shallows.

"Probably just one of the lifeboats." Terven said dismissively.

"It sounds kinda familiar though…" Daychaser seemed troubled, and Jackson looked over at him questioningly.

"Probably nothing…" Daychaser met Jackson's gaze and shrugged although the nervous look didn't leave his eyes. "Just be careful if you're planning to go ashore with them."

"We need you to come this time. You have to explain what is going on!" Leavan said. "I don't think our father will listen to us."

"If you hear an explosion, get back here, so I can take you to safety, or it'll be both our hides." Blade snapped.

Jackson nodded before he helped the kids towards the beach. "The spell I cast will wear off when we get out of the water." Jackson called as the kids fought their way through the waves to the shallow beach up ahead.

"Got it." Henri said while Jackson tried to use his water magic to block the worst of the waves from crashing down on them as they scrambled up the sheltered beach. As they stumbled past the last of the waves, Jackson had to slide his way under a slight overhang where he dried himself off enough for his legs to change back, much to the fascination of the other kids.

"You do have legs!" Donner shouted over the wind.

"And your clothes changed too." Leavan pointed out.

"There isn't time for that, we have to go find our parents, they will be so worried." Kayla grabbed her younger siblings' hands and ran through the rain towards a large stone building that was a bit further up the shore.

While they ran, Jackson was surprised to note that he was taller than the other kids as they hurried towards the dark wood door of the building. Kayla hurriedly threw the door open, making a group of tired and stressed looking men and women flip around.

"MOM! DAD!" Terven yelled.

"Mommy, Daddy!" Danna cried when the adults came running over and cried out in relief as the kids were engulfed in hugs and kisses. Jackson hung back, looking around the doorframe nervously.

"You kids are in serious trouble." The man who was Terven and Leavan's father, Chief Norven, said sternly. "You know better than to run off without telling us where you went."

The man's wife hushed him while she inspected each of the kids. "There will be time for that later. Are you kids ok? How did you find us?"

"Did you find who you were looking for?" Grandpa Toceth interrupted.

"What on Mythos are you talking about Toceth?" Chief Norven asked. "Why would the kids be looking for someone?"

"He saved us again Grandpa!" Donner said, pointing to the door, "and he came back with us."

"Who saved you?" Donner's dad, Dotonal, asked as everyone looked over to where Jackson was peering in.

Jackson slipped back slightly at the gasps of the adults when they saw him and Toceth gave him a friendly smile and waved him in. "Come on in Jackson, we won't harm you."

Jackson took a tentative step forward, trying to ignore the surprised expressions of the adults as he moved into the room.

"The boy who saved Terven and Leavan?" Chief Norven asked in a hushed voice.

"Yeah, he found us when we were out to sea in the boat and saved us by making it so we could breathe underwater when the boat sank!" Donner grinned, his comment making the parents of the kids visibly pale.

"Mercy. Were you kids that close to being drowned!?" Donner's mothers cried.

"Jackson and his ocean creature friends found us and brought us here." Kayla said.

"YOU!!" Jackson froze when Dillox came flying through the crowd, his eyes burning. "You're the one who stole the orb and my artifact!" He pointed at Jackson accusingly. "You're nothing but a thief!"

"He only stole the artifact because you stole it from the monster!" Donner cried indignantly. "Which was why the monster's been attacking us all these years!"

"Preposterous." Dillox feigned insult. "Why would I steal something from that horrid creature, tell your foolish kid to mind his own business." He said to Donner's parents whose expressions tensed.

"The boy also stole the Orb of the Basilisk which only proves he's nothing but a lowly thief." Dillox continued.

"Commander, this is Defsli. Can you hear me?"

Dillox was cut off by his own voice.

"This is scorspent spy Defsli, can anyone hear me?"

"This is Commander Slavson. Where have you been Defsli? You better have news for me. We've heard nothing from you since your message about the Growingstar Tribe."

"Oh, I have news Commander, news I'm sure you'll love to hear."

"…I'm listening."

"I am with the Spherefang Clans who are trapped on some hidden islands with no way to escape."

"They shouldn't even still be alive. You were supposed to have set off the shadow holes if we weren't able to make our move in time…"

Jackson held the memory crystal high so everyone could hear while he gave Dillox, who had gone white as a sheet, a tight stare.

Jackson let the message end as he held the broken button up in his other hand. "This is a message from Dillox to Toxicshade commander Slavson can you hear me? I've found a way to get your boats through in four days time, can anyone hear me."

"And you call me a thief." Jackson said icily.

"Why you horrid little!" Dillox was cut off when he had to dodge the strike of a bright purple magic snake.

"You traitor." Toceth's eyes were flashing. "After all the kindness we showed to you and your brother this is how you repay us?"

Dillox sneered. "You should've died years ago for daring to refuse the Emperor, and when I'm done, you'll have nowhere to hide." With a yell Dillox pulled out a large pouch and stabbed it with a shadow dagger.

"GET DOWN!"

Jackson covered his eyes when a huge plume of smoke filled the room and he heard Donner yell in fright.

"He got Donner!" Danna screamed as a roll of thunder shook the building. "He's got Donner!"

Jackson stumbled out the door and jumped out of the way when a group of men came charging out of the building.

"NOT ANOTHER STEP OR THE BOY GETS IT!" Dillox snarled as he pointed a shadow blade towards Donner's throat while he hoisted the boy into the smaller boat Daychaser thought he'd recognized earlier. Another roll of thunder coincided with a large wave that swept into the dock, causing the small boat to rock precariously.

"Let him go Dillox!" Chief Norven demanded.

Dillox laughed darkly while he cut the rope tying him to the docks as the ship began to move off. "Or what? You'll all be dead soon enough."

Jackson pushed his way through the adults as the rain cascaded down around them. "Donner!" He yelled. "Do you trust me?"

Donner's terrified eyes gave Jackson all the confirmation he needed before Dillox tightened his grip on the lad. "And what can you do?!" He yelled while lightning flashed across the sky and the boat began sailing out to sea.

Instead of answering, Jackson made Donner vanish into his bag, causing Dillox's arms to come together and his blade to slash his forearm, making him roar in pain.

"WHY YOU LITTLE!" Dillox hollered as he grabbed a wand and pointed it towards the group of people. The wand darkened as the mages in the group all readied themselves.

"It's a shadow eater spell." Toceth whispered in horror.

"Good to know." Jackson ran forward. As the spell fired, he brought his hands together at his side, a bright ball of energy forming around them before he hurtled it forward in a bright sphere of light that crashed into the dark beam!

BOOOOM!!!!

Everyone hit the ground as the explosion shook the ground below them and Jackson lifted his hands off his head and looked up. He slowly got to his feet while Dillox gave him a look of fear mixed with rage.

"You know light magic?" One of the men asked breathlessly.

Jackson didn't respond when Dillox ran to the other part of the ship and directed the boat in the direction of the canyons. Jackson balled his fists and ran towards the dock, diving into the raging water and barely waiting for his tail to return as he rushed after the boat.

"Daychaser!" He yelled while he rushed after the boat.

"What's going on?" Blade and the others suddenly appeared next to him.

"Dillox tried to hurt one of the kids, he's in the boat and is heading for the canyons. He might have the pearl in that ship!" Jackson didn't need to say another word before his friends quickly joined the charge. Jackson thought he saw a dark shape sail through the depths below them but shook it off as he focused on catching up to the small boat that was getting thrashed around in the waves, like a cork when the tide comes in.

Startide made an enraged quarking sound before she shot upwards and smashed into the boat, making it teeter even more to the side. Jackson felt something and called out. "Dive Startide! He's getting a spell ready!"

Everyone dove only seconds before a number of dark spears hit the water near where Startide had come up.

"Here comes a big wave." Blade shouted over the roar of the storm. "Get ready."

"Dive deeper!" Daychaser called and rushed over to Jackson, who grabbed onto his fins as they darted away while the shadow from a monstrously sized wave soared over the small boat! The wave cascaded onto Dillox's boat with a mighty crash, shattering it apart! Jackson and his friends were tossed about in the churning water as pieces of wood and the flag of the ship were scattered into the sea.

Once Jackson stopped spinning, he saw Dillox glaring daggers at him while he held a strange plant over his mouth. *Diver's flower.* Jackson thought as he and Blade regrouped and charged towards the man, whose eye slitted and shadow energy wove around his free hand.

Dark tendrils formed around Dillox before he lashed out at Jackson, who threw up a light barrier just before the tendrils smashed into it! The force threw him back in the water and made his shield drop, forcing him to spin out of the way when more tendrils slashed towards him! Jackson righted himself as four long shining white blades appeared at his side which he sent slashing into the tendrils, making the shadow magic dissipate into the water!

While Dillox readied another spell, Jackson fired a couple light arrows at the man, who barely dodged away before he shot a barrage of shadow orbs!

Jackson darted away when the shadow orbs charged after him while Blade zipped behind Dillox and lunged! Blade's bite missed its mark as Dillox barely managed to duck away only for Blade to whack the man's back with his tail as he passed! The impact knocked the diver's flower from Dillox's hand while Jackson destroyed the orbs chasing him with some beams of light.

"Heads up!" Startide called to Blade when some of the wreckage from the boat twirled through the water around him and Dillox.

"I'll kill you all!" Dillox somehow managed to scream. "And the Toxicshade will take care of the rest!" Dillox's eyes were flashing darkly, and Jackson readied himself for another assault when a dark form came barreling up from the depths, right as the floating debris from the boat were swept in front of him!

The swirling debris blocked Jackson's view of the Huntress's jaws clashing around Dillox while thunder boomed above them. A strip of torn cloth was all that was left of the man as the Huntress dove into the depths with her prize as more thunder rolled overhead.

Jackson let out a long shaky breath as the Huntress vanished, his body trembling.

"You ok?" Daychaser asked as he and Jackson's friends came swimming over.

"I… I think so." Jackson said quietly, having gone a bit limp in shock.

"Hope he didn't have the pearl on him." Blade said, while he looked in the direction the Huntress had gone. "Or we'll never get it."

"Oh, for currents sake, can we talk about that later?" Startide made an exasperated sounding whistle.

"No better time than the present." Blade quipped.

"Let's get you back to the sanctuary, you look exhausted." Daychaser said, nudging Jackson in the opposite direction.

Jackson **was** utterly exhausted, but weakly shook his head. "Donner's in my backpack."

"Oh stars, then we'd better get back to shore and then to the sanctuary." Startide rolled her eyes and sighed, "but let's hurry please."

The wind had picked up considerably once Jackson finally managed to crawl ashore, after getting battered by the waves on his way in. The rain came down in thick sheets, and he was faintly surprised when his tail switched back to legs as he dragged himself up from the waterline.

He stumbled his way towards the building, hearing someone shout before some men ran over to him. The kids' parents and Toceth all crowded around him as they helped him into the shelter of the building where he was wrapped in a warm blanket by Chief Norven's wife.

"Where's Donner?" Danna asked as everyone gathered around.

"I have him." Jackson smiled tiredly, and the adults exchanged worried looks.

"Did Dillox hit you with a spell boy? Donner's nowhere to be seen." Chief Norven pointed out worriedly.

"Just a second." Jackson's chest was heaving a bit from fatigue as he slipped off his backpack and put it on the ground in front of him. He slowly formed the symbol in front of him, his shoulders sagging in relief when Donner suddenly appeared next to the bag, looking around with wide eyes.

"Am I back now?" Donner asked quietly before his parents shouted with joy and scooped him up in a hug!

"A spacekeeper bag, I haven't seen one of these in years." Toceth said, looking the bag over wisely while Jackson slumped against the wall with a sigh. "Where did you get that?"

"A family heirloom." Jackson said quietly, his eyes closing as he rested a second.

"Where's Dillox?" Someone asked Jackson after a minute or two and he cracked an eye open to find everyone had gathered closer so they could hear him.

"A shark he tried to kill ate him." Jackson said feeling too tired to be tactful.

There was a gasp and Jackson leaned forward with a moan.

"So he's... gone?" Chief Norven asked and Jackson nodded.

"He won't trouble anyone ever again." Jackson said quietly.

"We don't know how to thank you." Donner's Mom said. "If it weren't for you…" She shuddered.

"Don't-don't thank me yet, we're not out of the whirlpool." Jackson slowly stood. "I have to get back to my… friends. Without the black pearl Dillox stole, we have to figure out how to contain the magic causing this storm." Jackson winced as multiple rolls of thunder shook the building.

"The kids told us about that. Is it really as bad as they say?" The chief asked.

Jackson nodded. "It could be worse actually… I didn't tell them everything."

Any comment was cut off by Donner who wiggled free from his mother's tight embrace and ran up to Jackson and held out his hand. "Is this the pearl? Dillox had it strung around his neck!"

Jackso's jaw dropped open as he stared at the large black pearl that was in a small clear casing connected to a long thin cord. "That's-that's it! Donner you're amazing!"

"Donner, how did you get that?" Toceth asked.

"It hit me on the head when Dillox grabbed me. I yanked it off him by accident when I was struggling to get away when he was dragging me out." Donner said proudly.

Jackson held the pearl almost reverently. "I have to get this to the canyon now!" Jackson shrugged off the blanket and went rushing to the door.

"Wait Jackson, this storm is getting horrible, it'll be too dangerous!" The chief called.

Jackson paused for a second when a bolt of lightning struck a nearby palm tree with a deafening roar! There was a loud cracking sound and Jackson stared in horror at the tree, which had been turned to stone.

Another clap of thunder shook the ground and Jackson noticed a couple other trees that had also been turned to stone. "I have to go now!" He shouted. "Look at the trees, the Shattered One must be losing control of the magic!"

He pointed at the trees before he turned and charged towards the sea, running headlong across the docks as he fought his way through the wind and rain and slipped, landing on his back with a painful crash. Dragging himself onto his hands and knees, he rolled off the dock into the water below with a splash.

"I have the pearl!" Jackson yelled into the water, hoping his friends could hear him while he made his way into deeper water. Within seconds he faintly heard their calls as they came rushing towards him.

"Did I hear something about the pearl?" Blade asked.

"I have it, we gotta get it to Lorgeo now!" Jackson held out his hand triumphantly.

"You need to get back the sanctuary!"

Jackson turned as Spinescale and Deepbite fought their way over to them "Lorgeo is losing control of the magic! It's only a matter of time before it goes whirlpool." Spinescale called.

"But I have the pearl." Jackson repeated as Startide and Daychaser joined them.

"Then let's move. I'll take it there." Blade said, opening his mouth for Jackson to put the pearl into.

"I'm coming with you. There's no way you could fight off the magic to get this to Lorgeo, but I should be able to." Jackson said with more confidence and energy than he had.

"Jackson no you can't—" Startide started.

"We don't have time to argue, Blade lets go." Jackson said, grabbing onto the shark's fin.

"We'll follow along." Daychaser said, although he looked like he wasn't convinced Jackson was making a good choice. "Just hurry."

Jackson nodded before Blade torpedoed into the water towards the canyon while more thunder roared above.

They had only gone a short distance when Jackson felt magic gathering around them. "BLADE HARD LEFT NOW!"

CRACK!

Blade dodged left just as magic charged lightning coursed through the water only inches away! Jackson watched wide eyed as the immense, jagged boulder the lighting left in its wake immediately began sinking in a host of bubbles.

"Hang on, more rocks falling from the sky up ahead." Blade dove deeper.

Jackson braced himself when he heard loud splashes above them while more thunder crashed above! Huge chunks of rock cascaded through the water ahead of them and Jackson closed his eyes while Blade grunted as he darted between them. While Blade dodged and dashed between the rocks sailing into the sea from above, Jackson tensely hung on for dear life, crying out warnings whenever he could.

"DODGE RIGHT!" Jackson yelled when more magic gathered above them. Blade skidded out of the way just before another bolt of lightning zapped through the water, creating another jagged rock formation to their left.

"That was too close." Jackson whispered to himself while Blade dove beneath another boulder, which grazed Jackson's tail as they whipped out from under it.

"Careful Blade." Jackson whimpered when they saw the strange light of the barrier faintly glistening up ahead.

"That's what I should be tellin you." Blade shoved him forward urgently.

Jackson swam forward as quickly as he dared while more magic energy arched through the water a dolphin-length away. He went up to the barrier and shouted out for Lorgeo, only for his calls to go unanswered.

Carefully he stuck a finger through the barrier and yanked it back when magic immediately began to attack it. He swam alongside the magical force-field until a bright bolt of lightning suddenly illuminated the canyon and he spotted Lorgeo. The crystal golem wasn't very far from where Jackson was pacing and was tightly holding the star Jackson had taken back from Dillox, his face contorted in pain while magic crackled around him.

"LORGEO!!" Jackson yelled, trying to get the crystal being's attention. Jackson looked from the pearl to Lorgeo and back again before he closed his eyes and took a deep breath. He opened his eyes and quickly backed up, formed a light shield around him that he infused with earth magic and all the water magic he could drain from the ocean's tear. He winced before he braced himself, letting out a yell as he dove through the forcefield!

The force of the canyon's magic made Jackson's barrier partially collapse while he forced his way through the wildly flying energy! As Jackson dodged around the swirling energy to Lorgeo, he failed to notice his tail glowing brightly when he came up to the crystal golem.

"LORGEO!" He screamed as the canyon's magic began breaking through his barrier.

Lorgeo opened an eye and looked over at Jackson in shock.

"THE PEARL!" Jackson flung the pearl towards Lorgeo with his water magic just as his tail was hit by the rogue magic that broke through his barrier, immediately turning his tail to stone!

Lorgeo's eyes flipped open, and he snatched the pearl in his hand before jamming it into place! A blast of energy exploded from the star, throwing Jackson back while plumes of dirty water and wild streaks of magic shot in all directions! A second pulse tossed Jackson out of the canyons and his vision blurred as the stone encasing his tail reached up towards his chest before he slipped out of consciousness.

CHAPTER SEVENTEEN

SURPRISING CONNECTIONS

J ackson. Jackson!"

Jackson groaned and opened his eyes slowly. "Wha-what?"

"Oh thank goodness he's alive." Startide called triumphantly.

"He's gonna wish he wasn't, when I'm done with him!" Falganous snapped.

Jackson winced, backing away from an irate Falganous nervously before he looked around. "Uh… Where am I?"

"You're back in the sanctuary." Seanel said, looking both relieved and furious. "Where we should've locked you up to keep you safe in the first place!"

"If Jackson hadn't returned the pearl, it's doubtful he would've been safe even here once the magic broke free." Koiwae said, coming to Jackson's defense, even though he looked a bit rattled himself.

"I know that, but what he did was just too dangerous!" Seanel said adamantly, bellowing in agitation. Jackson had never seen the whale median look so shaken before.

"But necessary." Oceaono intervened before Fulrion could speak. "Even if we didn't like it." He rubbed his head. "Still. Jackson

I swear, if you ever put yourself in danger like that when hundreds of lives are not on the line, I'll let Falganous and Fulrion rip into you until your blood turns cold."

"Have half a mind to do it now…" Fulrion grumbled through gritted teeth, making Jackson shiver.

"How long have I been asleep?" Jackson asked, trying to change the topic.

"Almost two days." Spinescale got a mischievous look in her eyes, "and finally, it was you who missed out on some interesting things. Not me, Deepbite, or Startide."

"After you gave the pearl back to Lorgeo, he cast a spell that re-absorbed the magic he had set loose and cleansed much of the magic in the canyon that had gone whirlpool after Dillox stole the star-pearl." Startide answered, shaking her head in wonder.

"He unpetrified your tail too, it wasn't lookin to good." Blade said.

"It also freed every creature and person who had been petrified since Dillox took the artifact." Daychaser got a wry smirk. "Although, Lorgeo quickly re-petrified the men who helped steal the artifact in the first place. He helped the other men to their ship that had been petrified before they sailed to the islands where the clans were."

"So the kids Uncle?" Jackson asked hopefully.

"He and the other men returned on the ship, there weren't that many of them anyway." Blade seemed to shrug. "Although why there were still petrified creatures down at the bottom of the canyon is beyond me."

"Most of those who are left were petrified by the Great Petrifying or the magic connected to it." Shavral said solemnly. "Lorgeo could do nothing to restore them, it would be too dangerous for him alone to try."

"But why not?" Jackson asked with a concerned frown "Does that mean we can't help them?"

"Fear not child." Sharval began. "There is always a way. However, there is something strange about the magic of the Great Petrifying that has made undoing it... unique."

"Because of how the spell was cast, we know it will need to be undone all at once." Seanel added. "Trying to do small portions at a time, will likely kill or petrify the person trying to do it."

"That is going to take a lot of power..." Koiwae gave the medians a long look. "Have you figured out how to go about doing that?"

"We might have a couple ideas." Falganous replied a little too quickly, making Koiwae raise a brow suspiciously.

"It is something we are still trying to figure out." Oceaono sighed. "We were hoping you or Lorgeo might have some ideas."

"I may..." Koiwae flicked his fins thoughtfully. "However, I'll need to know more about what we are dealing with, but that can wait until later. Now Jackson..." Koiwae said turning to face him. "Lorgeo has told us that the ships Dillox was trying to contact have never appeared. He also said that, due to this recent surge of energy through the system he built, the whirlpools are likely to grow a bit over the next week or so before they shrink back to their usual size. Therefore, the canyon pass will be blocked for a time until Lorgeo can get things back to normal."

"Which means, starting tomorrow, your training will continue here." Oceaono finished. "We planned to teach you what you needed to know at the Starkelp Strand Sanctuary, but since you're here and we can reach you, we will start part of your training in the morning."

"In the meantime, I believe you have something you need to return to the Spherefang's." Docion said with a smile.

"Oh yeah, the orb." Jackson sat upright on the sandy bottom. "I completely forgot."

"The Huntress is going to escort you to shore here in a few minutes while we talk to your friends about their training." Sharval said kindly.

"Their training?" Jackson looked over at his friends and gave them a mischievous smile. "Glad to know I'm not the only one."

Daychaser and Startide smiled while Blade just huffed, although his eyes sparkled a bit.

A few minutes later Jackson was led out of the sanctuary by the Huntress herself, who proudly escorted him towards the harbor.

"You gonna be ok pup?" She asked as he swam towards the docks.

"I should be, thank you so much for escorting me here, Huntress." Jackson said, giving her a small bow.

"Don't be a stranger once ya start your training." She said, giving him a grin before she turned and quickly vanished into the deep.

Jackson took a deep breath and slipped under the docks before he crawled up the sandy beach to wait for his legs to turn back. While he waited under the pier for a moment, he had an idea strike him and he brought out a deep green shirt out of his bag. Once his legs returned, he slipped on the shirt, grabbed the post next to him, and hefted himself to his feet.

When he came to the road leading into town, Jackson hesitated nervously once he saw the walls and buildings of the village not far ahead. He swallowed the lump in his throat anxiously as he walked down the short path to town, only to jump when he heard someone shout and a bell started ringing wildly.

"What on Mythos?" Jackson skidded off the street and jumped into a big bush to hide before he suddenly heard Deepbite hiss.

"Get back out there you silly, the town's been waiting for you to show up!" Deepbite poked his head out from the foliage. "They're waiting for their orb too, so get moving."

"How long have you been hiding there?" Jackson demanded in surprise.

"Long enough. Now hurry up, we don't have all day." Deepbite lunged at Jackson with a hiss, making the boy stumble back out onto the road in shock. Jackson gave the snake a tart glare before he anxiously walked up the road, stopping as he neared the gates of town.

It seemed the entire village had come out to meet him, and Jackson's jaw dropped when he noticed Toceth and all the other mages were all dressed in their nicest venom robes.

"JACKSON!!" Donner broke through the crowd and raced towards him, only for his older brother to run out and nab him, dragging the squirming and grinning mischief-maker back into the throng.

"You have done us a great favor, young Jackson." Chief Norven said as he, Toceth, Donner's dad, and some other men and women who's clothing marked them as clan leaders, took a few steps forward.

"You have helped us and our families even when you were under no obligation, and have saved us from the grasp of not only one, but many disasters." Toceth continued.

"As is the custom of our clans, we are to offer something to the one who, without need or obligation, hath saved us from destruction." Said an older woman who Jackson was surprised he recognized.

"But first, we do ask that you return something of ours." Donner's Father said firmly. "Something that my family has had charge over for generations."

Jackson gave a nervous chuckle, which made many of the men and women smile.

"Perhaps you would like to tell us why you took it as well." Toceth suggested kindly.

Jackson cleared his throat while he procured the sphere from his bag. "I-I didn't intend to take the orb." Jackson forced himself to raise his voice so everyone could hear. "I only grabbed it after I was shoved into it by Dillox, and it fell from its pedestal. I was so startled by Dillox's attack, I forgot to put it down and didn't dare drop it when I was being chased."

He walked over to the clan leaders and held out, not the orb, but the little button. "Once I escaped, I found this had been attached to the orb." Toceth reached out to inspect the button as Jackson continued. "A friend of mine, who knows something about magical items, said it's a device that siphons off magic from whatever it is attached to and converts it to another. Dillox was using it to make the Orb of the Basilisk retaliate and send off enough magic to act as a beacon so the Toxicshade could try to follow it to you."

Jackson vaguely noticed a few people pale at the mention of the Toxicshade while Toceth handed the button to the other leaders.

"We... had no idea Dillox had sabotaged the orb in such a way." Donner's father looked pale. "Thank you."

"Now, if I may?" Toceth smiled, holding out a hand for the orb.

Jackson looked at the man's outstretched hand for a moment before he took a deep breath. "Actually, most noble Toceth, I mean no disrespect but..." Jackson said as the man's eyebrows raised. "Before I return the orb, I have a question for you and the rest of your clan leaders."

There was a murmur of surprise and Toceth nodded, although Chief Norven and Donner's father's eyes slitted suspiciously.

Jackson let out a slow nervous breath. "In my family we have a question only those we know as friends or allies know the answer to..." He had to press on before his nerves got the better of him. "I would like to ask this question of you, as I feel you may know the answer. The question is this: 'What does a star, its light a-green, become when planted, to eyes unseen.'"

"It can't be!" One of the leaders exclaimed as a gasp ran through the crowd.

Toceth's hands shook when Jackson held out the orb. "It-it grows to be a majestic tree, that adds each member another leaf." The old man's voice was shaking while Jackson placed the orb into his trembling arms.

"My grandpa, Spencer Growingstar, spoke well of you. Toceth Spherefang." Jackson smiled, untucking his shirt to show the symbol of his family crest.

"I knew I recognized you!" Toceth's voice was almost a whisper.

"But how? Where did? But who?" Chief Norven completely lost his formal air once he saw the symbol on Jackson's shirt.

"Is Spencer really your grandfather, young man?" The old woman Jackson had recognized earlier asked as she came forward with an anxious look.

"He is, Great Cousin Zelli." Jackson grinned while the woman's eyes widened when he said her name.

The chief finally seemed to find his tongue and called for order when many of the clan leaders had begun swamping Jackson with questions. "One at a time, I can't even think straight!"

Everyone immediately backed away while the chief pinched the arch of his nose while he seemed to try and think.

Toceth patted the man on the shoulder as he handed the orb to Donner's Father. "It would appear that we have some catching up to do with Jackson Growingstar." Toceth's voice rang loud and clear. "The ceremony will end a bit early today while the Clans Council has a brief meeting with Jackson, our cousin."

The clans slowly dispersed, and Jackson was led through town to a small garden where benches were placed in a semicircle around a single stool where a speaker could sit and talk to those around them. Jackson was urged to sit on the stool while the Clans Council and Chief Norven and his family crowded into the benches, the chief giving Toceth a brief "thanks" before taking his seat.

"What a way to completely undermine all their formalities." Deepbite chuckled while he slithered up next to Jackson, curling up on the stool. "Spinescale will be so upset she missed this."

Toceth noticed Deepbite next to Jackson and gave the boy a knowing look. "A friend of yours, Jackson?"

Jackson gave a quiet laugh, "Yes, you could say that."

"How is my dear cousin Spencer, Jackson? After we fled, I feared I'd never hear of him again." Zelli asked, taking her seat next to Toceth and holding his hand.

Jackson opened his mouth, only to find he couldn't get any words out before he closed it, looking down at the ground. He became painfully aware of everyone silently watching him as they realized something was wrong.

"Oh, dear." Zelli came over and grasped his hands reassuringly. "What has happened?"

Jackson fought back tears, a few escaping despite his efforts. "My Grandpa... my family are... are no longer where I can be with them."

Zelli grasped her aged hands around his comfortingly as there was a concerned murmur among the others.

Jackson sniffed and wiped his eyes on his shoulder before he managed to look up at the rest of the leaders who were watching with deep concern and sympathy. "After my grandfather warned your clans and you fled for the eastern continent. Dillox and his brother told the emperor everything about what my tribe had done in the hopes of getting rewarded, and a bounty was put on us."

Jackson heard Zelli's quick intake of breath.

"We were able to escape and eventually found a safe place. We'd been living there until this last year when we were found again." Jackson looked out to sea as tears fell from his eyes. "Grandpa and the Tribe Council made the choice to hide the tribe and have Grandpa use Mass Petrification..." He took a shaky breath. "I... chose to leave and find a way to free them before it was... was too late."

Jackson wasn't prepared for the warm hug he was suddenly swept up in by Zelli and Toceth, who would be his great-cousin-in-law. He let himself cry for a minute as the others came over to lend their embraces before he pulled back, wiping the water from his eyes.

"You poor dear, have been traveling alone all this time?" Zelli asked, putting a gentle hand on his cheek.

Jackson shook his head. "I've made friends with the ocean creatures; they've been helping me."

"Your grandfather was a great man." Toceth said gently. "I'm sorry you have been put in such a horrible position."

Jackson shook his head. "I chose the path I'm on." Jackson realized he sounded a lot older than he was. "My family didn't put me in this position, they actually didn't really want me to leave. I don't even think most of them beyond my grandparents and parents know I'm gone."

"I wish I found that comforting." Toceth said ruefully, shaking his head while he and his wife backed away.

"You should stay here with us." Henri suggested. "Maybe we can help you find a way to help your family."

"I'm afraid we have no way to undue Mass Petrification my boy." An older mage said. "It's one of the hardest spells for an earth mage to cast, and only a master earth mage can cast it effectively."

Jackson shook his head. "I already know someone who can teach me the spell to free my family."

"Who is this, someone?" Chief Norven asked.

"Uh…" Jackson looked over at Toceth. "What do your clans know of the ancient water nation who were called the Sonaeko?"

CHAPTER EIGHTEEN
RELIVING A DREAM

A while later, Toceth was rubbing his head after Jackson had explained some of his journey. "So, your friend is one of the last Sonaeko left, and he and the other remaining Sonaeko have asked you to help them in exchange for teaching you how to free your family?" Toceth repeated.

"That's about the size of it." Jackson confirmed, having left out the very important facts covering the whole nation being stuck in stone, the weird warning about things growing worse in the seas, and basically anything he feared might make Toceth and the other leaders so afraid for him they would try to keep him from returning to the sea ever again.

"I can't believe there are still water magi's left, after all these centuries." A female mage said.

"Are you sure there isn't something you aren't telling us?" Chief Norven's wife asked, looking concerned.

Jackson shrugged. "There is a lot I'm not telling you, but I don't know if I should." He smirked shyly.

"Because you're worried we might not let you leave for fear you might get hurt no doubt." Toceth gave Jackson a stern look.

Jackson could only shrug, although he managed to smile sheepishly.

"Thought so." Toceth sighed. "Jackson, I'll admit that if you were on this journey for other reasons, we would keep you here where you are among family and friends and would be safe..."

"However," Zelli added, giving Jackson a conflicted look. "If your grandpa gave you permission, and his blessing, there isn't much we can do…"

"Well, we could do something, but I'd never risk angering Spencer by doing so. He'd make me own up to it in this life or the next." Toceth said wryly, "and I'd rather not take my chances."

"But you could stay for a bit, right?" Kayla asked.

"I don't know. I'm not even supposed to be at these islands at all… I was supposed to be somewhere quite far away from here." Jackson frowned. "I know that as soon as Lorgeo says the magic in the canyons is stable, and the whirlpools have shrunk back down, my friends and I will be leaving for the Starkelp Strand."

"It must've been the Creator's will to bring you here." Zelli said warmly. "Because of that, you and your friends were able to make sure your grandfather's efforts to protect us weren't in vain, and now we can dwell here in peace."

"I do wish there was a way we could know what is happening to our relatives and old friends back in our homeland." Chief Norven said solemnly. "I would like to know what happened to Mavous, Justven and the others."

"I just wish I could've—Wait who?!" Jackson's eyes bugged out.

"My younger brother's Mavous and Justven and some other men from our clans left right before we fled. They volunteered to help the Toxicshade in some of their efforts with the hope that it would appease the emperor." Chief Norven seemed lost in thought and didn't notice Jackson's shock. "They were sent on a mission right before we received the warning from your grandpa. I… why are you staring at me like that?" Norven gave Jackson a perplexed look.

"Mavous and Justven are YOUR brothers?" Jackson gaped.

"You know them?" A woman who looked like Norven's mother pushed her way up towards Jackson. "Do you know how they are doing? Are they ok?"

Jackson only managed to make a slight gurgling sound in his throat, feeling utterly stupid as he tried to say something intelligent and failed miserably. "They... Uh... What?"

The older women gave him a slightly perturbed look. "Good fangs, Jackson! Are my sons ok?"

"Are **you** ok, Jackson?" Donner asked. "You look like I did when a snake whipped me across the face."

Jackson could only sit back on the stool and stare while he struggled to find his words. "So that's... That's why the cockatrice liked them." He finally said.

"The cockatrice?" Chief Norven questioned.

"Af-after my grandpa cast the spell, I took refuge with a cockatrice flock we were friends with while the Toxicshade destroyed the village and searched the valley." Jackson was still stunned. "The flock was attacked by a battalion of the Toxicshade not long after I got there."

The older woman had an outraged look cross her face. "My boys helped to attack a cockatrice flock?"

"Uh well, that's not quite what happened..." Jackson went on to explain the whole scenario, from Justven defending Greatcrower, the little revolt of the other mages, to Jackson's help in healing Justven before Mavous accused his tribe of killing the Spherefang's.

"The last I saw them, they were part of the group that chased me into the sea..." Jackson said quietly. "I don't know what happened to them after that, this is the first time I've really been on land this long since."

"Well at least they've kept their honor." Norven's mother said, although she still sounded disappointed. "But they should've known better than to trust the emperor's claims. I raised them better than that!"

"Now, Calnoa." Great Cousin Zelli patted the other woman's hand. "The only thing they knew is that we vanished, and our cities were laid waste."

"Still, they should've known that Jackson's tribe would never do such a thing." Calnoa said stubbornly before she walked away.

"Oh dear…" Zelli watched the other woman leave worriedly.

"It's ok Zelli, she's just worried." An older gentleman who was slightly bent with age came over and patted Zelli's shoulder. "Don't worry about her. I'm just relieved our sons still have their honor and have ousted out one of those arrogant shadow dukes."

"Here's hoping they'll do it to a few more." Another man called smugly.

Jackson spent the rest of the day visiting with Toceth, Zelli, and the other members of the Spherefang Clans, learning he was related to quite a few of them, including the kids he'd met. Around dinnertime all the clans gathered for a large feast in his honor which greatly embarrassed Jackson: although he relished the delicious food he'd been missing out on for months. As evening fell, he saw Spinescale come slithering over to find him and smiled down at her.

"Hey Spinescale, time to go?" He asked while people watched him and Spinescale curiously.

"Yep, and you're really going to need your sleep if you're gonna handle the schedule Oceaono and Koiwae are putting together for you." Her eyes sparkled mischievously.

Jackson groaned. "Are they really going to be training me that hard?"

"Nope, worse." She smirked.

"I take it this means it's time to say goodbye?" Zelli asked with a sad smile.

"Yeah... my Sonaeko friends are going to start teaching me how to undo petrification spells before my other friends and I head out." Jackson reluctantly got to his feet.

"It was wonderful to see you dear." Zelli said, wrapping him in a hug. "If you can, come back to visit us soon."

"And hopefully you will be bearing good news about your family. You and your tribe are always welcome." Toceth said, patting Jackson's shoulder in a fatherly way.

"You should bring them here if you are able to free them." Chief Norven came over to shake Jackson's hand. "We would be honored to have your tribe join us here."

Jackson felt some tears prick his eyes. "Thank you." He said quietly. "I will if I can, and I'm sure my family would love it here."

"Come back to visit soon!" Donner came rushing over, followed by the other kids. "You need to teach me how to speak snake!"

"Oh, please no, I'll never get a moment of peace." Spinescale hissed in dismay while Deepbite snickered.

Jackson laughed before saying goodbye to the other kids and was just turning to walk down to the dock when he heard someone running up behind him.

"Just a minute young man." Calnoa said, grabbing his hand and placing something in it. "If you somehow manage to see my sons again, give them this right before you leave them." Jackson looked down at a strange spiraling venom crystal. "Don't give it to them a moment before, just give it to them as you leave." She instructed, "and don't let them ask you any more questions, just leave and don't look back."

Chief Norven came up with his father and put a gentle hand on his mother's shoulder, looking at Jackson with some tears in his eyes. "They'll know what it is Jackson, everyone in our family does. Just make sure they get it and let them know you were instructed to give it to them."

Jackson looked down at the stone with a puzzled look before he nodded and put it into his pack. "I will."

"And take this with you too." Toceth and Zelli came over with a small chest which they gently handed to him. "A little something to remember us by."

"And to thank you for helping our clans." The chief smiled.

Jackson slowly opened the chest to see a large purple diamond-cut gem, with a light green crystal snake with dark purple eyes coiled around it. Small waves of magic slowly undulated across its surface and the snake seemed to grin at him before he closed the chest. "I…" He shook his head as tears came to his eyes. "Thank you, I'll treasure it."

The others smiled while he put the chest in his bag. "Be careful out there." Toceth said when Jackson gave him and Zelli one last hug.

"I'll try."

He heard Daychaser and Startide whistle from the now calm waters of the harbor and turned to see them and Blade swimming around waiting for him. As he started down the docks, Jackson noticed one of the buildings along the shore looked hauntingly familiar. He froze when the memory of the dream he had at the outpost came flooding back to him.

"You found your family." A gentle and warm voice said as a soft breeze wisped by Jackson's face, drawing his gaze to a bright ray of sunlight breaking through the clouds. He swore he saw a small glowing dove that smiled warmly at him before vanishing into a beam of sunlight.

Guess I did, didn't I? Grinning as he looked back one last time, Jackson smiled at his new friends and relatives. A phrase his Grandpa used to say floated through his mind as he turned back. *"Sometimes the Creator sends a messenger and peace to help us when we need a bit of guidance, understanding, or comfort."* With a thoughtful smile Jackson waved goodbye before running down the dock, diving nimbly into the water.

"Ready for tomorrow?" Blade asked with a cocky smirk while the sun sank below the horizon. "Cause I'm trainin ya, we gotta get ya swimmin faster."

"Oh, bother." Startide rolled her eyes. "Blade, Koiwae said he might have us race Jackson once he learned a few new spells that help him travel quickly underwater. He didn't say you'd be training him."

"That's what I heard." Blade flicked his fins dismissively. "I'm sure ya just missed somethin."

"Riiiiight." Startide replied sarcastically as she turned to Jackson. "Anyway, it sounds like Koiwae and Oceaono have something they want to talk to you about."

"Let's just hope it's something good." Daychaser grinned. "We got a ways to go if we're gonna help restore the Sonaeko and your family."

"We're all going to be busy." Spinescale added, although she looked excited while Deepbite just shook his head wryly.

"You're telling me." Jackson laughed while he and his friends swam off towards the sanctuary, blissfully unaware of a huge storm that was beginning to form to the north. "You're telling me."

GLOSSARY

ARCHIPELAGO — (Ar-ki-pel-a-go) A group, or chain, of islands.

BEAKED WHALES — Also known by ocean creatures as deep divers or diving whales, beaked whales are an unusual group of whales with very pointed beak-like snouts. The males often have protruding tusks on the side of their jaws. There are many different species that vary in appearance, behavior, and size. The black-backed diving whales Jackson meets resemble a larger version of earth's Andrews beaked whale.

BILLOWFINS – Billowfins are a species of magical fish that was once plentiful before the great petrifying. They're deeply tied to water magic, something that is evidenced by their liquid-like fins and tails. The way their liquid-like fins move is considered calming and serene by many people, as are the billowfins themselves, since they were often very calm and thoughtful creatures.

BOOK OF THE SONAEKO — A sentient magical book that holds the secrets of the long lost Sonaeko Nation. Jackson is able to summon it so he can learn more about the myriad of things the book has chronicled. It's like the water magic version of the internet... Well kinda, I mean it's different in that: the book's actually self-aware and has a bit of an attitude, there's no real search function beyond asking the book, and it has a particular hatred for bookworms… And no, I mean the magical Mythonian species of worm that sometimes eats books, not people who like to read books!

BUTTERFLY FISH — Unlike earth butterfly fish, these fish actually have fins that look like butterfly wings. However, they aren't pollinators so don't let them anywhere near your sea-lilies, unless you want the butterfly fish to eat them…

CADOLIN — (Ca-dol-in). Also known as seawolves, they are an aquatic creature that's a mix between wolves, dolphins, and whales. They have four powerful flippers they use when swimming at a normal or slow pace and need higher maneuverability. They use their tails for long distance and high-speed swimming, but at the cost of maneuverability. Please note, they don't find it funny if you treat them like a dog or try to get them to play fetch, it'll end up with a game of chase… You'll be the one getting chased, and likely bitten… Ask me how I know.

CHIEF NORVEN — (Nore-ven). The current Chief of the Spherefang Clans, the father of Henri, Kayla, Leavan, and Terven.

COMMUNICATION CRYSTAL — Magical crystals used by the Sonaeko to communicate with each other over long distances. They're usually found in large towns, cities, outposts, or other places where the Sonaeko dwelled. They can vary in appearance, but are often shaped like large orbs, and many creatures refer to them as communication orbs. I've been wanting one for years, but the only one I found was in the ruins of a Sonaekian town… I felt a bit sheepish just taking it, and who knows who I might accidentally contact if I tried to use it!

CURRENTS — In the world of Mythos there are two types of currents, the currents of water that flow through every ocean, and the magical currents of water magic that course along with the actual physical currents. Many ocean creatures and water magic users can both send and hear messages, warnings, voices, and other more magical things on the currents of magic that flow through the seas. However, when the magic of the oceans is out of balance, the currents can fail in their flow or become hampered. If that is the case, please refrain from sending invitations for parties, holiday get-togethers, game nights, or sleepovers on the currents, or you might end up with a strange assortment of party-crashers...

DISHONORED — If a creature is dishonored, it effectively means they've chosen a path of darkness and evil. Dishonored creatures are cut off from the good magic of the world, though many are still able to use dark forms of whatever magic they could've used before. They are also able to somewhat hear things on the currents, especially if the currents are out of balance and weakened.

DOCION — (Doe-see-on). The large dark blue-gray dolphin median. He is perceptive, calm, composed, and patient. He is also a diplomat who specializes in working with interspecies communication.

DRAGONTURTLE — Immense turtles that have a host of dragon-like traits and can breathe a hot steaming blast of magical energy from their mouths. They're often cantankerous and dangerously smart and sailors dread running into one on the open ocean. One attacked my friend's pleasure boat once when he sailed too close to its favorite kelp patch... My friend survived, but his boat didn't!

FALGANOUS — (Fal-gain-us). The dark green and orange dragonturtle median, his bite is worse than his bark, trust me on that.

FLATHEAD SHARKS – What some ocean creatures call hammerhead sharks. They're largely similar to earth's hammerhead sharks, though size, color, and patterning can differ.

FULRION — (Ful-rion). The dark brown leocampus median. He is an expert in many things, just not manners or patience. There might be a heart of gold underneath his huge mane of fur somewhere... maybe. I hope so, cause I'd really like to see it sometime!

GARDENERFISH — A tan and purple species of fish that's similar to earth's damselfish species. Like some damselfish species, these fish are known for "raising" patches of algae which they feed on. They're perfectly decent creatures until you mess with their algae... at which point, does the phrase "GET OFF MY LAWN!" mean anything to you?

GONE WHIRLPOOL — Gone crazy, going wild, uncontrolled.

HOOKJAW FISH — Mythonian salmon, but unlike earth salmon, the non-breeding adult males' jaws are hooked even when they're young. To me it looks like they should speak with a strange accent... I mean, you can't have a jawline like that and not have a unique sounding voice, right?

GLOSSARY

IRONMAMBA — An ancient evil empire that started the Steelserpent War, the war which led to the disappearance of the Sonaeko nation.

JEWEL ISLES BLACK DOLPHINS — While there's a large net of species that are called "black dolphins" by Mythonians, the ones around the Jewel Isles are species similar to earth's pilot whales.

KOIWAE – (Coy-way) The billowfin guardian of the Jewel Island Sanctuary. Koiwae is a wise, thoughtful creature who has looked over the Jewel Island Sanctuary for… many years. I wouldn't ask him how old he is though; however, I'm guessing at least two hundred and sixty, maybe more…

LEOCAMPUS — (Lee-o-camp-us). A creature with the front half of a lion and the back of a shark, they live in large prides that dwell in seagrass prairies and other underwater habitats. The roars of adult males can travel for many whale-lengths underwater, helping the prides to establish territories and communicate with one another. However, those roars can also bust your eardrums if you're too close, so if a leocampus pride looks ready to begin singing the song of their people, you might want to put a bit of distance between yourself and them… If you don't… Well, I hope you have access to some good healing spells.

LORGEO — (Lore-gee-o) A mysterious, solitary character.

MISTSURGE OUTPOST — A Sonaekian outpost Jackson and his friends stayed at for a time, before the magic in the outpost failed.

MOONSTONES — Mythonian moonstones are magical stones innately tied to light magic. Like the moon reflects the light of the sun to provide us light during the night, moonstones use actual light to make light magic that can then be used by magi and magical creatures. They usually glow a soft white and look stunning in pieces of jewelry. I once had a necklace with a moonstone pendant... once... Actually, I got it back now, those nymphs finally fessed up after I called them out!

NATURE EMERALDS – Green gemstones that are connected to the magic of nature. They gather nature-based energy and magical power from the world around them, and can help make gardens flourish. I personally have two, one for my underwater garden and one for my land-based garden. No, they aren't for sale, don't even ask.

OCEAN'S TEARS — Teardrop shaped water-magic-based gemstones that pull magic from the water and currents around them. Magi and water magic wielding creatures can easily access the magic found in the gemstones, helping them cast larger and more powerful spells.

OCEAONO — (O-see-on-o). The sapphire golem leader of the Sonaeko Medians. Serious, calm, humble, and determined, he is a capable spellcaster and leader.

GLOSSARY

OROCA — (Or-o-ca). The honorable Mythonian version of earth's orcas and killer whales. The white markings and patterns are often more extreme and unusual then seen in earth's orcas and killer whales, and both Mythonian oroca and killer whales often get larger than earth species. The term oroca always refers to honorable members of the species, while killer whale refers to dishonored and wicked members, confuse the two terms at your own risk.

ROYAL WHITE – A Mythonian shark species that is similar to earth's great white sharks. However, royal whites get even larger and are often lighter in color with dark markings. Most royal whites grow lighter in color with age, but their skin doesn't change color all at once, instead turning lighter in thin stripes which blend together over time. They're only slightly terrifying… slightly… but they're also awesome looking!

SANDTYR — (Sand-tire). A brown to cream colored species of shark that resembles earth's lemon sharks. They have a long, large dorsal fin and can have a variety of patterns, from a scattering of speckles and spots to thin light stripes. There are two closely related species known as Darktyr and Deeptyr. Deeptyr sharks are a gray color, while Darktyr are a dark bronze-brown with glowing green eyes, making them fabulous to have around during spooky holidays.

SAPPHIRE GOLEMS — (Saf-ire, gol-ems) An ancient species of gemstone or crystal golems that were members of the Sonaeko Nation. They're highly intelligent and powerful magic users whose bodies are always made from magical blue crystal in varying hues. Unsurprisingly, they usually love sapphires and often have jewelry or accessories made from them. While I'd never counsel you to bribe anyone, if you're already friends with a sapphire golem, it'd be wise to have a stash of sapphires on hand as gifts for holidays and special occasions.

SEANEL — (See-nel). The small but wise whale median and Oceaono's old friend and mentor.

SHARVAL — (Shar-val). The shark median. She is a large dark gray shark with a white belly and large scars running down her left side and is a war veteran and old friend of Docion. She doesn't say much, but when she does, you'd better listen.

SIDE EYES — Mythonian flounder, they are largely similar to earth flounder. Both their eyes are, unsurprisingly, on one side of their head, which makes finding a pair of glasses that fit right a horrible challenge.

SONAEKIAN — (So-nay-key-an). A member of the Sonaeko Nation.

SONAEKO — (So-nay-ko). An ancient elementalborn nation that was known as the nation of the oceans and rivers.

SOUNDING — The term used by sea creatures that means echolocation, or the use of sounds to "see" the world around you. If that sounds strange, you should give sounding a try yourself, or maybe don't… Am I the only one who finds it weird that something can "see" what's going on around it by hearing it?

SPACEKEEPER BAGS — Extremely rare and special bags that are connected to large rooms, caves, or chambers that can be reached through the bag by special magical symbols and spells. People or creatures can teleport items and inanimate objects into the bag with those magical symbols. However, they can't teleport people or other living creatures into the bags without their permission or trust. They're also called spatial bags. I really want one... but they're way too rare, and I can't afford the price.

SPELL BLAST IT — A phrase that basically means, "shoot," "drat," "dang it," "darn it," "oh come on," etc. Jackson usually shortens it to "spells."

STAR OF THE SEA — A mythical, mysterious, and magical gemstone that seems to be connected to the magic of the seas and the Sonaeko Nation. It seems to have chosen Jackson to guard it, but what is it exactly? And why don't the medians talk about it more? I wanna know!!!

STEELSERPENT WAR — An ancient war that resulted in the destruction of many nations and is connected to the Sonaeko Nation vanishing. It's also called the Great War and was started by the ancient Ironmamba Empire.

SUNLIGHT STONES — Magical gemstones that are said to be connected to the power and magic of the sun. They shine brightly during the day and dim during the night. They are often used in underground—or underwater—cities and buildings.

THANK THE CURRENTS — An ocean creature phrase that basically means, "thank goodness," or "thank heavens."

THE SUN TOUCHING THE SURFACE OF THE SKY — A sea creature phrase meaning noon, or the middle of the day. There are different forms of the saying, like "when the sun touches the sky's surface," but they all mean the same thing.

TOCETH — (Tow-seth) A older man who was the past chief of the Spherefang's. He's married to Grandma Zelli, and is Bennor, Danna, and Donner's grandfather.

TOXICSHADE — A corrupt and wicked empire that has been waging war with nations all over Mythos. They've placed a bounty on Jackson's tribe and are trying to destroy them.

UNICORN FISH — A beautiful cream and white fish with a stunning spiral unicorn-like horn growing from its forehead. I've heard that if you catch one under a full moon and place it in a pool of healing magic, it'll turn into an actual unicorn! ...Or maybe it'll just stab you because they don't like being out of the water... huh, either way, you'll end up needing some healing magic.

VENSTORN — (Ven-storn). Four-legged creatures that look like a cross between an immense greyhound or horse and a serpent. Venstorns are often kept as riding mounts and familiars for people from the Venom Nations and a few other nations in the northern continent. They are intelligent and sly, and don't take kindly to being mistreated or abused and have a venomous bite to back their displeasure. They nip and bite to show both affection and dislike... so if you're planning to befriend one, good luck figuring the two out. There are a number of different varieties like racing, draftfang, royalspine, and the more normal wild type venstorns that have high amounts of endurance. All venstorns are omnivores, and eat a wide variety of things, including leaves and grasses. They live in large packs, commonly known as quivers, though adult males often wander around the quiver's territory by themselves.

WHAT IN THE CURRENTS — What on earth? What? What in the world?

ENJOY THIS SNEAK PEEK OF

BOOK THREE

MYTH✸S SEAS
DANGEROUS DEPTHS

For more information on upcoming novels in the Mythos Seas series, please go to Mythosseas.com!

CHAPTER ONE
SPELLS AND STUDIES

J ackson took a tight breath, his features tense in concentration while the body of a large, petrified sea turtle glowed faintly before him. His head was throbbing as his magic wove around the creature, and if he was above water, he would certainly be sweating like a venstorn on race day. After a few more minutes, Jackson winced when he felt a sharp pain shoot through his hands as his magic flickered. He yelped when his spell broke with a flash, throwing him backwards into a large seawolf that squeed-yipped in surprise as they tumbled backwards!

"Not again." Startide—a large oroca with an intelligent shine to her eyes—said in a way that reminded Jackson of an older sister. "The same thing happened last time."

"Should'a waited till we found somethin smaller." Blade, a fast, tough looking shark with dark sly eyes watched with a bored, slightly amused expression.

"Sorry about that Daychaser." Jackson apologized to the seawolf before he looked down at his hands and groaned. "Spells…"

He whispered, holding his petrified hands up in front of him.
"Remind me why this happens again?"

"Undoing a petrification spell always has the added danger of
backfiring if you are not successful." A large, magically glowing fish
who had long billowing liquid-like fins swam over to look at
Jackson's hands. "It doesn't look too terrible this time, young
Jackson, and this gives you a chance to try and remove the spell
from something much smaller than this turtle."

Jackson sighed. "I know, but isn't there a smaller creature I
could try working on Koiwae? I mean, after I'm finished freeing my
hands." He carefully began freeing his left hand from its granite
glove.

"The Huntress should be arriving today with some other
petrified creatures that Lorgeo found near the canyons." Koiwae
said, looking over at the pile of stone animals lying next to a patch of
billowing seaweed. "I specifically asked her to have Lorgeo send
some smaller ones this time."

"Thank goodness." Jackson said as the stone around his left
hand cracked and vanished away.

"I'm sure you'll get the hang of it soon enough. Even if your
hands keep looking like the rocks Deepbite and I like to sun
ourselves on." Spinescale, a purple and yellow winged sea snake
who usually had a mischievous sparkle in her eyes, snickered.

Jackson rolled his eyes and focused on restoring his other hand
as Koiwae came over to watch.

"You really are doing quite well. You have only been at this for
a couple days, but yet you've made great progress." Koiwae flicked
his fins approvingly as Jackson's second hand was freed. "I'm sure if
that storm hadn't prevented us from getting our fins on some smaller
creatures before now, you'd have already freed a number of
animals."

"Should I try again?" Jackson looked at the stone turtle warily. "We've been practicing undoing petrification spells all morning."

"Let's take a short break from petrification spells." Koiwae looked to the far end of the cavern thoughtfully. "I want to see how your quick-current spells are progressing after Oceaono's lessons yesterday."

"See if ya can keep up with me this time." Blade turned to face the far end of the Jewel Island Sanctuary's main cavern. "I'll even go easy on ya, just to be nice."

"Count me in too." Daychaser said, taking his place next to Blade.

"Ya think ya can beat me Day-dolin?" Blade asked in a haughty voice.

"No, but I can still try." Daychaser smirked. "Why? Scared someone's gonna be faster than you someday?"

"Oh, for the love of sea serpent scales. This is supposed to test how fast Jackson can go when he's using his magic to create a current that speeds him forward." Startide flared her fins out in exasperation. "It's not a competition."

"Only because I'll win." Blade smugly mumbled through his gills.

Spinescale giggled. "I think you better get moving Jackson, or Startide might end up trying to eat Blade before you can get to the other side of the cavern."

Jackson shook his head and joined the "line up" between his friends. He had just started forming his spell when Blade suddenly shouted.

"ONE-TWO-THREE-GO!"

Blade and Daychaser shot off, sending Jackson spinning around in the water! "Gah! Hey!" Jackson hurriedly righted himself, cast the spell, and flew after them! Blade was already in the lead as he torpedoed forwards, leaving Daychaser far behind while Jackson slowly gained on him.

Once Jackson caught up to Daychaser they maintained an almost even pace as they barreled onwards, until they reached the other side of the cavern. The two friends quickly touched the wall before they flipped around, racing back to where the others were waiting.

The race between Jackson and Daychaser seemed close as they neared the finish-line, both of them fighting to get in the lead. Suddenly Daychaser let out a triumphant squee, and with a few mighty strokes of his tail he surged forward, leaving Jackson in the bubbles. The seawolf let out a short victory howl as he swept past the finish, twirling to a stop by Startide, and beating Jackson by a good whale length.

"Haha!" Daychaser crooned, giving Jackson a smirk. "Beat ya."

"So, ya'll took so long, I managed to grab a snack while I waited for ya to catch up." Blade quipped, gulping down a fish as he lazily swam past Daychaser, having crossed the finish line a long time before the others.

"Uhuh…" Jackson rolled his eyes, though he smiled good naturedly. "Well, I might do a bit better next time if I had a little warning before you two sent me spinning around in the water, I had to completely restart my spell."

Blade huffed, still looking smug. "Tch, details, ya should've been more alert anyway."

"Despite all that…" Koiwae spoke up, coming over next to Jackson. "You may need to adjust how you form the spell, young Jackson." Koiwae carefully inspected the magic around Jackson that was slowly dissipating away. "I think you need to put a little more focus on how the current forms. Why don't you try it again…" The fish gave Blade and Daychaser a wry look. "This time, **without** anyone blasting past you, and making the test 'not a competition.'"

Startide and Spinescale snickered when Daychaser got a sheepish look on his snout while Blade just huffed. Jackson shook his head and smiled before he returned his focus to forming the quick-current spell again.

It took three more tries, and a bit of direction from Koiwae, before Jackson was able to form the spell to billowfin guardian's liking. Once Jackson finally formed the spell right, and made a quick trip around the cavern, Koiwae made him demonstrate the vortex and water shield spells he'd been learning.

"That should be enough for now, young Jackson." Koiwae said later, after Jackson had successfully formed a medium sized whirlpool around himself. "How are you feeling after all that?"

"I feel fine, a bit winded but fine." Jackson smiled, giving a tiny gasp.

"When it comes to doing magic, your stamina is truly remarkable." Koiwae shook his head. "Perhaps it makes up for your physical weakness."

Jackson winced, blushing a bit in embarrassment, not used to someone pointing out the fact that he wasn't strong or fast physically.

"Forgive me, I meant no insult." Koiwae apologized, looking ashamed of himself. "I should've thought before I spoke."

"It's ok." Jackson shrugged, rubbing his arm uncertainly.

"Your tone says otherwise." Koiwae swam over and caught his gaze, his eyes smiling knowingly at him. "I'm sorry young Jackson, but please do not fret because of your weaknesses. You are strong in many ways that are far more important than physical strength or endurance."

"I… ok, thank you." Jackson nodded but glanced down slightly until Blade suddenly spoke up.

"Hate to ruin the moment and all, but the Huntress is back." Blade interrupted Koiwae's praise when a large gray shark came confidently cruising into the cavern, her huge jaws loosely clamped around a bunch of small, petrified creatures. She eyed Jackson and his friends shrewdly as she drew near, opening her mouth to drop a small pile of stone creatures next to Koiwae.

"Thought I'd drop these off on my way through. Lorgeo said to take smaller ones this time." The Huntress sounded a bit bored. "You pups keeping busy? Been kinda boring out there lately since I helped ya take care of that shadow guy."

"We've had plenty to do." Startide said enthusiastically. "The medians and Koiwae have had a lot to teach us."

"Hm, I'm sure." The Huntress's tone made it blatantly obvious she'd rather not hear about it. "Well, I'm off to get my share of a small whale carcass that's floating around some of the southern isles; if I don't see ya again, have a safe trip."

"We'll sure try, and thanks for dropping these off for us." Jackson waved. The shark gave him a small grin before she coursed out of the cavern without a backwards glance. "Enjoy your meal Huntress." He called.

"How you ever managed to get on her good side, I'll never know." Spinescale gave the snake version of an eyeroll. "She's never that nice to anyone else."

"I've heard she's a bit soft for her pups, but that's it." Blade grumbled. "Beyond them, and Jackson, she's the uncontested ruler in these parts."

"Rules with a savage jaw." Spinescale added.

"Sometimes the tougher the creature, the softer the heart, as my Grandpodmother used to say." Startide said wryly.

"That's an oxymoron." Daychaser laughed as he went over and inspected the small pile of stone creatures. "Hey, these are a lot smaller."

A small current of water whisked the pile up from the seafloor, twirling it over to where Jackson and Koiwae were floating. Koiwae inspected each of the stone figures as they passed by him. Finally, he selected one, making the magical current of water sweep it over to Jackson.

"I would like you to try and free this fish, young Jackson. She's an old friend of mine who was petrified by the rogue magic that coursed through here after the Great Petrifying." Koiwae said. "You can tell by looking at the color of the stone encasing her that it wasn't the Great Petrifying, or its aftershocks, that froze her."

Jackson took the fish in his hands while inspecting the light grey stone encasing it. "The creatures petrified by the main spell and its aftershocks have a darker shade to the stone, right?" He asked, turning the fish around.

"Correct, and they have the faintest of brown and blue stripes around their forehead." Koiwae confirmed. "And remember, never to try and unpetrify any creature that had been frozen by the Great Petrifying or its aftershocks." Koiwae had an intent and serious look in his eyes. "The magic binding them is simply too strong and would petrify you completely, if it didn't kill you or the creature you're trying to help outright. The rogue magic that hit after the main spell should be safe for you to undo however…"

TO GET UPDATES ON FUTURE
BOOKS, CONTENT, AND LEARN
MORE ABOUT THE OTHER BOOKS
IN THE MYTHOS SEAS SERIES!

GO TO:

MYTHOSSEAS.COM

WE'LL SEE YOU SOON!

ABOUT THE AUTHOR

JEREMY J. DAVIDSON was born and raised in the beautiful, hot, and dry deserts of southern Utah, where he developed a love for warm weather, family, and creatures. Now living in the colder upper portion of Nevada's Great Basin, he still finds time to pursue his hobbies in writing, drawing, gardening, raising animals, and learning all he can about the amazing creatures of our world despite colder temperatures and snowy winters. He is the author of Mythos Seas: Call of the Coast, and the other books in the Mythos Seas and Mythos Seas Beyond book series!